Advance Praise for Miss Media

"Dorothy Parker meets Carrie Bradshaw in Lola Somerville, *Miss Media's* charming, disarming, and sly heroine. Lynn Harris' novel takes us into the bizarre—and alarmingly realistic—women's web-and-TV empire, Ovum Inc., with a keen eye, wry wit, and dead-on observations about the clash of the old guard with the new media. *Miss Media* is a fresh, funny, funky workplace fairy tale for the 21st century."
—Lori Gottlieb, author of *Inside the Cult of Kibu, And Other Tales of the Millennial Gold Rush*

"I remember when Lynn was bright-eyed and optimistic about the Internet age. She's funnier now."
—Joel Stein, columnist, *Time Magazine*

"Lynn Harris has created written a smart and side-splitting novel capturing our worship of pop culture, the ins-and-outs of what's in and out, and the crazy way life works when we're forced to discard the instructions. From its first page, *Miss Media* sucks us into its emotional, zany, and enjoyable spiral...upwards."
—Emily Franklin, author of *Liner Notes*

"*Miss Media* is an intelligent and laugh-out-loud take on how media people live, work, dine, and mate."
—Tracy Quan, author of *Diary of a Manhattan Call Girl*

Good Ink On Lynn Harris

"Harris is a charming and tart-tongued comedic talent."
—*Citysearch*

"Lynn Harris has done for the failing relationship what Jonas Salk did for polio."
—Dr. Katz, professional therapist

"Ms. Harris is a bright light on stage…her signature style combines her Yalie smarts, big heart, and verbal flair."
—*The New York Sun*

"She's a riot and an inspiration."
—*Zulkey.com*

Miss Media

Also By Lynn Harris

Breakup Girl to the Rescue! A Superhero's Guide to Love, and Lack Thereof

He Loved Me, He Loves Me Not: A Guide to Fudge, Fury, Free Time, and Life Beyond the Breakup

MTV's "Singled Out" Guide to Dating (with J.D. Heyman)

Tray Gourmet: Be Your Own Chef in the College Cafeteria (with Larry Berger)

Miss Media

A Novel

Lynn Harris

iUniverse, Inc.
New York Lincoln Shanghai

Miss Media
A Novel

iUniverse, Inc.

For information address:
iUniverse, Inc.
2021 Pine Lake Road, Suite 100
Lincoln, NE 68512
www.iuniverse.com

Cover design by Chris Kalb

ISBN: 0-595-28776-X (Pbk)
ISBN: 0-595-65860-1 (Cloth)

Printed in the United States of America

For Chris Kalb

Author's Note

Miss Media is a work of fiction. Any resemblance herein to companies living or ailing, good or evil, is not entirely coincidental, but also not entirely the point.

Acknowledgments

My deepest gratitude to the people who are personally responsible for my faith in humanity.

Betsy Fast, Chris Kalb, and Colin Lingle, for everything, always.

Judy Bornstein, Dixie Feldman, Laura Gilbert, J.D. Heyman (special thanks for the *Canon* fodder), Marjorie Ingall, Amy Keyishian, Michael Lee, Carolyn Mackler, Wendy Shanker, Juliet Siler, Paul Sullivan, Kim Williams—and all our other peeps from Team BG and you-know-where—for fighting the best of fights, speaking the *bon*-est of *mots*, and being the best of friends.

Hillery Borton, Claudia Cross, and Jan Kleeman for your expertise and loyalty.

David Adelson, for being better than anyone I could ever have made up.

And, as always, to my parents.

Brooklyn, 2003

1

Everything was round. Oval, more like. Oval-backed chairs, oval phones, oval video monitors, oval desks arranged in clusters. This was clearly no place for cubicles. The vast room's white outer walls curved smoothly up toward a single giant skylight. Never before had the hulking building, a converted cupcake factory, seemed to rise so close to the sun.

Somewhere in the glossy plasma below, Lola Somerville was taking her books out of boxes and trying to align them along the curve of an oval shelf—smaller books on the tapered ends, bigger ones in the middle. "Alphabetizing is so twentieth century," she tried to tell herself, silently missing the nice square milk crates back in her home office.

Her former home office.

Today was Lola's first day at Ovum, Inc.

Ovum, Inc. was where everyone and her sister (and, therefore, everyone and his brother) wanted to work. Ovum's programming and "content," on television and on the web, was for women—real women. Ovum promised the spirit and edge of smart, funny women's 'zines such as *Ms. Thing* and *Rack*, but with the benefit of resources such as money.

Yeah. Lola was sure she'd done the right thing.

Lola yanked her emergency scrunchie from her wrist and twirled her bra-strap-length hair into a bun. Rotini-twisty and marmalade-orange, her hair was the envy of the "mousy" legions. Even strangers told her so. "No no no," Lola would always reply, "I'd kill to have, like, normal, dealable hair!" but she was totally lying. Lola could pass for Nicole Kidman if she were two feet taller and had a different face—so her hair, she felt, made up for the fact that otherwise, one might describe her as "the hot girl's approachable friend." Skin the color of the crayon they used to call "flesh," roundish cheeks, mocha eyes, vestigial freckles. Lola loved to wear pink and orange and other colors forbidden to redheads, which was, her mother suspected, why she was still single.

Though she'd made a name for herself on the Internet, Lola had only provisional geek qualifications. Two years earlier, she had launched her first website with one hand on the keyboard and the other holding open the book *Hooray for HTML*! She'd originally conceived the website as a homegrown defense against the global domination plan of Dr. E. Ron Wilson, kabillionaire czar of the *Men are Pigs, Women are Nuts* self-help empire: bestselling books, CDs, classes, intimate apparel, a chain of Pigs, Nuts, 'n' Beans cafes, you name it—even a line of GPS-equipped automobiles ("So Nuts won't noodge Pigs about asking for directions!").

As it turned out, DrERonWilsonSucks.com had held Lola's creative interest for about three days. Then, it had occurred to her, why not kill with clueful-ness? A longtime magazine writer, reporter, feminist, and fan of guys, Lola had figured she could offer a balanced, inclusive point of view with an advice column of her own. She didn't need an advanced degree—after all, that mean Dr. Ruthless on the radio, her degree was actually in geography, and Lola, girl reporter, had exposed the fact that E. Ron had earned his Ph.D. (in "Speech") from the shady online degree provider ResumePadding.com. Solid research, common sense, ethical and socio-political principles, a general disdain for tacky behavior and some server space—that's all I need, Lola had thought, to establish a voice and make a name for myself. Right?

Right. AskLola.com had grown big fast, big enough for Lola to earn a little ad revenue and hire overqualified Kat to deal with tech stuff, and then overqualified Ted to help sort letters and research answers. But not big enough for a "workplace" other than Lola's crates and countertops, and the futon she used to flip into a couch when Kat and Ted clocked in. So when Ovum, Inc. had offered to buy her site—and, Lola insisted, her staff—the heady mix of flattery and salary was tough to resist.

The business plan: AskLola.com—as Ovum's own and only relationships "brand"—would have a direct link from Ovuminc.com's high-traffic hub. Kat would oversee the technical process of shifting to Ovum's server, but the only visible change on the site would be the words "Ovum, Inc. presents Ask Lola" along the tippy-top title. That, plus all the bells and whistles the team would finally have the technological and financial resources to add. And Lola herself would appear on Ovum television as their in-house relationships expert.

Lola had also been granted a modest number of stock options, which, after Ovum's knockout IPO, would help her (an only child) repay her loans from Bank of Dad and lift her to a whole new level of New York City takeout.

Fortune, validation, a soapbox: excellent incentives. But the most powerful pull of all, really, was Ovum itself. Lola wouldn't have sold her baby to just anyone nice with a checkbook. But Ovum! Ovum *got it.* Lola had actually worried a bit that alignment with such a woman-y place might alienate the male fans of her expressly co-ed website. She'd quickly seen, however, that Ovum wasn't *that* kind of woman-y—neither lavender-scripty Woe Girl, nor glittery vacant

Go Girl! It was the kind of woman-y Lola had been waiting for: mainstream, inclusive, smart, cool *and* well-financed. Finally. Finally, the really good guys don't have to be "alternative." Here, AskLola.com—and possibly Lola herself—could grow really, really big and strong.

"What on earth is the catch?" Lola asked herself for the billionth time. The answer suddenly hit her.

These fucking round shelves.

•

"Yo. Time for orientation, only I don't think they call it that." Kat, one of the few women on the planet allowed to wear a skirt over pants, snapped back the cover on her *Power Puff Girls* watch and walked toward Lola's desk.

"C'mon Ted, let's head over." Lola nodded toward a group of employees assembling around an oval conference table.

Ted adjusted his framed Cincinnati Reds 1975 World Series pennant and glanced at his new haircut in the muddled reflection. With an amiable grin and cheeks round as Ding-Dongs, he looked like the young Little League coach the kids loved and could walk all over. He followed Kat and Lola into the office's swirling nucleus.

People hurried all around, moving, joining and separating like molecules under a microscope. Trip-hop music pulsed faintly from somewhere. Cameras roamed about; although each show had its home base, the whole Ovum office was one big TV set. (This design concept was called "A womb with a view of one's own.") Maybe that was why everyone looked so damn good. For whatever reason, Ovum's employees were already known to be walking proof that people, particularly women, could be both smart and hot.

"You know," Ted said, "I pretty much see this orientation—"

"I heard we're not supposed to call it 'orientation,'" Kat wagged her finger. She had a smile that went up higher on the right and spiky dark hair with streaks that changed color with her mood—her racing stripes, Ted called them.

"Why not?" Lola asked.

"Guess we'll find out," Kat said.

Ted went on. "Anyway, this…meeting, this whole company actually, I see it as some sort of evil bakery. With me standing outside, nose against the glass, looking at all these women I can't have."

"Dude. Enough with the 'she's out of my league' number," said Kat.

"No, I mean because Lola will kick my ass."

"Me and what stepladder?" asked Lola. She was nearly a foot shorter than Ted, even when his Red Sox cap matted down his unbrushably dense dark-blond hair.

Ted was referring to AskLola.com's official position on—that is, against—flings at the office. Sure, the economy was booming the way it had been right before Lola had graduated college. (Right after, she'd had to wait out the slump waiting tables in nursing shoes.) Still, who wanted to worry if the person they'd gone home with the night before would respect them in the morning meeting? So, no random hookups with co-workers and certainly not with superiors. Lola would, however, green light serious—and decorous—workplace courtship. Hey, that's where you spend your time, and at least you know your crush has a job.

As they walked, however, Lola was too distracted to reassure Ted. There were far too many other things going on around her. Someone's robot cat was chasing a pink ball. The blender at the juice bar hummed; Lola smelled beets. Wait, wasn't that an Indigo Girl?

"They're playing on *Chyck with a Y* today," said Ted, referring to Ovum's flagship news/talk TV show. The song "Closer to Fine" was a standard on the CD mixes he made for heartbroken friend-girls with whom he was secretly in love.

"'Y' as in chromosome, as in 'See, relax, we like men,'" Kat explained.

"Right," said Lola, having heard nothing. The group reached the Tube, Ovum's dining/hangout area.

"Shiitake, fontina, or fiddlehead?"

A guy in jeans, an apron, and a toque was talking to Lola.

"I'm sorry, what?" asked Lola.

"Omelets to order for the new folks," Mr. Toque explained.

"Oh, my. Okay, um, everything? Thanks."

"Sure. Just egg whites, or whole?"

"Oh. Whole, please. You can even give me other people's yolks. Hate to waste," Lola said, turning to follow Kat's walleyed gaze toward the coffee urn. Oh boy. Peet's coffee. The best ever—this side of the Tiber, anyway. Normally you can't even *get* it in New York.

And in the middle of the conference table? A giant box of Krispy Kremes.

Yeah. Lola was sure she'd done the right thing.

"Here, I'll get some Peet's for us," offered Kat. "Lo?"

"Yeah, thanks," Lola said.

"Ted?"

"Sure."

"And how do you take your coffee?" asked Kat, gamely feeding Ted a straight line.

"Like my men."

Lola rolled her eyes. Too easy! "You're fired," she said.

"Sorry!" said Ted. "Haven't had my coffee yet."

Lola took an oval seat and glanced around the table. The group was mostly women, mostly in their late twenties or early thirties, diverse and attractive in a totally approachable, non-Condé-Nast sort of way. A thick silver packet adorned with a hologram of the Ovum logo lay at each place.

A few seats to her left, Lola recognized the trademark frumpery of Gilda Perez, the tack-sharp gender-issues columnist from Frisson.com for whom Ovum had created a head writer/producer job on *Chyck with a Y*. With no makeup, hair-colored hair, reading glasses, plain beige crewneck, she looked fantastic. Not because she'd made a successful, labored attempt to be anti-chic, but because she truly just didn't give a shit.

Gilda's hiring was one thing among many that reassured Lola about Ovum's intentions. So was the fact that Ovum had tapped Tammy Abedon—New York's wittiest and most charming female comic—for *Chyck's* plum host spot, even though she was not thin. Lola adored Tammy and thought she represented everything good and right and hilarious. She had chatted with her at various goody-bag parties and now hoped, high-school-giddy, that now the two of them would get to be actual friends.

"Welcome to Ovum, everyone!" Taking her place at the head of the oval table was Angela Chan, yet another ace-in-the-hole hire for Ovum. Black jeans, spiky boots, orange wrap, dark hair cropped close in a look that on anyone less formidable would have been called gamine or pixie. Angela Chan had been the media director at Planned Parenthood and a reporter in places like Bosnia. (It was she who'd shown the world that systematic cruelty to women was a military strategy, not just a fact of war.) She had worked in the White House at some point. Now she was VP of programming, if Lola recalled correctly. Apparently Angela also played bass and dabbled in extreme snowboarding. She'd been on the cover of *Time* when it broke the news that lesbians were in.

"Basically, we're just here to say hello and tell you how happy we are to have you with us," said Angela with a genuine smile. "I guess other companies would call this an 'orientation,' but we find that term patronizing. We just haven't had time to think of another name for it. Anyway, we hired you because you're smart, you're visionaries; we don't need to tell you where you are, what to do, or where you are going."

Angela laughed and tilted her head as she took a sip of her Peet's. "We're not the kind of network that thinks it needs to spell out for women how a 401k plan works."

Lola made a mental note to find out how a 401k plan worked.

"Main thing is," Angela went on, "we're really glad you're here. We're really glad we're *all* here to do this important—and fun—work for women and the people who love them. And when we're done at this brief meeting, please remember to take advantage of our 'podular' furniture system—the desks roll around so that you can interface with everyone around you."

Lola peeked down. Sure enough, the conference oval was on wheels. So was the coffee hutch.

"I also bring warm greetings—and immense regrets—from our founder and CEO, Madeleine "Maddy" North. She wishes she could welcome you herself, but she's meeting with the UN right now to see how Ovum can aid international efforts to support sustainable farming for female heads of households." Angela glanced at her watch. "Okay, gotta run. Any specific questions, I'll be glad to take them offline."

Offline? We're online?

"Cheers!" Angela was gone in a flash of pashmina.

•

Lola, Ted and Kat were back at their desks, hopped up on French roast and feeling downright smug. "Everyone here is so cool. Everything here is so cool," said Kat.

"I know, right?!" grinned Lola, sitting cross-legged in her seat as always, despite her mom's warnings about curvature of the spine. (Lola had read *Deenie*. She knew.) "But okay, let's keep setting up. We may be getting paid, but we still have work to do."

And checking on my Internet suitors counts as work, Lola silently reasoned. She pulled her wavy dyed-orange hair (from Clairol's "Frustrate Your Parents" line of home dyes) into a topknot, turned to her iMac (also orange), and logged on to PitchingWoo.com. Ping! There were three messages in Lola's PitchingWoo mailbox.

Lola's take on Internet dating was another of her well-known positions. Internet matchmaking should, she insisted, be part of any single's diversified dating portfolio.

And she had to practice what she preached, right?

On the one hand, Lola never referred to her own love life in her column. In fact, on her short list of public enemies were those women whose *oeuvres* were basically guy-bashing mini-memoirs of their own lame dates and loneliness, and/or lame dates and blow jobs. As Lola often pointed out—in a tone that Kat gently warned her could sound self-righteous—*her* column was for, and about, her readers. *Not* herself.

But on the other hand, Lola's column *was* about dating and relationships. She had to do fieldwork, didn't she? How else could she call herself an expert?

Lola clicked on the first message, from a young man who'd enjoyed her profile and wanted to introduce himself.

TO: Truffle

"Truffle"—an homage to Lola's favorite fungus, hunted by her favorite fauna (dogs and pigs)—was Lola's PitchingWoo username.

...About me, let's see: Dancing, story telling, hanging out in the record shop–these are the things that I've tried to cultivate.

Oh yes, the record shop thing takes *years.*
Delete.

TO: Truffle
FROM: CatMan
RE: Thanks for your note

Ah! She'd liked this guy's profile and had sent him a quick note the day before.

...Unfortunately, I am so NOT the "dog person" you mention in your preferences. Last summer, when a dog licked my face, I fainted.

Delete.

TO: Truffle
FROM: Boqueron
RE: RE: RE: RE: RE: BUFFY

Yay. Boqueron (a type of Spanish anchovy) was Lola's current alpha e-male. They'd been corresponding several times daily for several days, which is like seven years in Internet time. His profile read: "I own a glue gun, a power drill, and seven varieties of olive oil." He was witty, a strong e-conversationalist, had some sort of tech job, and was clearly an anchovyphile (a big plus for Lola and her salt-craving palate), with much to say about *Buffy the Vampire Slayer.*

Lola clicked, expecting another assemblage of astute pop culture insights and chatty biographical inquiries that were making it harder and harder for her to conceal her job description.

`Enough typing. Let's meet.`

Eee! Of course, now she'd have to start thinking about when and how to tell this guy she was *the* Lola. It was the only part of her job she really hated. Guys got intimidated. One had asked, "So will dating you be like playing football against a team who has my playbook?" She had to admit that he was clever. And also that it might.

Lola willed herself to log out, figuring she'd be coy and make Boqueron wait a few hours. Plus, she still had plenty of unpacking to do.

She picked up another handful of books—*Backlash, The Beauty Myth, Harry Potter and the Prisoner of Azkaban*—and realized her tippy-top shelf was just out of reach. Kicking off her clogs, she began to climb up on her desk.

Whoops! The desk suddenly slid to the left. The books clattered down; Lola bonked her arm on her computer.

"Riiiight. Wheels," she said aloud without looking behind her, still splayed, pratfall-style, on her desk.

"Yep. They'll roll right out from under you," she heard Kat warn, too late.

Yeah. Yeah. This was definitely the right thing.

2

"I'll have a dragon roll, one hamachi with scallion, and one spicy tuna, please. And edamame," said Lola. "Oh, wait, you have soft shell crab? Could you make the dragon roll a spider roll, then? Thanks."

Sushi Tuesday—Lola could get used to this. Every week, three sushi chefs moved their trays of glistening fish and sticky rice into the juice bar area. Kat, a couple places ahead of Lola in line, had already pointed out that the fridges in The Tube were already filling up with "seconds" that people were evidently saving for dinner.

"Thanks," Lola said, accepting her little oval tray and noticing a small sign at the end of the counter.

ANY REMAINING SUSHI WILL BE DONATED TO THE JAMIE LEE CURTIS BIRTHING AND REPARENTING CENTER

"Well, *that's* not the best idea," came a voice from behind her left shoulder. Lola turned. *Yee.* This must be The Talented Mister Right: equal parts Matt Damon and Jude Law, with a soupcon of Phillip Seymour Hoffman mischief.

"What do you mean?" asked Lola, smiling as she reached for a set of chopsticks. She could get used to him, too.

"Sushi's not a great idea for pregnant women."

Too bad he was married. Really, why else would such a girly factoid occur to him? In fact, Lola was surprised she hadn't though of it herself. (One of her favorite ways to torture her mother was to explain that the reason why she wasn't married—and bearing grandchildren—was that she simply could not go nine months without sushi. Mrs. Somerville's worries were thus so compounded—Spinster child! *Anisakidosis!*—that she wouldn't know where to start, so she would stop.)

"Oh, *right,*" said Lola.

"My brother-in-law actually went sushi-celibate in solidarity when my sister was pregnant," said Talented. "Now *that's* love."

And *that's* a ray of hope, thought Lola. Cheekbones, cleft chin, good shoes—and ah, no ring. Flaw, please.

"I'm Miles Farmington, by the way. You're—"

"Lola Somerville," she said, at the same time he did.

"I'm a fan," Miles explained. "You helped me through a bad breakup."

Flattering! And it's so awesome that we work together! Oh, wait, the opposite. "Oh, great! I mean, I'm sorry. Ha ha, I mean, thanks," Lola said. "What do you do here?"

Please say, "I temp."

"I work for Fern."

Hell's bells! Fern Gellar was the VP of Technology, basically the only woman currently in the industry with the credentials for that title. She was one of the first women admitted to Systers, the influential electronic mailing list for female engineers with membership strictly limited to the cream of the techno-crop. Ovum had wooed her from Microsoft, who had wooed her from Sun Microsystems, who had wooed her from Yahoo!, who had wooed her from a vigilante hacker cabal. "I basically run the technology project management department. Developing features on the sites, adding broadband, streaming, that whole thing," said Miles.

"Oh, cool. We should talk—"

"—about how to add video and other goodies to your site."

"Definitely," said Lola. "That would be great."

"I know where you sit. I'll come find you." Miles waved and headed off just as Kat appeared on her way back from the Tube.

"Wow," said Kat.

"Right?" Lola said. "Oh, well."

•

Kat dropped off an extra plate of sushi at Ted's desk. Usually, the only fish he'd do was tuna (white, not light), and vegetables were a challenge. But since they'd ordered sushi a lot when they worked at Lola's place, Kat had trained him to eat crab stick and often used it as a Trojan horse for cucumber.

Ted thanked Kat.

"Dear Diary," Kat said. "A great day. I got Ted to eat omega-3 fatty acids plus green vegetables."

"Dear Diary," said Ted, "A great day. I confirmed that if I keep pretending I don't like good food, Kat will continue to bring it to me."

Lola made room on her desk for her sushi and tackled the "DO?" pile of advice-seeking letters that Ted had culled for her.

Dear Lola,

I really think this new girl's the one. We both love chocolate, puppies, and great movies...

Ooh, do you also both watch *E.R.* and fear fire?"

Would that it were that simple.

•

Meanwhile, Kat and Ted were huddled around Ted's computer with Douglas, one of Miles's underlings. Douglas was demonstrating the new filtering system he'd worked around the clock to develop for Lola's now-tripled volume of letters, to make it easier for her to work around the clock to answer them. Lola's team had wanted to roll all their desks together and set up the systems simultaneously, but their power cords didn't reach. Whoever had masterminded the "podular" system had forgotten that Ovum's desktop computers were not wireless.

"Curses!" came Doug's voice. Lola glanced over—screen freeze. "Ow, Vulcan Nerve Pinch," he said, pressing Control, Shift, Command, Return, Escape, Power, and "U" simultaneously to perform some sort of extreme restart. Kat and Ted looked on admiringly.

Douglas was cute, even though Star Trek references are to single men as cats are to single women. Tall, maybe over six feet. (Lola, at 5'2" in wedges, thought anyone over 5'8" was over six feet.) He had clunky glasses, floppy hair. Lola had a sense that he was the boy equivalent of the librarian who, at the end of the video, whips off her spectacles and hairnet and starts shaking her money maker all over the shelves. Maybe he'd be good for Kat. If Kat didn't have her long-distance thing with that arty boy Clive. Lola worried about that. Anyway.

Lola went back to her pile of letters, resolving not to mess around with PitchingWoo.com until she was done.

•

The din in the office decrescendoed abruptly to a hum. Good Lord, where did the day go?

Every day at precisely four PM, all the TV monitors in the office switched automatically from Ovum's own programming to DSBC (the Disney-Seagram channel). It was time for *Penelope!*—the most popular talk show in any and all media heretofore invented throughout the universe.

The uberguru Penelope had first begun to draw attention as spokesperson for NOW during the battles of the earlier 90s: *Planned Parenthood v. Casey,* William Kennedy Smith, Anita Hill, Paula Jones. She was the first pundit to articulate the issues of gender and class at work in the Tonya Harding/Nancy Kerrigan incident. Penelope's feminist credentials—normally, of course, a dark mark in the mainstream—seemed to have been mitigated by various other achievements, including her bestselling line of cookbooks *(Cooking with Power);* her chart-topping pop albums featuring collaborations with Madonna, Andrea Bocelli, the Buena Vista Social Club, Reba McEntire and exiled Iranian pop diva Googoosh; and the fact that whenever she got arrested in the act of defending a women's health clinic, her mugshots circulated as pin-ups on the Internet.

Penelope was indeed a beauty. Her real parents' identity was unknown—she'd grown up in foster homes in Fargo—but according to her ethnic makeup of record she could have been, were she two generations younger, the love child of Mariah Carey and Tiger Woods.

Bottom line: when Penelope said "Jump!" people said, "Where can I buy one?" There was talk of a run for president.

And every day at 4 PM, everyone at Ovum pretended to work while watching *Penelope*—for research. While purists and cynics dismissed her as a McGirlPower sellout, no one could deny the end result: Penelope defined the issues for the masses.

Today's topic: The International Campaign to Ban Landmines. "What we endeavor to do is to take an issue and 'put a face on it' for you," Penelope was saying. 'Today, that's a painful task, as our guest—a young farmer from rural Croatia—was severely disfigured when a mine exploded near her home. We'll also show you how women and children are the disproportionate victims of these hidden killers—and—okay, I'm not supposed to say this, but...we'll show you how you can combat Senator Helmsley Vestibule's efforts to get the UN to ignore this dire situation."

"That poor Penelope is so unattractive, and not at all a catch," said Kat. "Oh wait, the opposite. So when's she gonna marry that guy?"

Kat wasn't talking about the senator. Penelope's frequent target was the cranky and powerful old-timer known for heading up the new Senate subcommittee on

Gender Relations and, speaking of gender relations, being a strong proponent of generous endowments (as in top-heavy interns, not National Arts). No one really knew why his wife Harriet stuck around, or what she'd seen in him in the first place. They'd met on the Hill, but she hadn't worked since their third date. Then again, Lola was well aware that some women stayed with men for far less than senatorial perks.

What Kat was wondering, Lola knew, was whether Penelope would ever marry her long-term boyfriend, the heartthrob tennis champ Leo Cameroon. Speculation about why the two hadn't yet tied the knot ranged from "she's his beard" to "he's her beard." Either way, Lola had a feeling there was more to it.

"They'll never get married," said Lola. "That would be boring, like if Mulder and Scully hooked up."

Though Penelope gossip was normally irresistible, that was about all Lola felt like saying at the moment. She put on her headphones—the universal symbol for "do not disturb"—even though she didn't bother to stick in a CD. No time for *Penelope!* today; she felt like quitting before midnight for once.

She paused, staring at the blank New Document that was to be this week's column.

Okay, first just one quick PitchingWoo.com check.

Score! A note from Boqueron before she'd even answered him.

```
I spoke too soon, I'm afraid. This week is already
a total meltdown. Let's stylus each other in for
next, for sure?
```

Sigh. But fair enough; Lola didn't have time this week, either. She wrote him a quick note back in agreement.

Ping! One more message.

```
FROM: Da Bard
RE: HI THERE MA CHERE
IS IT A CRIME / TO WRITE MY PROFILE IN RHYME?
```

Yes.

Delete.

Lola logged off PitchingWoo.com.

But before she could retackle her WORKwork, Ding! Instant message from Annabel, Lola's best friend since seventh grade. While everyone else was going new media, Annabel had gone old school and taken off to spend a year doing community service with AmeriCorps and meeting hot rock climbers in

Montana. She called it her "Junior League Abroad." Lola missed her terribly, but at least Annabel was online pretty much whenever she wasn't on belay.

annabel2k: whassup? they giving u free sushi now or what?
hernamewaslola: every tuesday.

3

URGENT

OVUM-WIDE MEETING

Today

4 PM

in the Incubator

Frappuccinos (with added calcium) will be served

For company-wide communications, Ovum used the old-fashioned system: flyers in the bathroom stalls. (E-mails posed too high a risk of being forwarded to the hungry-for-anything-at-Ovum press.) Otherwise, Ovum's restroom was anything but dated: it was sleek, white, infused with varying "motivational" scents (depending on the time of day/week/month)—and co-ed. Lola called it the Ally McBathroom. She and her team had all gotten used to it faster than they'd expected, perhaps because the hourly right-to-their-desks deliveries of spring water (regular or caffeinated) kept them in there a lot. (Also, Lola and Kat couldn't complain about the vast and varied unbleached tampon supply.)

"Wonder what the meeting's about." It was Miles, arriving to wash his hands right next to Lola. Hell's bells! Lola thought crazily, now he knows I pee.

"Maybe they're announcing a big merger with FairerSex.com," Lola kidded, referring to the company that would be Ovum's competition if Ovum covered such issues as bikini stress and "man-pleasing moves."

"Ha! You know I used to work at FS, right?" asked Miles. "It was all women in edit and fashion, all men on the tech side. Lame. Actually, the structure really hasn't changed that much. They should call it LearnedHelplessness.com."

I love him, thought Lola. See, it's not just his eyes.

"Yep. I worked there, too." Tammy Abedon, host of *Chyck with a Y,* had arrived at the sink on Lola's left. "Until they told me that if I wanted to move from head writer to host of one of their Internet radio shows, I would have to lose weight. For a *radio* show."

"That makes total sense," said Lola. "Oh, wait."

Miles smiled and shook his head. The three exchanged more thank-God-we're-*here* pleasantries and parted ways.

•

Lola headed back to her desk, detouring around Susan Sarandon's entourage as she tried to think of ways to stop thinking about Miles. Today's ambient music was a live jazz band (all-female); evidently the idea was to get employees to think freely and improvise.

Kat and Douglas, either inspired or oblivious, were busy updating the AskLola.com message boards to accommodate the increased traffic. They looked cute together: Kat, Doug, and all those new visitors.

Quick PitchingWoo check. Lola clicked and skimmed.

OCCUPATION: First Officer, Starship Enterprise

Delete.

ME: Handsome, physically fit, look a bit like David Duchovny.

Oooh!

My hobbies include reading, songwriting, ventriloquism.

Delete.

Okay. Now, for real, it was time to make a dent—before urgent-meeting-o'clock—in the never-shrinking letter pile.

Dear Lola,
At school, I'm part of the cool geek crowd, if that makes any sense. I mean, we're smart, but

it's not like we have our own online gaming characters or anything. Anyway, would you believe it, my girlfriend—I mean, my ex—dumped me for the captain of the football team. Evidently I am trapped in some Freddie Prinze, Jr. movie.

Lola, it hurts to see them together. How can I get this girl back for being such a bee-atch, not to mention a cliché?

—SWD (Dweeb) Seeks Revenge

Lola laughed out loud. God, kids are smart.

Dear Dweeb,

Here's the thing about revenge. You think it's gonna make you feel good, but it doesn't. You think it's gonna teach someone a lesson, but it doesn't. Revenge is TACKY. Revenge makes you look bad. And when you look bad, you feel worse. Do you really want Jennifer Hate Hewitt to think you're the psycho hose beast ex from hell? (Do you really want the captain of the football team to kick your ass?)

So better yet: don't let 'em see you sweat. Let her wonder why you don't seem upset about the breakup. *That* hurts. See? Revenge, schmevenge. You're above that. Hold your head high, and you'll get yourself on track for that other cliché: the one where the geek gets the girl.

Love,

Lola

Not bad, Somerville. Proofread, spell check, save. Next.

Oops. Lola's Palm Pilot beeped its 3:55 reminder for the 4:00 company meeting.

Waaait! Four PM was *Penelope!* o'clock. Surely the staff would mutiny. Then again, who couldn't use a Frappuccino? Lola shrugged. She and her staff joined the general migration toward the Incubator.

"I'm glad they're serving Frappuccinos, because I love them but I can't order them with a straight face," said Ted, stopping to tie his sneaker. Someday I'll get Kat to teach him about shoes, thought Lola.

The Incubator was the vast central conference area, near the staircase up to a mezzanine that was to be the twenty-four-hour day-care area (still under construction, assorted permits pending). The meeting room was encircled by curved white normal-height walls, which of course didn't come close to reaching the ceiling far above. Every surface in the area, including the oval table up front, was made of write-on white board and the chairs were all equipped with special pens. This was to encourage (and record) non-linear, spontaneous thinking, especially when employees gathered for a brainstorming session (officially known as an Exercise in Fertility).

Employees were still pouring in. The staff had actually already outgrown the Incubator's seating capacity; Lola, Ted, and Kat, like several others, found spots to lean against the walls. Frosty plastic cups were being passed around. Lola noticed that the jazz band was on break. She fixed her gaze on Gilda Perez's right shoulder as a way not to look for Miles.

Angela Chan was making her way to the front of the area, adjusting her wireless microphone. The large oval video screen behind the front table flickered to life, showing a time code against a dark blue background. The crowd hushed; the only sound in the room was that of straws in slush. If we're missing *Penelope!* this better be good.

"Hi, everyone." Angela was one of those people who could wear those calf-length cardigan sweaters that would look like hell on, say, Lola. "Since I know how busy you are, I'll get right to the point. Well, actually, Maddy will get right to the point." On cue, Madeleine North appeared on the video screen. She was in some sort of nondescript studio, wearing a beige suit jacket accented with a batik scarf, no doubt a gift from an Indonesian artists' community she'd helped in some way.

"Hello! Greetings from Palo Alto," said the screen Maddy. "So sorry I can't be there today, but I'm out here trying to nail down some very important distribution deals. Still, I wanted to be the one to deliver some pretty mind-blowing news about someone who's going to become part of the Ovum network. It's something that's been in the works for a while, and we finally came up with an arrangement that will make everyone happy—and that just may permanently change the face of television programming for women. So without further ado, women and gentlemen, please welcome...Penelope."

Gasp.

Penelope herself was walking toward the front of the room, smiling her $37 billion smile. She looked impeccably understated in a plain white shirt and pumpkin silk pants. Greeting Angela with a peck on the cheek, she turned to face the crowd.

"Hello, Ovum!" she exclaimed. Not knowing what else to do, someone—was it Miles?—started clapping. Soon the whole room was cheering. Penelope beamed, said a few words to Angela, and then made a convincingly modest shushing gesture to the crowd, who obeyed.

"Thank you! Thank you so much, truly," said Penelope.

Said Penelope! Lola, Kat and Ted stared at each other. Penelope! Words—even stunned looks—failed. It does not get huger than this.

"That's right, I'm one of you now. My show will be on your channel; my website on your server," Penelope continued. "I am grateful for the opportunity I had at DSBC—I really was able to push the envelope," Penelope went on, her voice rising. "But fuck envelopes! I want to push the *issues,* free and unconstrained by The Man."

Ted glanced at Kat and Lola as if to say, "Did she just say 'fuck envelopes'?" Lola nodded, cracking a smile.

Penelope reached preacher level. "So now. I. Have come. To work for. The WO-man!"

Applause. Incredulous looks. Even Madeleine, via videoconference, seemed to sense that it was time and began to clap herself.

4

Like everyone else in the office, Lola and her team were debriefing in their "pod." "I mean, as long as she means that whole thing about being able to be edgier here. As opposed to this meaning that *we're* going more mainstream," Lola was saying. "Hah, can you see that? '*Chyck with a Y,* featuring Harriet Vestibule.'" Lola cracked herself up. Her colleagues smiled and nodded vaguely. They were still coming down from the Penelope high.

"Maybe Leo will dump her for me," mused Kat.

"Or me," said Ted.

Beat.

"Sorry."

•

Lola had two voice mails. One from her landlord noting that she hadn't used the gas in weeks and wondering if she was dead. The other from her mom asking if the Penelope rumors were true. But first, Annabel, who had just logged on.

hernamewaslola: you're not going to believe this
annabel2k: what now, fondue friday?
hernamewaslola: penelope
annabel2k: she finally having you on the show?

Ah, Lola's pet peeve. E. Ron Wilson's publishing imprint, Pigs and Nuts Books, was owned by a subsidiary of Disney-Seagram. When Penelope did shows about relationships, she pretty much had to have Dr. Wilson as her "expert"—barely masking her distaste when she did. So, Annabel actually had an even better point than she realized.

hernamewaslola: maybe she will, now that you mention it—SHE JUST JOINED THE OVUM NETWORK!—her show, her site, EVERYTHING!

annabel2k: ***NO WAY***

hernamewaslola: way.

•

As promised, Lola had her own weekly segment on *Chyck With a Y,* where she got to dish with Tammy about a relationship issue of the week. She adored it. Before now, the only advice the "pundette" had ever been asked to give on television involved either a small number ("Five Ways to Make Your Summer Fling...Love in Fall," "The Three Keys to a Perfect Marriage," "Party of One: Totally Alone in the World—and Loving It!") or a huge exclamation point ("Trend Flash: 90s Women Love Casual Sex!") That, or comments on the basic theme "The Gender Wars Explained: We're Bitter Because Men Keep Not Marrying Us."

On these shows, Lola had tried to find a way to balance her desire to promote her website—and, she hoped, enlightened viewpoint—with her desire not to die of shame, or boredom. Each time, she'd challenged herself to come up with advice that did not involve recommending the use of either bubble bath, or "I" statements—as in, "I *feel* that you're not hearing me." Of the latter approach—a pet of E. Ron Wilson's—Lola had written, "I *feel* that I sound like a jackass."

She'd also tried, when she could, to place things in the bigger picture. Women enjoying casual sex? "These survey results—instead of leaving women trapped in the old Heidi / Ho complex—point to the nuance and breadth of women's sexual choices and motivations," Lola might say. "But we shouldn't take them as license or mandate to think, 'Hooray! Now we can be all, Wham, bam, thank you...dude! That's a pyrrhic victory. After all, the spurious promise of the sexual revolution..." She'd press her luck until the host glazed over, or interrupted. ("So what's the best thing to wear for casual sex?")

Lola had, after all, always believed that the NEWSnews offered far better insights than "research" commissioned by the toothpaste people ("97% of respondents say that fresh breath is key in good kissing!") or, actually, that love and relationships were in many cases what drove the NEWSnews to begin with. As she had once written in her column in an open letter to the commander-in-chief: "Relationships run us, and some of us run the world. So we might as well handle them right, yes?" She was sick of relationships being treated as fluff rather than bedrock.

So Lola's *Chyck* segment was basically the cable show she would have done in her basement if she'd ever gotten around to it, only with much better production values and Tammy as the host. She even got to suggest the topic and work with her team and *Chyck* producers to develop the scope. And within a couple of months, she had the process, and her presence, down pat. Does it get better than this?

Today, for example, Lola was set to debate *News America* columnist Simon Snood, who had recently written that women should quit being so picky and waiting for their impossible ideal of the perfect man because the longer they tarry, the more likely it is that their babies will have birth defects.

I am going to have a freaking field day, thought Lola, leaning down to change out of her Pumas and into her TV shoes. Geez, every day here is a field day, in a big way—a bigger way than she'd really had time to let sink in until, for some reason, right now. As Lola sat up, goofily, she pinched herself. Ow. Yep, well, if this is dreaming, the Spielberg people must be behind the special effects. And if not, God, is this what you call arrived? Am I "set" at 29? And not even in that wonky Science Fair, Pre-Med, Med School, Doctor, check check check check kind of way. Is it actually possible that I could have realized dreams I didn't even realize I had, just by following my heart?

hernamewaslola: yo. everything rules right now. just had to say.
annabel2k: right on. ☺!!!!!!!!!!

And when you have arrived, whatever that means for you, isn't that when the right guy does, too? Isn't that the healthy way it happens? When you're not looking for a boyfriend to spackle in the gaps you haven't filled in yourself? When you've got all your ducks in a row…except one really cute duck? Isn't that what Online Lola tells people all the time? Yeah. It's finally my time, she told herself. Everything's coming together. I mean, if this isn't *it*, then what is?

Phone. Makeup. (Ovum had tried, earnestly enough, to have the talent appear *au naturel*, but they had to concede to the focus groups that without it, everyone on camera looked really, really bad.) "Lola! You're late."

"Sorry! I'm on my way!" Indeed, Lola thought.

•

Lola, Simon, and Tammy sat in the oval-backed armchairs of the studio area they called the Salon, adjacent the actual VW Bug used for Ovum's auto mechanics show, *The Shop*. The Salon was a simple open-air platform with changeable colored lights underfoot that Tammy had nicknamed her mood floor.

Stand by; three, two, rolling. Cue Tammy. "We've all got intimacy issues, but only Ovum has *Intimacy Issues* with our own Lola Somerville of AskLola.com!"

Lola smiled. "Hi, Tammy. Thanks." Hee, hee. Lola wanted to swing her feet in glee. Look at me. I am king of the world, in a world where women get to be king. And men do too, only they do not feel all threatened by the women who—oh. On TV. Paying attention.

"Our guest today is *News America* columnist Simon Snood," Tammy was saying. "Welcome, Mr. Snood."

Snood. Hee hee. Dude. Snickerdoodle. Doody. God I love my jo—Oh. On TV. Paying attention.

Snood—bespectacled, pale-skinned, unintentionally tonsured—could have been anywhere from thirty to fifty. Was he baby-faced, or crabby beyond his years? Impossible to say.

"In his most recent piece, Mr. Snood expressed his concern that single women have crossed the line from 'maintaining high standards' to being downright picky, and they're doing themselves—and possibly our society, am I right?—a disservice."

Ovum employees passing by slowed down to listen as Snood boldly began to champion his lost cause, and Lola finally, silently, gathered her wits. "Between thirty and fifty percent of high-achieving women in America do not have children," stated Snood, the studio lights tiddlywinking off his round glasses. "The longer they wait, the more likely it is that their babies will have birth defects—and thus that we will live in a once-great nation of undcr-achievers."

Lola was more than ready now. "Mr. Snood, do you think that women just stand around and 'wait' to have children the way they wait for the bus? Do you actually think that the women who really want to have children aren't making an effort—as in, trying to balance making a living and making the acquaintance of a worthy prospective dad?" Lola asked, adding, "Or co-parent?"

"That's just it—perhaps women need to stop fetishizing the concept of balance," Snood replied.

I shall have nightmares about this guy saying "fetish," Lola thought.

"Perhaps they do need to focus more—and more realistically—on finding a mate," Snood went on. "When women try to 'have it all' they put us all at risk."

What are you even doing here? Mr. Snood, fire your handlers.

"It is true, isn't it, that later births can carry higher risks for all involved?" asked Tammy, trying to be fair.

"Yes," Lola and Snood said together. Snood forged ahead, sort of. "Amniocentesis is not a panacea."

While you're at it, fire your thesaurus.

"So as long as women continue to be so picky…."

"Picky, Mr. Snood? About the person we're going to spend the rest of our life with?"

"Well, I'm certainly not saying—"

"I'm not sure what you *are* saying, Mr. Snood, because six months ago you wrote an editorial blaming women's 'low standards' for our nation's high divorce rate." (Ted, and Nexis, you are the man. Men. People. Whatever.)

"Miss Somerville," Snood cleared his throat and placed his hands stiffly on his seersuckered knees. "Every thirty-something single woman I know is waiting for her knight in shining armor to ride down Madison Avenue in his Porsche and whisk her off to the Hamptons," he said.

"Lola?" Tammy asked.

Lola looked Snood in the eye. "Madison Avenue goes *uptown*."

"That's our show for today," said Tammy.

Lola felt triumphant, almost. That was a little too easy—unfair, really. At least she hadn't stooped to point out that her opponent was not himself wearing a ring.

Apparently, though, Snood didn't hold a grudge. After the show, he asked her out.

Lola politely declined. Not just because Miles was coming toward her.

"Hey. You kicked ass. Of course, you always do."

Why do guys always look so perfect in just a white shirt and jeans? Not just when they're complimenting you?

"Thanks," Lola said. "But come on! Fish in a barrel."

"Maybe," Miles said. "But he's clearly not *that* stupid."

"I guess not—"

"I mean, didn't he just ask you out?"

OhGodOhGod. "Yes! Indeed! He has the genius of ten men!" Deflect with humor. Leave now.

"So you're going, right?" Leave soon.

"Back to work? Yessir."

"No, to the party." Leave pretty soon.

"Party?"

"Oh, you haven't seen the company-wide e-mail yet."

Company-wide *e-mail?* Must be something they *want* to leak.

"Ovum's throwing a bigass party this Saturday in honor of the whole Penelope thing."

"Oh, cool."

"Yep. It's gonna be here, and apparently they're getting that great salsa singer India, and—get this—Madeleine North herself may actually show up!"

"Hah, right! But wow, they must have had this in the works for a while."

"Yeah. So anyway. I'll see you there, huh?"

"Of course!"

"With Snood as your arm candy, right?"

Eeeuw. "Of course!" Lola laughed. Helped her choke down the rising fear.

5

"Lola? Lola. You have *got* to see this," Kat said without turning her head. She and Douglas were working on something or other. "Sorry Doug, but this is a Code Red."

Lola walked over. "Here, Greta just IMed me this link," Kat said. Greta was in Miles's department; she coded stuff for streaming. "*Look.*"

Lola peered at the screen. She saw a fuzzy mass of black and white sort of like an ultrasound. Please don't tell me Kat's old enough to have pregnant friends who think this is interesting.

"Wait, they're just too close to the camera," Kat said. "Here we go."

What suddenly materialized was hands-down, the Lord God King #1 ultra turbo uber most adorable thing Lola had ever seen: a mother panda cradling her

Newborn.

Panda.

CUB.

Of course! She'd just read about this: the successful birth at the San Diego Zoo—and the 24-hour *Panda-cam* in the den. This was even better than *Real World: San Francisco.* It was quite possibly the best use of the Internet ever. Pandas were now up there with dogs and pigs. Kat and Lola were riveted.

Ted looked over their shoulders. "We really need to find Lola a boyfriend," he said.

"Ted!" Lola protested.

"Someone's at least got to give you a stuffed one of those," Ted replied.

"Search all cars going the wrong way on Madison," Douglas winked.

•

hernamewaslola: yo. http://www.SanDiegoZoo.org/Panda-cam.html RIGHT NOW
annabel2k: hold on
annabel2k: OMIGOD. I'm swearing off television.

annabel2k: and books.
annabel2k: and men.

•

Dear Lola,
I snooped on my boyfriend's Ebay account and found that he's been bidding on an engagement ring. *Lola, he is getting my ring on Ebay!* How do I stop him?
—Going, Going, Gone?

Dear GGG,
You don't. Girl, that's what you get. For your ring, and for snooping. Not that snooping can never be justified, but here's the thing: once someone's doing it, something's *already* wrong. What drove you to dig in the first place? Insecurity? Greed? Lipstick on his collar? Your reasons may not be terribly serious, or at all deal-breaking, but still: there's a matter of trust here. I don't care if he gives you a ring from a gumball machine; mine *those* depths before you say yes.
Love,
Lola

•

One down. I'm allowed to read PitchingWoo now. Two notes.

FROM: Moscow on Hudson
RE: Howdy!
Hello! I am single Russian gentlemen looking to correspond with nice lady and improve my English. Your profile looks very appalling to me.

Lola laughed out loud. Forward to Annabel, Kat, Ted—and oh, why not, Doug—and…*delete.*

Ooh.

FROM: Boqueron
RE: RE: RE: RE: bizzy this week
Yeah, recycled subject line still applies this week. I am so sorry. Not like you're exactly on vaca either, I know. And I'd try to jam something in but I want to do our meeting more justice than some 11 PM rendezvous where we'll nod off in our lychee martinis. But wait, I have an idea: how about some enchanted...Sunday brunch? This weekend? Lemme know.

Hey, that works, thought Lola. It's the morning after the big Ovum party, but whatever. At this rate, when else? Resisting the urge to advanced-search Zagats.com for "Romantic + Brunch," she dropped him a quick "Sure!" note back and willed herself to leave the time and place up to him.

•

hernamewaslola: so what should i wear to this big party at which i want to look good for me, not for others, and in particular not for others who are superiors whose names are like the word "kilometers," only not metric?
annabel2k: nothing?
hernamewaslola: ok.
hernamewaslola: and over that?
annabel2k: ha ha. ok, the lil blue cynthia rowley. with the boots.
hernamewaslola: right, duh. thanks. ps *finally brunch with* ***BOQUERON****...**at 11:30 the next am!***
annabel2k: who-hoo! yes, and good distraction from "meters"
hernamewaslola: right.
annabel2k: where brunch?
hernamewaslola: cafe reggio
annabel2k: cute. i'll be up—call from restroom!
hernamewaslola: always do. ok, column now. ciao xoxo
annabel2k: xoxo

•

Dear Lola,
My boyfriend rules. Adorable, kind, funny, successful, worships me. His one flaw—which is almost, but not quite, balanced out by the "worships me" part—is that he's a little squirrelly on the marriage thing. (A lot squirrelly. It's been five years.)

Meanwhile, I'm ready. Rrrrrrready. I'm ready to forsake all others—and...I'm ready to bail if he's not. Well, I'm ready to say "I'm ready to bail" to *you,* Lola, a semi-stranger who doesn't know who I am and can't hold me to it. Whether I'm ready to say it to *him,* I don't know.

Lola, I am horrified to think of myself as The Girl Issuing the Ultimatum—hell, I'm having trouble seeing myself as The Girl Who Wants to Settle Down and Breed in the first place. Have I become a walking stereotype?

And speaking of walking, what if I tell him I'm walking and he says, "Close the door behind you?" Help!

—Ultimatum Frisbee

Ooh, killer letter. Top of pile. Good eye, Ted. And good grief, Mr. Snood, see? We. Are. Freaking. Trying.

Finally, even *I* am actually trying. Right?

That very moment was the first time it had ever occurred to Lola that maybe, all along, she *hadn't* been trying. Her love life, thus far, would hardly give rise to the low drama of her Tramp Lit step-sistren. Hah, can you imagine? "Dear Diary, Today I had another unfortunate but non-toxic breakup with a Perfectly Nice Guy toward whom my feelings remain cordial," Lola penned in her head. "But not to worry! When I'm ready to give it another sporting try, I'll date That Mensch, for three months. And then, see above." Soon to be a major motion picture.

Hmm. She looked up. Doug was gone. "Hey, Kat? Can you come here for a sec?"

6

"Is it the panda?" Kat asked, scooting over on her chair.

"No. Well, sort of. No."

"Okay..."

"Kat, do you think I've been too picky?" Lola asked.

"What, you're thinking of saying yes to Snood?"

"No, seriously."

"Lo, you're not starting to think you're so old it's time to *settle* or something, are you?"

"No, it's not that. That's"—Lola pretended to check her Palm Pilot—"June. But seriously. I mean, I've dated all these pretty great guys."

"PGGs. Yeah."

"Hang on." Lola opened her snack drawer. "Sweet or salt?"

"Salt," said Kat. Wasabi peas. "Thanks."

"Have I not given them a chance?" Lola asked. "Am I missing something, or sabotaging something, or...something?"

"I don't know, Lo. I mean, I really don't think so."

"I mean, I really have been totally focused on work for the last few years...could I be using that to, you know, avoid commitment? Am I gonna be that 'Oh my God, I forgot to have children?' lady in the cartoon?"

"Well, you are totally focused on work, but you do love it."

"Yes, it is my first love," Lola said. "Well, actually, my first love was the theater. And okay, second was Hughie Zampitella, in fifth grade. So work's the closest possible third. Certainly the biggest since middle school." She crunched on a handful of peas. "Anyway, so Kat," Lola frowned. "I'm thinking maybe I bury myself in my work as a way to avoid forming lasting relationships."

Kat thought for a sec. "Or maybe so far your work has actually been more interesting and satisfying than the people with whom you'd otherwise be forming lasting relationships."

"...Oh," said Lola, taking a second to catch up.

"Plus Lo, you know, for someone in your line of work, love *is* scary."

"Oh wait, the opposite," Lola goaded.

"No, Lo, not the opposite," insisted Kat. "First of all, come on, every day your letters remind you how rotten things can get, and how relatively lucky and spoiled you—unlike, say, Nina Sambuca—have been."

Nina Sambuca was the bad-girl author of the best-selling pharma-memoir *Xanax Planet.* She was Lola's Tramp Lit arch-nemesis. She had been, anyway, until the writer Blake Fox at Literati.com had exposed her book—not to mention her weekly blow-and-tell column at Frisson.com—as fabrications. Of course, the *mea culpa* column Sambuca wrote in response had set all-time page view records.

"But thing is," Kat was saying, "when you're the expert and all, you *can't* get it wrong in your real life. 'Can't' in quotes, I mean."

"God, do you think that's it? That I've been going through the motions but actually playing it safe?"

"I don't know, Lo. I mean—

"Kat, Snood's not right, is he?"

"For you? No," said Kat, popping a pea in her mouth.

"No, really. Am I waiting for someone outlandish, someone way too totally impossibly perfect? So that that way I'll never meet anyone with whom I'd actually have to try and make it work, so then I don't have to risk failure or commitment or—"

"Lola Lola Lola Lola—," Kat put her hand on Lola's knee. "I don't know if it's that deep. I mean, *you* are very deep, of course. And yes, as I said, your job puts some pressure on you. But geez, the love thing is totally scary for everyone, and partners are hard to find in general. Why do you think I'm holding on to one in Prague? Plus look, it's not like you've got some kind of insane *checklist* or anything."

"Um, Kat?" Lola glanced behind her to her left, then to her right, and lowered her voice. "I have a checklist."

"Nuh-uh. An actual checklist?"

Lola was taking a small, worn piece of paper out of the pocket inside her Palm Pilot cover. "Mmhmm. I made it with Annabel in college."

"College? And you still have—?" Kat's eyebrows had practically dislodged her barrettes. "Okay, let's see."

Kat unfolded the paper.

MR. LOLA SOMERVILLE
(in no particular order)
SMART
FUNNY
GOOD TASTE
GOOD PERSON
DOG PERSON
MATURE
CUTE
FINANCIALLY STABLE
HAS OPINIONS
CARES ABOUT WORLD
MASCULINE/ATHLETIC BUT NOT MEATHEAD
HAS OUTSIDE INTERESTS, HOBBIES
NOT PICKY EATER (BONUS: ANCHOVIES, SPICY ETC)
FEMINIST, WHETHER HE KNOWS IT OR NOT
ALSO HATED "LES MIS," OR AT LEAST "TERMS OF ENDEARMENT"
3-5 YEARS OLDER

Kat looked at Lola. "Are you nuts?"

"It's asking a lot, huh?" Lola sighed. "I guess you're right. Checklisting myself out of the market."

"A, I didn't say that, and B, are you nuts?"

"Wait, so what do you mean?" Lola asked.

Kat tossed the checklist in the recycling pail.

"Hey!"

"Picky? You're not picky enough! You sound like that guy with the—you know, that 'we both love chocolate, puppies, great movies' guy? Lo, *any* guy you'd be attracted to in the first place, even a teeny bit, would have most of those qualities."

"Oh. Okay. Right. So?"

"So? So your checklist doesn't really narrow things down. It's all givens, not pluses. If someone fits your checklist *and* doesn't work out, it doesn't mean anything—except that you dated a total PGG that you didn't happen to click with soulmate-style."

Lola thought about that. "Oh. Okay. Right. So, like, I have high standards for Fundamentally Good Guys—as well I should—but beyond that if nothing sparks, or works out, it's not me."

"Right," said Kat. "It's *you*."

Lola frowned, puzzled.

"You, *plural,*" Kat said. "Not a match."

"Ah. Gotcha," said Lola.

"Don't worry, Lo, you're fine. Seriously. Okay? I gotta finish coding. Thanks for the peas."

"You're welcome, Kat," Lola said. "Thank *you.*"

Lola watched Kat scoot to her desk, and then turned back to her work, leaving the checklist in the wastebasket.

She had a copy at home.

7

Lola's party clothes were easy to spot, as they were pretty much the only items left hanging, forlorn, in her closet. The work clothes that usually kept them company were strewn across her bed, her desk, her stereo, her dish-drying rack. Earlier, when she'd reached in for a water glass, Lola had discovered the o.j. carton in the cupboard, full. And her loafers in the sink.

Things had gotten even crazier at Ovum since implementation of the new policy requiring executive producers to attend all marketing, business development, and technology strategy meetings (intention: to promote "empathy," "collectivity," etc.). So at this point, home was just where Lola kept her stuff—which stuff was where was another story.

No time to clean now, though—she had to meet Kat and Ted in 45 minutes, and she was still pretty much napping. If I just wear these sheets as a toga, I could stay here ten more minutes, thought Lola. No, flannel too frumpy. Lola reached for her fuzzy stuffed Giraffe (her clean little secret) and gave herself five more minutes.

•

Lola arrived five minutes late to meet Kat and Ted at their rendezvous point, the yellow door of the warehouse-turned-gallery across the street from Ovum's studio. Fortunately, Kat and Ted were evidently more like ten minutes late. Drat, Lola mused, I could have stopped to lay out my First Date Outfit (Brunch Variation) for tomorrow. Oh, well. Lola peeked inside the gallery, spotting a mop in a gray janitor's cart. Could be art, could be cleaning. You never know.

"Hey!" Lola heard behind her—Kat and Ted. They exchanged hey-you-look-greats all around. Even for Ted, who was wearing his best same thing he always wore: jeans and a polo shirt. Kat was wearing an adorable emerald mini-dress that you'd never guess she'd fashioned from the kelly-green frock she'd had to wear as her cousin's maid of honor. Lola, having obeyed Annabel, wore her china blue Cynthia Rowley mini-dress with orange flower-shaped beads: a Loehmann's coup. She'd passed the savings along to her full-priced mod boots.

"Shall we?" Ted asked. They joined the crowd streaming toward the front doors, recognizing virtually no one except a couple of girls from animation, and wasn't that that guy from that band? The Smashing Blind Lemon Melon Pumpkinheads?

Once past the various checklists and checkpoints and headsets, they stepped into the curved-walled elevator. When the doors opened, it was as if someone had transformed the office into a swanky, funky nightclub. Actually, that's exactly what had happened. Some sort of hotspot-cum-Internet café, actually, because everyone's computers were of course still right out there on the desks. That made Lola slightly nervous to see waiters (men only) carrying trays of satays and mysterious blue cocktails; there were bars and food tables set up near the mailroom and the Incubator. The crew had rejiggered the studio lights to blink and flash along with the music of the fresh-from-the-Lilith-Fair punk-folk band Chattel, who were warming up for Puerto Rican salsa sensation La India. After all, Latinos were the Next Next Big Thing, after lesbians. The place was already packed—who *were* all these people!?—with even thicker clusters waiting their turn for one of three body-henna artists. Hey, there was Joan Jett talking to Rebecca Lobo. You couldn't miss the 6 foot 4 hoops player. Or the giant egg up on the *Chyck* platform, between the video screens, behind the band.

Giant egg.

Lola gaped. All she could think of to say was, "There's a giant egg there."

Kat nodded. All she could think of to say was, "Let's get a drink."

"Here's one," said someone else. A hand with a complicated Dick Tracy-ish watch popped into Lola's vision, bearing a tumbler sloshing blue. Lola knew that voice. That voice, and also the voice in her head saying, "Crap/Yay!"

"Hey, Miles," said Lola. "Thanks."

Sip.

"Hey, no problem. Great dress. Betsey Johnson?"

Is he gay, or just perfect?

"Nope, Cynthia Rowley."

Just then, a server swung by with a tray of blue drinks for the others, and Douglas showed up with pixie-cut Greta. A look from Ted made it clear that Lola was to find out if Douglas was WITHwith Greta. Actually, Lola wondered if Doug was sweet on Kat. Or if he knew that Kat had that long-term boyfriend, her college sweetheart Clive, who was off doing some sort of spoken word thing in Prague.

Greetings all around. "Some party, huh?" Doug said. "Beats the hell out of Cheetos and Coors back at BetaTester.com. Oh and hey, there's a killer Saint-Andre over with the cheeses. It's like butter. Don't miss it."

"And a manchego that's great with figs." Miles added. Did he *know* Lola snacked on dried figs all day at her desk?

Sip. Sip.

"Yum," said Lola, realizing she'd just drained her mystery drink. "In fact," she said, looking hard at Kat, "Let's go get some. I better eat something before I have another one of these." But look, the waiter was back. "Okay, *while* I have another one of these."

Sip.

Just then, though, the band clanged its last chord and Angela Chan ran up to the platform in boots no one else could possibly run in. "Hello, everyone! Welcome and thank you for coming tonight!"

"Angela? Where's Maddy?" Miles asked.

Lola shrugged and shook her head.

Sip.

"I've got a very special message to bring to you tonight from our founder, Madeleine North!"

The video screens blinked from the Ovum logo to Maddy's face. She was in some sort of nondescript room, dressed down in a denim shirt. "Hello, everyone," she said. "It's a proud night for me, but it's also been a tough night for me. Earlier today, my daughter, Betty, was injured playing rugby." Silence, or close to it. "Her head and neck took a bit of a twist in a fall. We were quite worried for a while, but it turns out—thank goodness—it's just a strain. She's resting, and she's gonna be just fine." Applause. "So even though this company's like my second child, Desmond and I felt that we just couldn't be away from our first baby upstate tonight. Thank you all for understanding." Everyone understood, of course.

Maddy touched her earpiece. "But never mind me—hey, I just work there. The person you really want to see is our guest of honor…". Applause, even as Maddy went on. "You know her well—now let her get to know you! Please welcome—and I love that I can say this now—*Ovum's own*…Penelope!"

Heads turned right, where Angela had come from before, and then back, to the egg. The front was sliding smoothly open. Out stepped Penelope.

Uproarious applause, both for Penelope and good new-fangled human ingenuity. All Lola could think about, of course, was the on-stage cocoon scene in—

"*Spinal Tap*," Miles said, leaning in close.

Sip. Sip. Sip.

•

Despite the lure of cheese and figs, Lola had somehow not yet made it to the food table. She'd been foiled in her bold attempt to fjord the dance floor, which had filled up the instant India began to play. Miles was there dancing. (He was actually coordinated. No comment.) As were Lola's buffers, Kat and Doug. Greta and Ted had gone off to try to figure out how the egg worked.

India, true to her "crossover appeal," had started out not with pure salsa but with some Latiny pop, much of it in English. Freed from having to channel moves from the movie *Lambada!,* Lola tried extremely hard to affect an effortless "What, me dancing?" style, without of course looking too laconic or wooden, but also without...all right, Somerville, just relax. Just obey the No Hands Over Head Rule, and you'll be fine.

Lola knew well that the blue drinks were beginning to do their black magic, because the more she drank, and the hungrier she got, the less she cared. Cheese good, yes. But drinks good too. Dancing fun. Miles. Mmm. Sip sip sip.

Kat made her way over. "Ooh! This is my favorite India song. 'I just want to-oo hang arou-ound you...'" she sang, sneaking a closer look at Lola.

"Okay, Lo, seriously, we really need to feed you now. Your brunch isn't 'til 11.30 tomorrow. Sorry Miles, I'm cutting in for a cheese break!" Kat called out merrily, taking Lola's arm. And charging right into Penelope and Leo Cameroon, who were making the rounds.

"Oh! Sorry! Um, hi!" Lola and Kat said.

"Pleasure to meet you," said Penelope. "This is Leo Cameroon." Duh! But cool that she didn't just assume we knew.

"I'm Lola and this is Kat. We're with AskLola.com," ventured Lola.

"Of course! You give excellent advice," said Penelope.

"Thanks," said Lola, and that was about all there was to say. They were pretty much yelling over the music, anyway. Waves and nods goodbye. Lola and Kat stood there and silently counted. Nine, ten. "She knows me! She knows me!" Penelope a safe distance away, Lola did a Riverdance jig/end zone boogie. "Who hoo!" Sip! Sip! Getting sippy widit!

"Ooh!" Kat reached into her bra, where she kept her teeny cell phone. She peered at the screen. "Ooh! It's Clive." Prague boy. She looked apologetically at Lola. "Go ahead!" Lola smiled.

Now which way is the food? Who's moving the walls? Oh, that waiter's standing nice and still right next to me. Sure, one more. Thanks. Sip.

Miles came into focus from the blur behind him. "One more dance before the after party?" Dance? After party? Palm in the small of my back? Okay, yeah.

Sipsipsipsipsip.

•

After party. Lola knew exactly where she was—Darts, the dive bar two blocks away at the dive bar Darts—but had no idea how she'd gotten there. And no recollection of leaving Ovum. She never had gotten one of those figs, had she? Oh, well. Lola just felt buoyed along and content, like a leaf on a brook. A fizzy stream. Mmm. Fizzy brooky. Brooky brunchy. Brunchy soony.

Oh. Lola tried to sketch out a clever plan to knock out the middle man and go straight to brunch from Darts, really really early. But the thought of hefting the forty-five-pound Sunday Times to while away the hours just made her sink further into the skanky couch, which at any moment might swallow her like the toothy plant in *Little Shop of Horrors*. Leavy soony. Fizzy brooky.

Douglas was there. And Miles, next to Lola. Kat had left exhausted, amidst assurances that everyone would make sure everyone got home safe. Ted, the designated teetotaler, could do the job. He was around somewhere—with Greta?—probably playing a unique game of billiards improvised around whatever balls the table was missing. Smooshed and slumped on the limp-springed sofas, they chatted and laughed about God knows what until last call. At some point Lola thought she noticed that Miles's right hand had ever so lightly touched her knee.

"No worries, I'll put her in a cab," Miles was saying. Everyone was getting up. They went outside and waved to Ted and Doug, who said they felt like walking. Miles hailed a taxi.

•

Ow. Head. Ow. Awake now. Eyes closed. Ow.

Something in Lola's head pounded like a strait-jacketed lunatic hurling himself against the walls of his cell. Ow. Where's Giraffe? Pat, pat. Here's something soft. But not fuzzy. And a little bony.

This is not Giraffe.

It is a human hand.

Attached to an arm coming from somewhere behind me.

And wearing a complicated Dick Tracy-ish watch.

Which says 11:07 AM.

8

HELL'S BELLS!

Lola had to think fast. She tried, but it hurt.
She switched back to slow. Simple questions.
Where am I?
 I am home. Good.
Where am I supposed to be?
 At brunch with Boqueron. Bad.
Who else is supposed to be here?
 No one.
Yet who else is here?
 Giraffe...
Mmm hmm, and who else?
 Um, whaddaya mean, who else?
Lola, for God's sake, fess up, you're the only person having this conversation.
 All right, all right.

Miles is here.

Yes. And how did he get here?
 I don't know.
Think harder.
 Ow. I really don't know.
Okay, pass. Next question. What happened once he got here?
 I don't remember.
Okay. Check for clues.
 All right. First I shall calculate our spooning coordinates: Lying on right side. Left arm pinned under Miles's arm. No visible clothing on same. Shit. Scanning other side of body. Okay. Right arm pinned under self. Right hand smashed under own thigh—touching dress.

Dress.

I am still wearing my entire dress.

Excellent! Bravissima. Now what?

Oh, God. Brunch. Can't eat.

Not the point.

Right. Also can't blow off Boqueron, i.e. die alone and childless.

Correct.

Okay. Must unpin self and call Boqueron.

Ah, yes. But you don't have Boqueron's cell phone number.

Oh, well! In that case must stay in bed with Miles and repeat last night, whatever it was, because it is not fair that I do not remember it, and it obviously cannot happen again. Which is why it must happen before we get up—because then it will still, like, count toward last night.

Lola sat bolt upright. Her evil thoughts had jerked her awake like a Peet's French roast, size Big Ho.

Miles, in turn, was jerked awake like someone who'd been spooning someone who'd suddenly sat bolt upright.

"Hey," he said, sleepily, adorably, repulsively. Already Lola was trying to self-administer aversion therapy.

"Hey," Lola said. "Sorry."

"Hi. Um, look, I should—". Not a dreamy curl out of place. No gross stickum in eyes. God dammit, could he at least please smell like Morning Boyfriend?

"Yeah," Lola said, attempting a pleasant but noncommittal smile, as if to say, "Hey, last night was fine, but not. I mean, it shouldn't have happened, but I'm not going to freak out on you because it did. And just because we slept together—I mean SLEPTslept, of course—does not mean that I am now scripting in my head the column about us in the *Times* wedding section. In other words, I am neither easy nor psycho. And just for the record, it is unfortunate that women still feel that they must pry themselves out of those pigeonholes. Anyway, we will both act completely professionally at work, as if there had never been any sort of congress between a young woman who knows better and her superior."

Quite sure that she had made her intentions clear, Lola spoke. "Actually? I amsototallylateforbrunchwith...my aunt. Tell you what? Take your time? Make yourself totally at home? There's an extra set of keys on the hook by the door. Just lock up and give them to me tomorr—I mean, drop them back through the mail slot?" Check plus.

"Wait, where's your brunch?"

Curses. Okay, Lola, *lie.* "Café Reggio." Never been a good liar.

"No way, I live right down there on Sullivan—and I have to be home in time for a noon videoconference with Maddy, et al. Let's split a cab!"

Say, Lola? You are having a conversation with Miles, who has no shirt on, in your bed. Just wanted you to notice that.

Okay, now you can panic.

"Oh, I don't think—." Yo Lola, there is no logical reason why not. Plus, hey, you're never gonna share a Cab of Shame with this man again, so you might as well take advantage. Call it closure. You just have to move *fast.*

"Why not?" Miles moved to throw off the covers.

Oh God.

Okay. Pants. Okay.

"Sure, right, why not? Lemme just, um, powder my nose." Lola leaned down to sweep a few items of clothing off the floor—whoa whoa whoa, HEAD RUSH, come up slowly, toss hair gently—and disappeared into the bathroom.

"I look like ass," she said to the mirror. It didn't argue.

She brushed her teeth, clipped up her hair, brushed on mascara and lip gloss, and changed hurriedly into the jeans and cropped baby-blue sweater she'd grabbed. On her way out, she skidded her feet into her black square-toed loafers, the first shoes she saw. For the first time in history, the "I didn't spend hours planning this effortlessly 'casual' outfit" look had been achieved sincerely.

"Ready?" she said, back in her room.

"Yep!" said Miles. He'd made the bed.

•

Of *course.* The Andorra Day Parade. Fifth Avenue was totally shut down; the cab engine might as well have been, too. They were at a total standstill.

"My aunt's gonna kill me," Lola said miserably.

"Why don't you call her?" asked Miles, reaching for his StarTac.

"She…doesn't have a cell phone."

"Well, why don't you call the restaurant?" asked Miles, reaching for his Palm Pilot.

Lola perked up, then slumped back. How was she supposed to convey to whoever answered that "a woman who appears to be waiting for someone" was actually code for "a guy I met on the Internet but can't describe now as I am currently in a taxicab with the superior I hooked up with last night"? She did officially believe that it was legal, if not advisable, to date more than one person at once, at first; hey, it worked for the Brady sisters. But somehow it seemed indelicate to be dropped off at P2 by P1. And somehow she just didn't want to explain.

She was trapped.

"Oh, you know, it's okay. She'll be so buried in the crossword, come to think of it, that she won't even notice I'm late."

Miles frowned slightly. "You sure?"

"Yeah." Thin smile. "She'll enjoy the downtime," Lola added inanely, not wanting to sound inconsiderate about making someone wait. Though what did she care what he thought, anyway?

It was 11:43. DamndamndamnDAMN. Lola turned her watch to the inside of her wrist. Checking it only made the cab move slower. She imagined that the sweat on her brow would soon start condensing on the windows, which would *really* give the wrong impression. What had she done to deserve this? Okay, a lot. Was that gross feeling the "I am sabotaging any chance at relationships" feeling or just the "I have no idea what or how much I drank last night" feeling? The latter seemed pretty credible. Whatever.

Miles, to his credit, was managing to maintain jaunty chit-chat about everything except the huge rhinoceros head sitting on the seat between them. The one wearing the big rhinestone necklace, like something Kat might wear. The one that said, "HELLO! YOU TWO JUST SPENT THE NIGHT TOGETHER."

11:57. They inched. They crawled. They made it about twenty blocks, the longest mile in Manhattan. They chuckled, a little too hard. They neared Washington Square Park.

They finally couldn't stand it anymore.

"Look, I—" they both began.

"We—" (Jinx.)

"Last night—"

"I really don't think it's a good idea for that to happen again," Lola—finally beating Miles to it—said as warmly as she could.

"Neither do I," Miles replied. (Lola's brain: "Phew." Lola's ego: "WHAT?!")

Miles went on. "Next time I'd rather take you out on a real date."

•

Lola sprinted to within half a block of Café Reggio. Hung over, 45 minutes late, sweaty—really attractive.

She glanced around the charmingly shabby hasn't-changed-since-the-beat-poets Village café. Couples, pairs of men, groups of women, one strollered family on a tourist visa from the Upper West Side. There were two single men in the entire place. One had a long white beard and a stack of yellowed newspapers at his side. The other had a copy of the *New Yorker—aha?!*—and, Lola discovered as she watched, a girlfriend just on her way back from the restroom.

Lola stood in the door. She had primly thanked Miles for the kind invitation and told him to check with her Monday at work, where her calendar was up to date. The words "at work" had echoed in her head in that Satan voice in *The Exorcist.* Meanwhile, at the café, someone started to steam milk for a latte. Lola heard her love life—and, were word to get out about this, her credibility—vaporize with that same harsh whoosh.

9

Lola figured if she scrunched down small enough at her desk, Kat might not see her.

"Happy Monday, boss!" called Kat.

Hell's bells! Should have crawled under. Should not have worn bright pink and orange checked sweater.

"Hey," said Lola, barely turning around, making a loud display of typing busily.

"How's Ping-Pong?" asked Kat as her Mac chimed on. They both had the Panda-cam as their start-up page now. The zoo hadn't named the little one yet, so Douglas, after teasing them both about their obsession, had suggested Ping-Pong. Not bad.

"Still asleep," said Lola. It was, after all, like five AM in San Diego. Lola had come in early to immerse herself in work—like *that's* an escape!—as her home, too, was haunted. The rest of yesterday had been a wash: she'd called Annabel immediately ("I am calling you from the Café Reggio bathroom, but I'm so not on my date…") and together they'd composed the contrite e-mail to Boqueron. Lola had spent the remainder of the day trying—and failing with flying colors—to avoid checking for his response. Nothing so far. Finally she'd slept, crookedly, on the post-futon Grownup Couch she'd bought with her Ovum windfall. She could hardly even look at her bed. It still held Miles's faint outline, like the Duvet of Turin.

Right, trying to immerse herself in work.

```
Dear Ultimatum Frisbee,
```

"So what'd I miss after I left Darts?" Kat again.

"Not much, I don't think," answered Lola.

Kat rolled up a chair, disco-ball earrings swinging. She wasn't getting the idea. Or maybe she was.

"So you and Miles shared a cab home, huh?" Sleater-Kinney was doing a sound check somewhere, so fortunately no one could have overheard a thing.

"How did you know that?" Lola hissed, stunned.

"Aha," grinned Kat. "You just told me."

Lola couldn't help but smile. "That's why I hired you," she sighed.

"You guys talking about Lola and Miles?" It was Ted.

Lola threw up her hands. "What, did someone send out another company-wide e-mail?"

"Come on, Lola, you know Kat and I share a knowledge base. Except she speaks HTML," said Ted. "Kat just told me she had a hunch, that's all. No one knows anything. We get how serious it is."

Lola's eyes widened.

"—I mean, how seriously important it is to keep it quiet," Ted replied.

"But isn't it?" wondered Kat.

"Isn't what what?" asked Lola.

"I mean, you guys have real intentions, right? We know you'd only get into something at work that you were pretty serious about," Kat said, clearly doing her darndest to sound like she wasn't lecturing. "He does seem pretty cool."

"We'll see," said Lola, doing what she imagined was "smiling enigmatically." Anyone who wasn't Kat, or Annabel, would think she meant, "I have embarked on something too miraculous and ethereal to explain in earthly words." Kat, however, would know she meant, "I am not ready to talk about how badly I may have fucked up."

•

Can't concentrate.

Two messages in PitchingWoo.com inbox. One from Boqueron. Afraid to read it, Lola clicked on the other.

TO: Truffle
FROM: nicestraightguy
RE: fabulous profile!
I'm a hetero, cute, well-dressed attorney. Outside the firm, you might find me watching a funky dance troupe, or shopping on 5th Ave. I love to read, everything from fashion magazines to *The Girl's Guide to Hunting and Fishing* to *Bridget Jones' Diary*...

Sorry, Lola thought, but I already have a date for the Judy Garland episode of *Biography*.

Delete.

Deep breath. Clickclick.

```
TO: Truffle
FROM: Boqueron
RE: Re: Hell's Bells!
Well, I was bummed, but I completely understand. I
had a late night myself, and you're certainly not
the first person in the world who's set her alarm
for PM instead of AM. So. Sigh. Shall we try again?
What works for you? "This week is already crazy for
me...". If that were a song, it'd be ours.
```

Okay, okay. Could be worse. Still, if he really wanted to meet, he would just freaking make time and make it happen, wouldn't he? Oh, wait, he did that. And I freaking made an ass of myself.

Speaking of which, where is Miles? Why hasn't he stopped by yet? Why can't he just leave me alone?

"Hey." Lola jumped. It was Douglas, looking a tad bleary and wearing a *Get Smart* T-shirt. Lola pressed a hand to her chest. "Hell's bells! You scared me."

"Sorry."

"No problem, I was just deeply absorbed in procrastinating." Lola attempted an unhurried—i.e. unsuspicious—click on her screen to hide Boqueron's note.

"Oh, I think I can help you with that, actually," Douglas replied. "I mean, with procrastinating. I was wondering if now would be a good time to set you up on that new sorting system. I know you don't really use it the way Kat and Ted do, but I thought it would be good for you to be able to access it and stuff."

"Oh! Um! Let me think." Lola fiddled around with her on-screen calendar, reading her meeting schedule under her breath. "Yeah, sure. Now's good."

Please God, don't let Miles come by when I'm here with Doug. Please God, don't let Miles come by when I'm not here.

"Great." Doug rolled up a chair from a small floating table. Lola mentally swatted an urge to reach over and chop off a lock of hair that kept falling in his eye. His hairstyle, or lack thereof, was a little trapped in the early 90s. Lola imagined that it would look much better cropped close than side-parted.

"…able to read even the mail that Ted's deleted. Are there other subfolders I should set up for just you?" Doug was asking. Lola tuned back in just in time.

"I'm sorry, what? Oh. Folders. Yeah. How about 'column themes,' like, for letters that, like, inspire column themes?"

"Gotcha." Click, type type, hair flop, click, type type.

Lola glanced over to the juice bar. Miles had just materialized at the counter. Lola inhaled sharply—quite audibly, apparently.

"Um, Lola?" Fortunately Doug was looking right at her. "You seem a little jumpy today. Are you okay? If you don't mind my asking."

"Am I okay? Of course!" Lola said, a little too emphatically. "I think this sound check is just rattling my nerves a little." She took half a breath. "Doug, help me out with something. You've been at Ovum much longer than I have, and I don't know other folks here that well yet. Do you have a sense of the attitude here toward office romance?"

"Wait, what?"

"Oh, I'm sorry, I mean, not, like—" Lola pointed back and forth between the two of them, braying a laugh. "I mean, well, I'm gonna write a column about it pretty soon., speaking of column themes." Mediocre bluff. He must know that you've written this one to death. "And I wanted to make the point that the permissibility would vary from company to company, depending on the culture."

"Oh, I see. Well, I don't think there's an official position on it up in the adminisphere. Of course, this place is pretty mellow about things like that, I guess. Let's see, not a lot of bed-hopping, that I know of. But that might be because everyone's always here."

Lola laughed a little too loud.

Douglas looked at her. "In any case, doesn't 'Ask Lola' say office romance is generally fine as long as it's a serious pursuit with a legitimate future?"

Lola reddened. "Yeah."

"I mean, you wouldn't want to let something potentially great go just because your W-2s come from the same place."

"Right. So what about you? You ever meet someone at work?" she asked, her inner editor for some reason asleep. "What? Lola! None of your business!" she quickly added, feeling obnoxious.

Doug laughed. "Yeah, once, but not here. Summer after college, in this teeny crappy little office where we both used to sit all day and test video games for bugs."

"That's a *job?*" asked Lola.

"Yeah," said Doug.

"But did you leave there totally hating video games?"

"Well…no," Doug said.

"Well, right, okay, I spent a summer working at Ben and Jerry's, and oddly, when I finished, I still loved ice cream," said Lola.

"There you go," said Douglas. "So I dated, if you can call it that, the girl who sat right next to me."

"If you can call it that?" Lola sensed that Douglas was open to chit-chat here. And she was open to not working. "Okay, gimme the big tell. What was her name?"

"We worked long hours and were really poor and we had to keep it a secret because the place was so small—six people in one tiny basement room—it would have weirded everyone out the door," said Doug. "Waterfall."

"Wait, what?"

"Her name was Waterfall. Shut up," Doug grinned.

"Douglas, *please* don't ask me to *not* tease you about that."

"Lola, I would *never* ask such a thing of you!" he said. "It's just that you should not commence teasing until you know everything."

"Go on," said Lola, sitting back.

"Since we couldn't really be all coupley at work, which is where we always were, we, um, created online fantasy gaming characters who were in love."

Lola stared, a smile forming faster than any jokes could. There were just too many.

"Yes, Lola." Doug stood up and bellowed, "We created online fantasy gaming characters who were in love, and I don't care who knows it." Of course, in the din at Ovum, he could have yelled, "Where are all those cute headset-and-clipboard girls when a man needs a cup of coffee and a lap dance?!" and no one would have heard a damn thing.

Lola took this in. "So Doug, what was your, what do you call it, 'character?'"

"I was a Ranger. She was a Druid."

"I see," said Lola. "'Together, you're Cops.'"

"Rangers have cool longbows and can detect poison," said Doug.

"Sounds like they're good to have around," said Lola.

"You're not even gonna tease me?"

"Not yet. Way too easy," said Lola. "I shall have pity on you, Ranger."

"Doesn't that make you a tease tease?" asked Douglas.

"Guess so!"

Douglas laughed and made a few more moves of the mouse. "Okay, you're all set." He touched her arm. "Gotta go. Hope that's helpful."

"Yeah. Yeah, it is. Thanks. Bye, Rang—wait, what was your fantasy name?"

"Forgive me, my good lady, but I am not permitted to reveal that which you ask."

"Geek," said Lola.

"Farewell," said Doug. He rolled his chair away just as Miles arrived with two cups of thick yellow juice. He set one on Lola's desk.

"You like yours with extra biotin, right?"

Doug glanced back.

Lola—Lolana, High Empress of Serious Pursuits (skilled in the Resurrection of Credibility and the Healing of Hangovers)—knew what she had to do.

She and Miles made a date for Thursday.

•

Dear Ultimatum Frisbee,
How come when men want to get married, they're settling down, but when women want to get married, they're giving in?

Hmm.

The letter "S" for Single is much less scarlet than it used to be, but that doesn't mean staying that way is Plan A.

Not bad.

You know, we can't win. They look at us funny if we're not married, and they look at us funny if we say we'd like to be.

I could really get into this one.
Hang on.

TO: tabedon@ovuminc.com
FROM: lsomerville@ovuminc.com
RE: show topic
hey, I'm kind of jamming on a big Lola Policy Statement on why women shouldn't be ashamed to admit they want to "settle down." can we do that for next week?

TO: lsomerville@ovuminc.com
FROM: tabedon@ovuminc.com
RE [2]: show topic
Hey, I love it but Angela just stopped by to remind me that it's almost the anniv of when the judge threw out the Paula Jones case. So she says we should use that as a peg to do something about how to handle **office romance.**

As opposed to *Oval* Office romance, ha ha—wait. Office romance. No way. Nowaynowaynoway.

Let's slate your other idea for June (open season on weddings). Hey, meantime why don't you pitch it to Penelope? Bet she'd dig it. She said to e-mail her anytime.

Lola felt sick. Sick*er*. I have to talk about this on TV with a straight face? She leaned back in her chair and looked up at the sky, making a big groaning stretching noise. Somebody up there clearly has it in for me.

"Kaaaaaaat? Why can't it be Sushi Tuesday already?"

"Didn't you hear? Sushi Tuesday is now a thing of the past."

Lola whipped back up, almost keeling sideways. "What?!"

"Mmm hmm. Now it's Tuna Melt Tuesday."

10

"Tuna melts rock!"

Lola and Kat glared at Ted.

"...which is so not the point!" he quickly added.

Lola and Kat shook their heads solemnly.

"Yeah, like what gives?" Ted went on. "Isn't Ovum more than flush? I mean, what about that party?"

"Maybe we blew everything on that big egg," suggested Kat.

"About the sushi, my mom probably wrote a letter about its perils," Lola said wryly. She resolved to bring her own lunch tomorrow in protest. Not quite a hunger strike, but it would do.

•

annabel2k: so what's the deal w/[kilometers only not metric]??
annabel2k: that was code
annabel2k: but you knew that
annabel2k: well?
hernamewaslola: [this line intentionally left blank]
annabel2k: u suck! come on!
hernamewaslola: IM not safe. will call u.
annabel2k: K.
hernamewaslola: so but wait, how's your love life? what happened with climber #1?
annabel2k:...i mean, WHOSE favorite movie is *Patch Adams?*
annabel2k: it just doesn't make sense.
hernamewaslola: ah. oooh. sorry.
annabel2k: eh, no bigs. stay tuned.
hernamewaslola: talk soon. xo

•

Dear Ultimatum Frisbee,

We can't win. They look at us funny when:

(a) we're not married ("What's wrong with you?")

(b) we say we'd like to get married ("How…retro!")

(c) We say we'd like to get married ("How…hard it must be to be a desperate, demanding man-trapper, a disfigured, limping loner driven to madness by the tick-tock of the Tell-Tale Biological Clock?")

(d) we say we'd rather not get married. ("What's wrong with you?")

So to hell with all that. What do *you* want, UF? A solid, lovely partnership? Well, you've got one, and it ain't broke. Or, a "legit" bond (with "legit" kids)? Well, this guy may not give you that.

Middle ground: your guy could be one of those who will groan and quake about commitment *even as he is trolling Tiffany's.* Steady, now. Ready, eventually. Best left alone to come through. Is he one of those guys? Ask your best friend, Gut Feeling.

But do remember what we said to "Noreen" http://ovum.asklola.com/advice/980203c.html:

<<Dear Lola,

Does my boyfriend of 13 years think I'm going to wait around forever for some kind of commitment?

—Noreen

Dear Noreen,

Yes.

Love,

Lola>>

So if you want to give an ultimatum, that's fine. *Brave,* even. Because *the person who gives an ultimatum is the person who has to keep it.* You could force the play—or you could lose him. If that's what happens, you're the one who's got to keep her word. But loss is almost always less sucky than limbo. So don't worry about The Right Thing to Do as a Woman, do what you need to do for *you*. Which is the same.

And let us know what happens?
Love,
Lola

•

TO: penelope@ovuminc.com
FROM: lsomerville@ovuminc.com
RE: show topic?
Hello, Penelope. This is Lola from AskLola.com. As I'm sure you're aware, I do a weekly segment (Intimacy Issues) on *Chyck with a Y.* Tammy Abedon suggested that I discuss with you the possibility of working together on a show about "the single thing"—why all the "Go, single girl!" messages have the side effect of making women guilty for admitting that while single can be fun, they'd prefer to be—gasp-married. The idea was inspired by a great letter I received from a woman ("Ultimatum Frisbee"—clever!) who wanted to give her boyfriend an ultimatum but who didn't want to be "that kind of girlfriend." Could we talk about building a show on that topic? I'd be very grateful. I think a lot of women who don't want to settle—for waiting forever—would too.
Thanks very much.
All best,
Lola Somerville

•

Lola hit the send button and picked up the phone. She really wanted to call Annabel, but she forced herself to place duty before dish.

"Hey, Tammy, it's Lola. I was wondering if we could talk about this week's topic."

Lola was determined to keep the segment's focus on legal issues and thus away from, say, her. Blushing on national television was a concern. And God forbid Miles should walk by while the they were rolling. The camera adds ten pounds of shame.

"Actually, Lola?" Tammy didn't sound like herself. "Could you come by my desk?"

"Uh, sure! Right now?"

"Yeah. Now. Thanks." Tammy hung up.

Weird.

"I'll be back!" Lola called to Ted, who had begun pulling together everything he could on the harassment lawsuits against Testostero.net ("hostile environment") and that skeevy ex-Senator Prindle ("quid pro quo"). At the moment, though, Ted was talking to Megan from wardrobe, who'd looked a little teary when she stopped by.

Lola made her way through the buzzing office to the *Chyck* production area. She passed three women in chadors with—was that Jay Leno's wife? Must be doing a segment about repression in Afghanistan.

Tammy was pretending to read the latest issue of *Rack*, but her reddened eyes weren't focused on the text. In signature Tammy style, she wore a hot pink and black houndstooth suit that said, "Yeah, I'm big. And?" From the nose down she looked great.

Lola rolled over a chair from a nearby empty desk. "Tammy? What's up!?"

"It's been nice working with you."

"What? What's going on? Are you leaving?"

"No. Well, part of me is—the big part."

Lola raised her eyebrows and waited for more. "I just heard. I'm not hosting *Chyck* anymore. Apparently I have been relegated to some sort of entertainment news segment. I'll be sitting behind a desk," said Tammy. "What am I, a crooked cop?"

"But I thought the focus groups adored you!" Lola exclaimed.

"So did I, but someone around here seems to be focusing on something else."

"This is nuts," said Lola. "What are they thinking?!"

"They've got to be, you know, downsizing," Tammy said, gesturing at her torso. That's all I can fathom."

"But that's illegal!" exclaimed Lola. "I've dated enough lawyers to know that!"

"Only if you can prove it."

"Maybe I can," said Lola importantly.

I have no idea what I'm talking about, she thought.

•

hernamewaslola: ok this is totally effed up

annabel2k: what?

hernamewaslola: tammy abedon was "relegated to desk job"
annabel2k: what? why? she's rilly popular. no?
hernamewaslola: YES! but i guess not with people who want to see only thin people! i mean that's gotta be it, right?
annabel2k: well if it is that is totally effed up. then why'd they hire her in the 1st place?
hernamewaslola: PR? to tease the fat girl? dunno.
hernamewaslola: i mean i'm totally bummed for her, but i feel like it's more than that! she was one of the reasons i came to work here! talk about a bait and switch! this place was supposed to be different!
annabel2k: i know. what ru going to do?
annabel2k:??
annabel2k: lo?
annabel2k: lola somerville?
hernamewslola: (thinking)
annabel2k: k.
hernamewaslola: maybe i'll anonymous-leak something to the press so someone else can dig up "the real story"
hernamewaslola: SHIT i can't believe i just put that in print, so much for "anonymous"
hernamewaslola: i better stop typing now

11

Damn. Lola had actually made a peanut butter and jelly sandwich the night before, and then left it at home this morning.

All right, I'll eat their freaking tuna melt, she thought. I've got bigger fish to fry. Haw.

Lola had briefly entertained a mini-conspiracy-theory that the wasabi-to-mayo move was an effort to plump them all up, Hansel and Gretel style, for the chopping block. She let it go when she saw the sign:

> **TUNA MELTS** (Dolphin-safe!)
>
> AVAILABLE WITH REDUCED-FAT
>
> AND/OR SOY MAYO AND CHEESE.

She grudgingly accepted her sandwich—"Full-fat, please!"—and then spotted her mark.

"Hey, Ranger Doug, can I talk to you?"

"Sure." He stopped, plate full. He was wearing a T-shirt bearing nothing but the area code 718, for Brooklyn. (Presumably. Queens, you still don't advertise.)

"Oh, I mean…not here. Sorry. And for more than a second. How about Darts, after work?"

Damn, now he's gonna think I'm flirting or something, but pods have ears. And she had to admit she admired his up-for-anythingness.

"After work? Okay, so like 11?"

"Sure. Great. Thanks. See you at the west elevator?" Douglas nodded. "Sorry to be cryptic," Lola whispered cryptically.

•

Back at her desk, Lola picked at her tuna melt. Until she got really, really hungry, and then she polished it off in three bites. She felt she'd made her point. Well, okay, she'd make her point next week.

annabel2k: `Panda-cam NOW`

Ping-Pong was batting a bamboo branch with her little paw. Unspeakably cute.

hernamewaslola: `<swoon>`

Phone.

"Good afternoon, Lola, this is Carrie Walters at *Chyck*." The show's alpha production assistant had a degree in early childhood education, which, if she ever actually used it, would probably firm her young charges' resolve never to grow up. Carrie was someone's niece, Fern Gellar's maybe, and she'd been tapped to run the day care center. But for now she was killing time—and, as she made clear to everyone, brain cells—in this job waiting for the center to be completed. Ted, oddly, didn't mind her officious manner—"There's just something about a woman with a headset."

"Hey, Carrie, what's up?" Lola glanced up at the mezzanine. Some sort of new tubing leaned against the wall where the center would be. But no one was working. Looked like it might be a while.

"Unfortunately, we've encountered a rather crippling—sorry, uh, big scheduling conflict with the studio. Would you mind taping your segment this afternoon."

No question mark there. Lola glanced at her calendar. "What time? In an hour? Well, I'd have to miss a branding meeting, but…" Yay.

Oh, wait, the polar opposite. UNYAY. This one was the office romance segment. And Lola hadn't quite finished constructing her deflector shields.

"Actually, Carrie? Is there any way we could do it tomorrow morning?"

"No."

"Oh! All right. Well, okay. I'll be in makeup at quarter of."

Lola turned to Ted. Megan looked like she felt better.

"Hey. Whaddaya got so far on the latest harassment stuff?"

"Just a bunch of dirt on Testostero.net. Facts on why the hostile environment was both hostile and an environment. As in, 'pervasive.' You know, public readings of filthy porn, like the Starr Report. Why?"

"Good enough," Lola replied. "Can you just write me a quick tip sheet on what you've got? I've gotta do my segment this afternoon."

"Already talking about office romance? But you two haven't even had your first date—"

Lola shot Ted the kind of look you shoot someone.

"—I'll just get to that memo, Miss Somerville."

"Mmm hmm. Thanks."

Hold the phone. Who the hell was going to host the segment?

•

TO: lsomerville@ovuminc.com
FROM: oestrada@ovuminc.com
RE: FWD: show topic?
Hiya, Lola! It's Olive over in Penelope's office! She forwarded me your show topic idea! Seems like she really likes it! She wanted me to ask you some follow-up questions! Well, actually, just one for now: so how would you respond to this "Ultimatum Frisbee?" I guess she just wants to know what direction the segment would go in! Please advise when you have the chance!
Thanks!!! ☺

•

"All set, boss." Ted handed her a memo. Lola never didn't get a kick out of having someone in her life who handed her memos.

"I love days when I feel like a real reporter," Ted said.

"Thanks, Clark Kent," said Lola. "Oh wait, he's a fictional reporter." She wasn't really paying attention.

"See ya." Lola headed for makeup, limbo-ing under a boom mike and glimpsing the U.S. Women's Ice Hockey team exiting the far elevator—in full equipment—like clowns, very tough and padded clowns, pouring out of a VW. They must be appearing on Ovum's women's sports show, *Sweat.*

Lola yanked her attention back to her pounding heart, whose aftershocks she was starting to feel in her forehead. Okay, deep breaths. No one knows anything. Anyway, that's beside the point. Just put your show face on and do the segment. You're just making up that you're busted because you feel guilty. It's just a coincidence. It doesn't mean anything. So get a grip, Somerville. As Ted likes to say, "when you're a dating expert, your entire love life is ironic."

Yeah, "ironic" in the Alanis Morrisette sense. Like, it just sucks.

All right, here's Tootie. Shut up, punch the clock, get to work. It's just work.

Tootie was the head makeup artist. Surely he—yes, he—had been referred by Cliché Employment Services. Huge queen. And Lola's pal—which, Ted joked, saved Ted himself from having to be gay.

Tootie took one look at Lola, pursed his lips, and did one of those snaps.

"Nerd!"

Lola looked down. Oops, her non-trendy sneakers. Lola walked the forty minutes to work, her only exercise these days besides fidgeting; she'd forgotten to slip into something less comfortable. Striped turtleneck tucked into last season's capris, which had been anathema to Tootie even when they were in. Of course, Tootie was into that thing where you cuff up your jeans practically to your inseam, so like he should talk. Admittedly, it was not Lola's most smashing ensemble, but she hadn't been planning on being on air. Plus she was a little preoccupied. Not to mention scraping the bottom of the closet, laundry-wise. Of course there was Miles to keep up appearances for, but now that he'd seen Morning Lola, she'd always look like Myrna Loy by comparison. Besides, she didn't want to look like she was all of a sudden extra-soignée every day. Lola had thought about this.

"Here, just lend her my jacket and the stripes won't glare." Someone had appeared behind Lola's seat in the makeup chair. Black suit, white skin, blond hair, red lips, like a colorized photo. Lola could see the newcomer clearly in the mirror. But not if this person turned sideways; she was too thin.

"Thanks, babydoll," said Tootie, busy doing imperceptible things to Lola's eyebrows with a tiny brush. "Lolita honey, get your feet out of your seat and sit up straight or I'munna turn you into Edward Scissorhands."

Lola obediently de-lotuspositioned.

"Right. Sorry."

"I'll send a runner for your real shoes. Under your desk?" Lola nodded.

"Lola." Jacket Lady came around the chair and extended a french-manicured hand. "I'm Stefanie Marlowe. Filling in for Tammy. Maybe permanently." She winked.

"Pleasure," Lola smiled, silently taking a solemn oath to loathe Stefanie for all eternity.

•

Stand by, three, two, and action. Cue Stefanie. "We've all got intimacy issues. But only *we've* got *Intimacy Issues,* with Ovum's own Lola Somerville. I'm Stefanie Marlowe, filling in for Tammy Abedon." Voice like butter for pastry. Cold.

"Today, on the anniversary of the district court's decision to throw out the Paula Jones case, we'll be revisiting the legal definition of HARRISment and what it means for gender relations at work."

Stefanie was polished, to a flinty sheen. And she pronounced it HARRISment. Lola hated that. Stefanie must pay. Bet she spells Stefanie with an F.

"Well, a lot of people got nervous when the courts were trying to define harASSment, but that's because they weren't reading what the courts were actually saying. Some of them thought, 'So I can't tell a woman she looks nice unless I want to tell it to the judge?!'" Lola calmly proffered her usual rap: decorous flirting, or even dating, does not a "hostile environment" or "quid pro quo" make; that if people would just settle down and be respectful, office romance and sexual harASSment would never overlap. She responded to a few questions about the Testostero.net case—thank you, Ted—and then delivered her Lola Policy Statement on when office romances are acceptable: "When you have a hunch that it could be something real: A hunch that comes from your gut. Not from your fourth eggnog at the office Christmas party."

Nice, Somerville. Got through that without flinching. Employee passersby were basically minding their own business. So far, so fine.

"So Lola. How can we, as women, best reassure men that it's still okay to ask us out at work?"

Lola blinked. When she opened her eyes, Stefanie was still there, which probably meant that she really had just asked that.

Lola took a breath and repeated, with most of the words changed, exactly what she had just said about the by-definition difference between decorous dating and harASSment.

Stefanie nodded. Then she leaned forward and hoisted the left half of her mouth into a smile. "Now, Lola. Have you ever had an office romance?"

Lola's heart dropped into her slingbacks and bounced back up, lodging somewhere in her throat. Had no one read this woman the rules? Oh, wait, there were no rules, just Tammy's unspoken, unwritten total cluefulness. Plus the fact that anyone who knew what Lola did knew that she talked about other people—her letter writers, celebrities, and the occasional *Buffy* allegory—not, ever, herself.

And, of course, the first breach at Ovum *had* to be on this topic.

Thinking fast, Lola dug an old wisecrack out of the hopper. "Well! I did work at home for many years. And there was a really cute Fed Ex guy. But I never got the courage to tell him he absolutely, positively, had to be there overnight."

Whew! And what a perfect segment closer. Obeying the director's cue, Stefanie wrapped up. Lola didn't want Stefanie to think she'd made her sweat. She hastily wished Stefanie luck, mumbled something about a meeting, and headed off.

Lola's gut was trying to tell her something, but, like a silent scream in a dream, it was mouthing words she couldn't hear.

I need some fresh air, Lola thought.

12

Yeah. Just a quick walk. After a quick check-in at the pod.

"Hey, I'm just gonna step out for a breath of fresh air. Need anything from the outside world?"

Kat, headphones on, waved "No thanks."

"Just love," said Ted, who was just saying goodbye to Amy from legal, who seemed to be clutching a picture frame.

"On it."

Lola reached into her pocket for her ultra-UV protection sunglasses, which she dutifully wore practically year-round ever since her mother had "caught" her on TV attending the U.S. Open without a sunhat.

Pocket.

Who moved my pocket?

Wait.

This wasn't Lola's jacket. It was Stefanie's. Lola had forgotten to return it. Which was convenient, as Lola had also forgotten to check Stefanie's pockets for something, anything: an evil talisman, turkey jerky, crack cocaine? Glancing casually around, Lola reached back in and pulled out a folded piece of Ovum memo paper.

OVUM, INC.
From the desk of Stefanie Marlowe

Desk?

```
- testostero.net
- tips for not crossing the line
- MF ?
```

Stefanie's crib sheet for the show.

MF. MF.

Hmm.

MF?

It didn't take long for Lola recognized those initials from, okay, for Chrissakes, a heart she had doodled.

Miles. Farmington.

Holy moly.

Think, Lola, think. It wasn't easy, given that someone somewhere was tuning a grand piano, plink plink plink like the soundtrack of *Eyes Wide Shut.* Think. Plink. Think.

Think. Did Stefanie know? Come on, she just got here, she's green—who could have told her? Could she have cornered me on purpose?

Plink.

I did not just think that. All right, Somerville, get a grip. Paranoid much? Please inform your ego that honestly, no one is as interested in your love life as you think they are. "MF" could stand for a million things. Something vulgar, sure. But also...More Fun! Maybe she was gonna ask whether blondes had higher harassment rates. Maybe Friday? The Testostero.net case was on appeal—the court might have something to say by the end of the week? *Mille-Feuille?* An outstanding type of pastry, worth mentioning anytime, really.

Plink.

Lola dropped Stefanie's jacket off, sans memo—since it means nothing, she won't miss it!—with Tootie. Bagging her plan to take a walk, she called Annabel instead. No answer. Drat. Lola left a message.

Then she tried not to think about the note, which was the same as thinking about it. Should she talk to Ted or Kat? No. Freaking out your staff is bad management.

Plus, they wouldn't freak out about the situation, because there is no situation. They would freak out about me, as I am being a nutcase.

Well. All the more reason to talk to Douglas tonight.

•

TO: oestrada@ovuminc.com
FROM: lsomerville@ovuminc.com
RE: [2] FWD: show topic?
ATTACHMENTS: UFanswer.doc
Hello, Olive. Thanks for your—and Penelope's—interest in this topic. To answer your question:

```
what would (or will) I tell "Ultimate Frisbee?"
Basically that if she wants more of an
official/explicit (legal?!) commitment, then she
will have to come up with a—graceful—ultimatum.
Not because he's bad, but because she's strong.
Here, I'll attach my full answer, should that be
helpful. Let me know what you think. Thanks again!
```

•

That distracted Lola for one e-mail unit of time. Restless, she opened Pitchingwoo.com's welcome page, but then stopped. She opened an e-mail to Annabel, then stopped. Time to quit deflecting and deflating scary things with humor and to actually mull over her decision.

It was, at press time, to pursue Something Real with Miles. That's what she'd hinted to Annabel in her recent voice mail. "The only way to make this work is to…make it work," she'd informed herself. "And you know that checklist I'm not using anymore? He totally whaled on it."

Going For—or at least With—It is the only way, Lola reasoned, to keep my

(1) word,
(2) professional/personal street cred,
(3) job? Nah. He's my superior, not my supervisor.
(4) mom from worrying that I will die alone and childless because of something she did wrong, and
(5) -self from worrying that I will die alone and childless because of something I did wrong.

On all levels, it was the principle of the thing.

Plus, the practice of the thing might be fun. More fun than, say, cordial dates in clean, well-lit public spaces, which was the basic story of Lola's late twenty-something love life. Things with her and Miles, she imagined, would actually have to be kind of *Mission: Impossible* at first—separate cabs, fake phone names—so that when she and Miles finally "came out," everyone would think, well, clearly they've proven that they can work together without weirdness.

Okay, I'm getting ahead of myself. But speaking of *Mission: Impossible.* Mysterious messages. If only I wasn't creeped out by Stefanie's weird note. Anyway.

Distract self.

TO: Truffle
FROM: SickOfBarScene
I would like to meet a woman who can gracefully balance her family, career and personal interests.

So would I, thought Lola. So would I.

Delete.

That was it. Nothing from Boqueron. That's weird. Her radio silence should, according to certain pink self-help books she refused to believe, make her all the more irresistible and him all the more interested. Odd.

•

Dear Lola,
I'm a 27-year-old guy in New York City. I'm nice, but I don't have that undateable Friend-Boy problem. I'm smart, but not unable to enjoy the dumber things in life. I'm cute, but not unapproachably so. I'm funny, but not loud funny. I'm outgoing, but not loud outgoing. I'm fit, but not neckless. I have a good and demanding job, but I'm not married to it. I'm mature, but still fun. I have a couple of exes, but no baggage I can't carry myself. I'm secure, but not arrogant. (Truly.) In short, I'd do pretty well on a choosy woman's checklist—and please don't tell me she doesn't have one—but I don't have a girlfriend.

What the dilly? I do meet people when I get out, and I've tried online, AND I've been open to fix-ups, but…things just never take. I do go on dates and stuff. It's not that they always blow me off—on the contrary—it's that everything always just *feels* off. Please do not say "Be yourself!" or "You just haven't met the right girl yet." I await your response eagerly, but not pathetically. Thank you.
—RD

Cute! And classic. A total DO.

•

Lola continued to fiddle while time crawled, actually getting through a good cull of her huge DO pile of advice. She also sat through two meetings with her best Meeting Face. She alphabetized many, many things. Her iMac desktop had never been so damn organized. Color-coded, even. Ping-Pong, meanwhile, slept soundly.

Finally it was 10:55 PM. "Come on, get outta here, you guys," she said to Kat and Ted, still working.

"'Out?' What is this 'out' of which you speak?" asked Kat.

"Legend tells of a great fireball that crosses the sky..." said Ted.

"That's crazy talk, old man!" Kat laughed. "No, seriously, Lo, just like twenty more minutes."

"Same," said Ted.

"All righty. But you guys better not be here when I get back. Well, actually, you better. Well, you know what I mean..." Lola called on her way out. "Bye!'

Twenty minutes. Good. Plenty of time to meet Douglas and get to Darts unnoticed. As much as she hated keeping secrets from Ted and Kat, she thought it was wise for now. She had entertained the notion of asking for Kat's technical help with what she had in mind, but Kat was more familiar with AskLola's internal system than with Ovum's infrastructure. Also, she didn't want Kat to get in trouble. Also, she didn't want Kat to tell her that what she had in mind was a really bad idea.

Lola changed into her untrendy sneakers and headed for the elevator. Doug was just arriving. They chitchatted about *Buffy* until they reached Darts, where they stopped at the bar for beers and then found a sawdusty table in the back, far away from other patrons. Lola crossed her legs up on the bench and kept chitchatting about *Buffy*, even though they'd really exhausted the topic for now, because she was nervous about what she really wanted to say.

"So Lola?" Eeep. "What's up?"

All right. "Douglas, this is going to sound nuts. But, well, weird things are happening at work."

"Yeah, that giant egg was something else."

"Hah, no, like, little weird things. Little things that could be giant. At least if you've been watching *The X-Files* since the first season."

"Like what?"

"Well, first this Tammy thing. You know about that, right? I just don't buy that she wasn't cutting it."

"You think it's a weight thing."

No dummy, this chap. "Right. Now I know, in theory, that they can hire and fire whoever they want, that they can cast whoever they think is 'right for the show.' That there's no actual discrimination unless you can prove it. Heck, maybe not even then. But Tammy's my friend and I just smell a rat here, a really skinny one. Especially because it goes against everything Ovum stands for, and especially because, well, have you seen who's filling in?"

"Not very clearly. She's so thin she disappears when she turns sideways."

Wow. "Hah! That's exactly what I thought."

"So besides that? She asked a bunch of really dumbass, totally non-Ovum questions in my segment, plus one that I thought was just plain annoying until I found this."

Lola produced Stefanie's crib sheet. Douglas looked at it and thought for a minute. Lola could practically see the cogs turning beneath his curls.

"MF?" Doug asked. "Ohhh."

"Yep." Lola cleared her throat.

"*Mille Feuille?*" Douglas offered weakly, and remarkably.

"Right," Lola said sarcastically, and—wow.

"I had a feeling," Douglas said.

"That what?"

"That he would like you."

"Oh! Oh. My. Well. Yeah. Thanks. I mean, but you know, it was just one nutty night. I mean, not *that* nutty! But you know…" She trusted Doug, but she still felt like downplaying.

"The party?"

"The party," said Lola. "That's the thing. I mean Doug, it's *exactly* what Lola, Online Lola, said not to do. Geez, *especially* with a superior."

"Well…you're not his direct report. And actually, Online Lola said '…after the fourth eggnog.' She made no mention of the fourth Blue Lagoon."

"Were you a Ranger or a Lawyer?" Lola laughed. "But anyway, so she actually asked me point blank if I'd ever had an office romance. Tammy would *never* have done that. Look, I'm paranoid enough about it in the first place, without being cornered on national television. If Stefanie were just clueless that would be one thing. But this note?"

"It is weird," Douglas said sincerely. "It really is. I mean, with all due respect, your love life is not a matter of national interest. So why? I don't know." He shrugged, at a loss. "At least I know why you're telling *me* all this. Oh, wait, the opposite."

"Look. First, Tammy gone, for no good reason. Then some random heinous stranger seems to know this big secret that could make me look really, really bad. I know it's probably just my ego talking, but my sixth sense is piping up, too. What if *I* were, like, *next?*"

Doug nodded.

"Alternatively, what if I have gone totally koo-koo?"

"Well...yeah," Doug said. "These all really could be just random shitty events, Lola. Plus, I mean, you are a catch, if you will. Why on earth would anyone here want to—?"

Because this job is too freaking good to be true and I still don't quite get that it is mine and I have to find a reason to freak out about it because that's what humans do to mess up their dreams.

Well, that, and because I really do have a weird feeling. The kind of feeling I always tell people to listen to, if not act on.

"Beats the hell out of me. I mean, I tend to assume people, and things, are fundamentally on the up-and-up. I would hate—hate!—to think that Ovum was, after talking that big game, basically...lame," said Lola. "But I gotta say, Lola always says 'Trust yourself,' and...I'm Lola."

Doug nodded again, then raised his hand. "I have a question."

"Yes, Doug?"

"Not that I don't care—I totally do—but you still haven't told me why you're telling me this."

"I'm not entirely sure, but I'm not gonna say anything to unduly freak out Ted and Kat and I'm not about to lay my inflated, self-involved paranoia on 'MF' before the third date," said Lola. "Plus—"

"Well, I'm happy to listen," said Doug.

"...Plus, didn't you say that Rangers can detect poison?"

"Yeah," Doug said warily.

Lola dropped her voice even lower, though The Charlie Daniels Band was providing plenty of cover.

"Can you, like, hack into the company e-mail system?" I did not just say that. This is not my life. This is not my job. Which are the same. So.

I've got to look somewhere, Lola had figured. Get something in writing at least about why Tammy lost her job. Also, and Lola was pretending to herself that this was less important, see if there's any chatter about her and Miles. It was a logical, if illegal, place to start.

"Oh boy. Whoa. Well. Wow. Okay. I mean, in terms of my skill set, I work more on building ancillary systems and applications, like your advice organizer, and that chatbot thing I developed?" Doug said. "Also, what you're talking about is completely illegal and scary. Could be a serious CLM."

Lola took a sip of her Brooklyn Lager and waited.

"Career-Limiting Move."

Lola waited some more.

"So when do I start?"

13

Lola had really thought that going to work in An Office would give her the security and serenity that she'd begun to crave, aghast, as she neared thirty. But instead, that lovely firm "set" feeling was giving way to "unsettled." Here she was, keeping college hours, wearing clothes from the hamper, masterminding cybersnooping, and heading into a proto-relationship that required *sneaking.*

Speaking of which, well, today for once she *wasn't* wearing clothes from the hamper. She was wearing clothes she'd barely remembered to pick up from the 24-hour dry cleaner (God bless New York): a dress-and-jacket ensemble that could "go from l'office to ooh-la-la!" with a quick accessory and shoe change (God bless women's magazines). Tonight, after all, was The Date. The first date of the rest of her life, if you think about it, which is why Lola was trying not to.

•

FROM: oestrada@ovuminc.com
TO: lsomerville@ovuminc.com
RE [3]: show topic?
Hi! Thanks for your message! Looks great! Bet Penelope will love it! Sounds like just her kind of thing! I'll be in touch when she gets back to me! Thanks!!! ☺

•

annabel2k: T-2 hours!
hernamewaslola: but who's counting? oh wait, i am
annabel2k: what ru wearing?
hernamewaslola: you know! you helped me pick it out last night!
annabel2k: just making sure

hernamewaslola: remember when we used to plan outfits for dances even down to socks?
hernamewaslola: oh wait we still do.
annabel2k: it's easy to decide what to wear to climb a rock. life is good here.
hernamewaslola: a HELMET.
hernamewaslola: sorry, channeling mom. Hey what happened with rock climber #2?
annabel2k: nothing yet. But that pitchingwoo dude called
hernamewaslola: and?
annabel2k: and i swear he was doing situps at the time
hernamewaslola: oy.
annabel2k: no bigs
annabel2k: ok anyway call me from the bathroom?
annabel2k: and if you take him home call me from your bathroom?
hernamewaslola: yep
hernamewaslola: i mean NOPE! will not!!!! We're starting over. like a *Real Couple*.

•

It was time. Exactly ten minutes after Miles's departure for the East Village, as planned. He was taking the subway; she, a cab. Can't be too careful. Earlier, he'd dropped off ten bucks for carfare in an office envelope. Nice.

Lola waved at Kat, Ted, and Ping-Pong and stopped for a quick glance in the bathroom mirror.

"Mmm, *girl!*" It was Tootie's voice—coming out of Douglas's mouth. Ha, ha.

"Whassup, Ranger?" This was not the place to discuss hijinks. Lola still couldn't believe she *had* hijinks.

"Hot date?" Doug went to wash his hands.

"Yeah, with *The West Wing.*" Douglas looked at her. "Okay, yeah…yes. Date," Lola said.

"Ooh! Who's the lucky man? Or wait, do we call them 'boys' these days?"

"Just some guy. Um, Martin." Yeah, Sheen. You dork.

"Why so sheepish? Oh, waaait, is he from the Iiiiiinternet?" Doug prodded, making boogey man gestures with his damp hands.

"Yes, as a matter of fact," said Lola.

"Hey, nothing to be ashamed of! I know a great advice columnist who'd back me up."

"Thanks." Lola smiled, fiddling pointlessly with her hair. She'd have to curl her eyelashes in the cab. Those contraptions scared guys. Guns didn't, but whatever.

"Where you going?"

"This place, *i?* In the East Village?" Yep, just "i."

"Oh, yeah! Sake bar. It's pretty authentic. No crab stick."

"Yum!" said Lola. "Allrooty, gotta go."

"OK. Good luck with Martin.com."

Lola laughed and waved on her way out.

"You do look great."

Lola grinned and waved again. "Thank you, Ranger."

"Get the smelts!"

"Bye, Doug!"

•

Lola had to walk back and forth a few times to find *i,* a teeny cellar joint marked only with a teeny slate sign with, yes, a teeny letter *i* in chalk. Still, she was a few minutes early. Enough time to change into the spectacular Pradas ($99 sale at Jeffrey—huge call-your-mom triumph) whose strap dug sharply between her toes like an oyster shucker.

Lola took the stairs in her sneakers, parted the bead curtain at the bottom, and entered a different world. Very dark, but not glum—more sexy speakeasy-ish. The only glow came from the backlit bar, a couple of neony fish tanks, and a few candles burning at some sort of shrine. Tremulous Japanese melodies wafted through the background. Among the crowded, crooked wooden tables it was darkness, more than space, that shielded you from your neighbors. This place *was* cool, not just trying to be.

I am the bomb, thought Lola, reaching into her bag for her shoes.

"Don't go changing." Whoops. Miles. Right on time, natch.

"Keep the sneakers on. They're cute."

I am a feminist who makes her own way in the world without following male direction or seeking male approval, Lola thought as she put away the Pradas.

"Okay."

"Shall we?"

They made small talk as they squinched into the table Miles had reserved. (*Reserved*. Point, Farmington.) Lola admired Miles's tailored cotton shirt. You know what looks great on guys? Buttons.

Menus came, Miles ordered some sort of sake and Lola pulled her legs into her lap as she furrowed her brow over the selections. This was really authentic Japanese bar food, evidently, with lots of eely squiddy things Lola was game to try, but not sure how to go about ordering.

"You want me to just pick some things?" Miles stepped in. "We ate tons of this stuff when I lived in Japan."

He lived in Japan? "Sure. I like everything except sea urchin," offered Lola. "You lived in Japan?"

"Yes, ma'am. Tokyo. A few years. Internet encryption technology stuff—pretty boring—but I'll tell you about it in a sec."

The waiter had come back. Lola glanced down at her menu while Miles did his thing. "Oh! And could we throw in one order of the smelts?" she suggested.

"Good call! Intrepid eater. I like that," said Miles, looking Lola in the eye while he poured her sake without spilling a drop. Yee.

Miles launched into his Japan story. Work schmork, he said; he and his buds climbed Mt. Fuji, golfed at midnight, ate squirming fish…Lola was rapt. Lived in *Japan.* Other guys she'd dated, or not, balked at going to *Brooklyn.* Goodness, what other fascinating stories and experiences did he have?

Their appetizers came—edamame, octopus, kimchee. Miles offered a small digression on Korean grace notes in Japanese cooking. Lola listened, and also watched his mouth move. Lips move. Lips. All of a sudden he stopped.

"Am I boring you?" he asked.

"Are you kidding me?" asked Lola. It was so nice not to have to Think of Questions.

"It's just that…no one's asked me about Japan in a long time; I haven't had the pleasure of thinking about it in a while. And I just feel like you…get it."

"Then bring it on!" exclaimed Lola, waving a chopstick and dropping a tentacle in her lap. Smooth, Somerville. She looked down.

Wait, what was—? A semi-circle of plastic was protruding from between her blouse buttons, like a tusk. Like a huge freaking plastic tusk. A huge freaking plastic *chest* tusk. What the—?

Oh, for God's sake. It was the underwire (under*plastic*, anyway) from the right side of her bra—an old one, worn to prevent hanky panky. Or to assure it, if you believe Murphy's/Bridget's Law. It had poked out of its sheath and somehow rotated itself out from Lola's top to greet the night.

Ohhhkay. No quick moves. Lola moved her left hand in toward her neck as if to play demurely with her pendant—not that she was wearing one. In the process, she let the heel of her hand slooooooooowly push the tusk to the right, back inside where it belonged.

Done.

Had Miles noticed? Evidently not. He was still, mirabile dictu, looking her in the eyes.

And evidently still talking about Japan. Hmm. Lola had missed some stuff. Oh God. Was he still interesting?

Hey relax, it's not like Mom's always riveted to Dad's linguistics stuff, and *they're* in love. Okay. All right.

Eventually the food came, along with more sake, and the conversation drifted from Japan toward other stories and experiences of Miles's. The Galapagos, City Year, couple of triathlons. He was really impressive. Lola was really...impressed.

Miles took a sip of sake, dabbed at his mouth with his napkin, and leaned forward. "I find you incredibly intriguing," he said.

I am a very mysterious woman because you haven't asked anything about me, thought Lola, her knees weakening all the same.

"Do you?" Lola asked mysteriously.

"Yes. Enough about me. Have *you* ever been to the Galapagos?"

Lola's eyebrows flew up.

"Kidding," said Miles. "Seriously. What made you decide to sell your baby and come to Ovum?"

All better. They talked about Lola's decision, about the office (both above-board and gossip), about what it was like to work there. At one point Lola excused herself to give Annabel the progress report, but her cell didn't work this far underground. When she came back, Miles—who had scored more sake—returned to the topic.

"How do you feel about some of the changes that have taken place since we've been there?"

Huh. "I mean, some things are different, maybe some stuff has gotten watered down a little, but it's still a far cry from FairerSex.com," Lola said.

"You still happy there?" Miles asked.

"Oh yeah, of course. It's amazing." Lola paused. "It's just..."

Should she gripe about Tammy? Nah, stay positive.

"Just what?" Miles pressed.

"Just...amazing."

"I'm so glad," he said. "Hey, can you keep a secret?"

If you count Annabel as me, thought Lola, "Sure."

"Fern's leaving."

Fern Gellar, VP of Technology. His boss. "Really?"

"Mmm hmm."

"How come?"

"She's gonna do the full-time mom thing."

"Good for her!"

"Good for me too, if you know what I mean."

"Waaaaita sec. Really?" Lola leaned in. "You're gonna take her job? Wow! Miles, that's really great." Oh *boy,* this thing had better work out.

"And can you keep yet another secret?"

"Three's a charm," said Lola.

"So's Angela."

"Leaving?" Ovum's big trophy? No way. NO WAY. "You're kidding. How come?"

"Same thing. Baby."

"But I thought she was a lesb—Oh."

This is all very odd, thought Lola. Nothing wrong with being moms (or having two moms, for that matter), but those women just didn't seem like the types to leave something while it was still building. Well, then again, who knows what their plans were—maybe they're launchers, not presiders. Who knows?

"Who's replacing Angela?"

"I heard they're bringing in some bigshot guy who's disillusioned with Disney-Seagram," Miles replied.

Guy.

Two women replaced with two guys. Hmm.

"Don't say anything yet, though, okay?" added Miles. "I just…I wanted you to be the first to know."

If you blush in pitch dark, do you actually turn red? "Thanks," Lola raised her sake cup. "Congratulations, Miles."

Clink.

Bzzz.

Mmm. Lola could actually *hear* the electricity between them.

Wait. Bzzz?

Bzzz. There it went again. It sounded like a radio station that wasn't quite tuned in, and it was coming from Miles's watch.

Lola stared. Miles rapped his wrist on the table, and the watch fell silent. "Percussive maintenance," he grinned.

"Wait, Miles? Why did your watch go *bzzz?*"

"This thing? Who knows. It's just some courtesy swag from an acquaintance in Japan. It does a lot of unnecessary stuff, like bleep me with tech stock updates," he said. "And not all that well, either."

Miles paid the bill, refusing Lola's Wallet Reach. She thanked him. They headed out to the sidewalk.

Solid date, Lola thought. A real DATEdate. Yeah.

"So how about a nightcap?" Miles was asking.

"Nightcap," huh? Lola thought. That could lead only one place.

"Thanks, but I'll take a rain check," said Lola. "It *is* a school night. I'd rather mix metaphors than alcohols."

"My loss," said Miles, touching her cheek.

Said Miles, touching her cheek.

Said Miles, touch—

Eeee. Long-lashed eyes, half-shut, moving closer. Oh. Lips, closer, too. Oh my. Now touching. Touching. Up on sneaker tiptoes. *Touching.* Soft, like kneaded dough. Soft. Dough. Does that Atkins Diet really work? Wait, what? HELLO, Lola. Miles. Is. Kissing. You. Pay attention so this time you remember, you dumbass. Mmm. Yeah. Noted.

Miles pulled away slowly, one arm still curled around Lola's waist.

"Thanks for dinner," she said. "Yay, smelts." Yay, smelts?!

"Hail you a cab?"

"Sure. Thanks." Cab pulled up, Miles handed the guy a twenty. *Damn,* he's good. He opened the door, placing a kiss on her forehead as she got in. She felt sort of blushy and fizzy and gooey and little. And also formidable, of course.

"Bye. See you tomorrow."

"Yes. Bye."

Slam. Lola gave directions and forced herself to look ahead. Waitwaitwaitwait. Okay. She looked back. Miles was looking back too. She smiled. Ohmigodohmigod, we actually did that thing where you both look back. Whoa.

Turning forward again, Lola settled into her seat, proud of herself for saying no to the nightcap.

Hell's bells, though; truth be told, saying no actually hadn't been *that* hard.

Why not? What is my problem? Just cold feet, surely. And why not? Been a long time since I've met a guy this good—whom I work with. Of *course* he's tripping those wires, making me skittish.

That's totally what Annabel would say. Lola took out her phone.

14

"Hey, did you see this?"

Kat had beaten Lola into the office. Not surprising, as Lola hadn't slept all that well. Between snooze button hits, she dreamt that she was trying to clean up her apartment and get ready for work, but everything she touched turned into a giant smelt.

Lola took a hot gulp of Peet's and wiped her lips with the back of her hand. "Is Ping-Pong learning sign language or something?"

"No, this," said Kat, beckoning Lola to her computer. She pointed to a press release newly posted at http://www.ovuminc.com/MediaCenter.html.

FOR IMMEDIATE RELEASE

NEW YORK—The women's multimedia network Ovum, Inc. today announces the departure of two of its highest-profile and most distinguished leaders, Fern Gellar, VP of Technology, and Angela Chan, VP of Programming.

Both have elected to pursue the home-based career of full-time motherhood.

"It is with both sadness and pride that we bid these visionaries farewell," Ovum founder and CEO Madeline North said by phone from the Philippines, where she is attending a conference on sneaker-factory reform. "They have raised a network; they must now raise a family. Their presence and their invaluable contributions will be sorely missed. Yet we also celebrate their exemplary choice proving women both powerful and human, their bold step demonstrating that women can have it all, just maybe not all at once.

"Due to the rapidly shifting nature of the new media infrastructure, we are unfortunately unable to preserve their jobs for their sometime return. Why, just months ago, the title 'information architect,' for example, didn't even exist; two months from now, it may already be extinct. These two visionaries will, however, always be welcome back, in some capacity deemed appropriate and mutually beneficial, upon completion of Ovum's state-of-the-art day care center."

Replacements for these two positions are yet to be determined.

Ovum, Inc. is a multimedia company whose web and television programming, including *Penelope*, reflects and enhances the multi-layered nature of women's lives.

For information and interviews, please contact Kim McMinnville, kmcminnville@ovuminc.com.

###

Meanwhile, Ted had arrived and had been reading over their shoulders. "Angela Chan? I thought she was a les—Oh."

"Wowee, right?" said Kat. "Weird that the we didn't hear directly right from the adminisphere, and too bad there's no props in there for Tammy."

"Totally," said Lola. "You know, I actually heard this last night from Miles."

"Oh right! Duh! For God's sake," Kat smacked her forehead, making the little butterfly clips in her hair go flap-flap. "How could I forget?! How was it?"

"It was…nice." Lola intended that as winking understatement.

"Yeah, but you're not wearing what you wore yesterday," observed Ted, disappointed. "My *God,* you don't already have a *drawer,* do you?!"

"No Ted, sorry, there was no Commute of Shame," Lola replied.

"So did Miles say who might be replacing Angela and Fern?" asked Kat.

"Yeah, actually," Lola said. "Angela, some guy from DSBC. And Fern, well, Miles is getting her job."

"Miles?! And did you say some '*guy*?'" Kat exclaimed.

Lola nodded with a sigh.

Everyone stared for a minute.

"Well," said Ted, looking up. "The ceiling *is* glass."

•

FROM: oestrada@ovuminc.com
TO: lsomerville@ovuminc.com
RE: RE: RE: RE: FWD: show topic?
Hi Lola! Unfortunately I've got bad news! Penelope was glad to hear about your idea, but she wanted me to let you know that she just doesn't think it's "right for her!" Sorry! ☹ Oh, but she says to please keep pitching! She thinks you're a great kid! Thanks!!! ☺

"Great kid"?! "Keep pitching"!? Lola hadn't expected a free ride, but what was this, Wiffle ball? There was also an Ovum-wide mandate (including clarification that the "man-" in "mandate" came from the Latin neuter past participle of *mandare,* to order) that all network shows and sites should make a good-faith effort to draw on Ovum's in-house talent first. So much for sisterhood!

All right, not so fast, Somerville. Don't go holding women to higher collectivey-er expectations just 'cause they're women. We're still running a business, making decisions we don't—and shouldn't—always have to explain. You must trust that Penelope, capable and formidable businesswoman and someone you should embrace as a mentor, knows what she's doing.

But wait, the opposite. She *doesn't.* This topic's "not for her?" It is *perfect* for her. Old genre—relationships, "commitment," yadda yadda—that people will never not want to talk about; but with a fresh, feminist-but-even-handed spin. Penelope does like to vary her shows between the hard stuff like, say, minefields in Cambodia, and the really hard stuff, like, say, minefields in relationships—and this one's ideal for the latter. *Especially* now that she doesn't have to nod along to that earnest bozo E. Ron Wilson…well, geez. I mean, you'd think…well, geez.

Harrumph, thought Lola. Well, she hasn't heard the last of me.

•

Somehow, between meetings (one marketing—in which they actually brainstormed possible "Lola" merchandise, including t-shirts, mugs, even Pez!—and one activism/initiatives), Lola managed to bang out quite a bit of her column. By 9:30 PM, Kat and Ted had turned on the AMC's production of *South Pacific,* with Jewel as Nellie Forbush.

"I'm having trouble suspending my disbelief for this production," Kat was saying. "I mean, yeah, musicals are traditionally heightened and artificial environments, but in this version they're playing it very straight, very realistic, and it's not really working for me."

"See, what you have to understand is that in those days, there were orchestras in the bushes," replied Ted.

Lola put on her headphones, took out a tub of sugary dried figs, and began her next move.

FROM: lsomerville@ovuminc.com
TO: oestrada@ovuminc.com
RE: more ideas
Hi, Olive. Thanks for getting back to me so quickly about my first idea. I totally understand. Just thought I'd zip over a few more while you all were fresh in my mind. Just briefly, how about:

- Dating "rules" are not about gender roles; they're about *manners*
- The new "no:" you should wait to have sex because that's more *fun* (teen show?)
- The curse of the "nice guy" (and girl "buddy")
- Teen show: What are double standards? Why are guys who do it cool and girls who do it "hoochies?"
- Can actual love come from virtual dating?
- Why was the new Woodstock so Tailhook?
- For a very special *Penelope*: the warning signs of teen dating violence

Okay, good, just two more and you can go home.

Lola suddenly sensed a presence next to her.

"Oh!" She turned and jumped, startled, catching her headphone wire under her elbow and yanking one of her earpieces into her eye.

"Miles, you scared me!" Lola attempted to remove the headphones, which caught in her hoop earring. Take it slow. Remain calm.

"Sorry," he smiled. "You were really concentrating. How's Ping-Pong?"

"Come on, how long were you standing there?"

"Twenty minutes. I like to watch. You working."

Shiver. Headphones off, placed a safe distance away on desk.

"Just kidding. Only a second or two. But you know what I like to watch even better?"

"Um, what?" asked Lola, failing to feign nonchalance.

"You *stop* working. How about a—?"

"Nightcap?" Lola leapt out of her seat and did her signature "HOORAY!" jig. In her head. Her actual body opened its mouth and said, "Aw, no, Miles, thanks, but I really can't tonight. I really need to get this done." She gestured toward her computer. "It's, like, an extra thing and I can't fit it in tomorrow."

Miles didn't even blink. "What if there were tapas involved? I know this place where they cure their own anchovies."

Holy moly.

"How about Friday?" said Lola.

•

hernamewaslola: I'm in big T for trouble
annabel2k: why?
hernamewaslola: kilometers? he * likes anchovies *
annabel2k: brb. must write maid of honor toast right now
hernamewaslola: right?! yah, out of nowhere he just mentions this tapas place that cures their own
annabel2k: wait so how did he know you like them? nobody likes anchovies
hernamewaslola: huh. lucky guess?

•

Lola suddenly sensed a presence next to her. Eeee! Bemused exasperation. "Miles, I *said*—"

It was Doug, holding a sheet of paper. "Hey," he whispered. "I think I've got something."

15

"Really?" said Lola in a stage whisper. "Well, Ranger, pull up a chair."

"It's not much," said Douglas, scooting in next to Lola. "I mean, I need to do this after hours, like there is such thing here in the first place."

"You're telling me."

"Also, turns out it's not about Tammy." Doug placed the printout on Lola's desk.

TO: lsomerville@ovuminc.com
FROM: newproducts@benandjerrys.com
Dear Ms. Somerville,

We are all huge fans of yours over here at Ben and Jerry's. Your warm, witty, and insightful responses to your advice-seekers are threatening to replace our ice cream as the comfort-to-the-lovelorn of choice! ;-)

It is with that observation that I write to request a meeting with you and your merchandising representatives at Ovum, Inc. Specifically, we would like to discuss the possibility of creating a "Lola" flavor of Ben and Jerry's with your likeness (and of course your input on flavor development).

Please advise as to your availability at your earliest convenience. We await your response with great anticipation.

Sincerely,
Jonas Ingall
Director, New Products

"A Ben and Jerry's *flavor?!* Oh, my God, that would be the best thing ever in the whole entire world!" Lola exclaimed. "I mean, that's better than a *stamp*! Oh my God, oh my God, oh my God. Let's see! Something with chocolate, I guess, though that's a bit of a cliché, so maybe with something interesting in it, something salty, but they've already done Chubby Hubby, so maybe instead of pretzels we use Cheez—"

Wait. Lola looked back at the paper.

"This is dated two weeks ago!"

Doug waited.

"And I never saw this! Why didn't it get to me?"

Doug finally spoke. "The version that would have gone from the server to your mailbox was deleted."

"On purpose?"

"Far as I can tell."

"Waaaait a sec. Who would want to do that? The soy people?"

"I honestly don't know."

"Could it be some sort of mistake? I mean, we were just talking about doing some Lola merch in a meeting the other day, but nothing even half this cool. This would be great for Ovum! It totally doesn't make sense."

"You're right, Lo. I don't know what to say—and I'm a Ranger," Douglas replied. "I can't imagine who wouldn't want you to see that. I mean, who wouldn't want you and your site to have that opportunity? Do you have any enemies? Geez, that sounds dramatic."

"No, I really don't; certainly not here, that I know of. I mean, I find Carrie pretty irritating, but that's ludicrous. And it's not like E. Ron Wilson knows I exist."

"Any ex-boyfriends who don't want to see you do well?" Doug inquired.

Lola thought about that for a second. "Well, the only one who really hates me is Henry, and I probably deserve it. But this is way out of his league. Last I heard, he still had a Commodore 64."

"Then he deserves whatever he got," said Doug.

"God, I can't believe I can't follow up!" Lola cried. "Whoever didn't want me to see this will find out that I did see it. And now Ben and Jerry will think I'm totally rude. Who'd have thought that after all my years of loyal butterfatty support, I would ever burn bridges with those guys? This is the worst."

Lola thought for another minute. "So Ranger, as long as it's not too risky,"—Douglas laughed sarcastically—"would you keep keeping an eye out? For this, and you know, we still got nothing on Tammy. Not to mention the whole Stefanie weirdness."

"You mean the way she spells her name?" Douglas smiled at Lola. "No, of course, sure I will." He waxed still more solemn. "But if I die, and I'm not around to look after you, promise me you'll rent *Army of Darkness*."

Lola smiled. He is adorkable. "Promise. Thanks, Doug."

•

Orange with chocolate. Did they have that already? Or what about chocolate with some sort of spicy something? Wasn't that supposed to be, like, a Mayan aphrodisiac? Coffee ice cream with crumbled biscotti. Hey, not bad. Malt balls. Everyone loved those. Chocolate grahams? Or something with fortune cookies? Something with ginger. Green tea with wasabi peas for crunch. Eeeuw, I must be really…

Lola plunged into sleep. She dreamed she was trapped in some sort of pint-sized container. A giant spoon came down and she only barely managed to hide behind a great big butterscotch chip.

•

Before she'd crawled into bed, Lola—still wide awake—had stayed up watching that week's *Buffy.* Huge drama: Buffy finally slept with her complicated and brooding boyfriend Angel, the "good" vampire who had been cursed (by a gypsy) with a soul. Cursed, because that meant he had a conscience and thus was tormented by guilt about all the terrible vampiry things he'd done over the centuries. But the curse also meant, of course, that he could love. Anyway, so they sleep together. And right there in bed, the very second he thus experiences true happiness, the curse is lifted. Which means that he becomes bad vampire "Angelus" again. Also, that when you have sex, your boyfriend might turn evil.

The episode gave Lola an idea for her next column theme (something like "When to Do it: The Last Word on the Third Date"). And she remembered just the letter to start off with.

Oh, wait. First finish that memo to Olive.

- Relationships and music: why our love lives have soundtracks
- Why are women waiting longer to have sex?

Please let me know what might interest you and Penelope. I have lots of letters and research, and of course, I've got more ideas where these came from.

Thanks for your attention.

All best,
Lola

•

Lola hadn't forgotten about last night, nor about Stefanie's crib sheet. Thing was, her questions and suspicions were vague and fluttering, like when you know you're getting a headache but you can't point to the exact place where it'll emerge. She didn't know how to pin them down, à la lepidopterist, in order to examine them. She also didn't know if she was squinting too hard to see connections where there were none. It helped, in terms of perspective, to have Doug on the case—if there were a case in the first place—but she didn't want him to think she was nuts. For the same reason, she didn't want to breathe a word to Miles. All she could do for right now was be very Zen (or at least somewhat *Celestine Prophecy)* about the whole thing and keep her mind and eyes open for thoughts and clues.

"Hey, Lola, gotta sec?" It was Kat, in a lilac faux-fur miniskirt. "How do you like these prototypes for the site redesign? This is the front page." Kat spread some printouts on Lola's desk.

Good Lord, Lola had almost forgotten. Kat had been polishing up the look and the navigation of the site; the design department had wanted to see the plans by the end of this week.

"Wow, they look great, Kat. So is this what the red will look like on the screen?"

"Pretty much. God, you don't know how long I'd fantasized about a huge dye-sublimation color printer like this one."

"You should see Clive more often," Ted said. He turned to Lola. "Sublimation? Sometimes it's too easy."

"Kat, it all looks killer. Walk me through the new nav later?"

"Thanks. Sure."

"Thank *you!*"

•

Lola dug up the letter that had popped into her head last night.

Dear Lola,
Thanks in large part to your column, I'm finally back in the dating loop after a gross breakup. Problem is, since I've been away for four years, I don't know how to treat sex anymore. It seems like everyone in New York City has sex on the third date. I have major mixed feelings about that.

One half says: HUH? SEX on your THIRD DATE?! HELLO HIV! HELLO HEARTBREAK!!!

The other half says: Girl, you are being prudish and stupid. People have sex all the time; use a condom and get over it!

Lola, which half do I follow? Please don't write something like, "Dearie, your first half is right, follow your heart, yadda yadda yadda," because my second half really is, well, lonely. And loud. Help?
—Good Girls Don't...Know What to Do Anymore

Welcome to my nightmare, thought Lola.

•

Lola had made plans that night for a late dinner with Rachel, an old high school friend whose husband was out of town. Rachel wanted to try Kitchen, the new place in the meat-packing district where you, the diner, select the combination of meat (or fish, or whatever), the preparation (roasted, braised, etc.), the sauce (purslane pesto, soy-persimmon lacquer, Zima reduction) and the sides (chayote, items involving the words *timbale* and *heirloom,* etc.)

I thought the whole point of restaurants was to let them do the thinking, Lola thought. Still, she was looking forward to spilling a little about Miles. Rachel, though happily married, made little secret of missing her dating days. Her fits of jealousy upon hearing of Lola's escapades on her Tuscany Tour '98 were, frankly, a victory for single women everywhere.

Kat was touching up her designs; Ted and Greta had gone to see *How to Make an American Quilt.*

"Come on, Kat. Wanna walk out with me? Actually, that's an order. You can finish tomorrow."

"Okay, gimme a sec."

The two headed for the elevator.

"So how are things with Miles?"

"No 'things' yet, Kat. Not even *a* thing. But, you know, I'm working on it."

"But, like, Lo, you *like* him, right?"

Lola took a second. "Like him? What do you mean? Of course I *like* him! Isn't that the point? The *like* thing? What's not to like?"

"Just checking." Kat smiled, then wrinkled her nose. "You smell paint?"

They looked toward the TV studio area. Some guys on the crew were repainting the Sweat set. Only they had just finished covering up the word "Sweat" on the backdrop. And changing it to "Glow." Lola and Kat looked at each other.

"This can't be good," said Lola.

16

Dear Good Girl,

Not so fast. There are, um, more halves to consider.

1. The other half of the couple, i.e. this guy. Do you actually *want* to sleep with *him*, or do you just not want to be "prudish?" The latter, as reasons to have sex go, is half-assed.

2. The other half of the date, i.e. the *after*-sex part. You want to have sex with him, but will you want to *have had* sex with him? Are you ready for the after-algebra (so many new variables!), the Morning Boyfriend, the cab ride home from East Skulk, the Scarf Syndrome? [a rollover feature made this LolaLingo definition pop up: *Scarf Syndrome: when sleeping with someone you're not that into nonetheless releases hormones that cause you to worry about whether he's dressed warmly enough, etc.]*

3. The other half of the glass, i.e. the full one. There are documented cases of couples who hit the sack the first night and leave only to register for new linens. Does this guy feel Bed, Bath, *and* Beyond?

4. The "ho" half of the Heidi/Ho complex. Some still swear that a guy's interest feeds only on the thrill of the chaste, the promise of play. There's an uncomfortable soupcon of empirical truth here. But if keeping someone's interest comes down to keeping him waiting, well, eeuw.

So consider all of these other halves—no Right answers, but those are the right questions—and see

```
where they get you. Bottom line: follow your heart,
but listen to your loins, too—keeping in mind that
even lusting can mean waiting. Wanting to,
reeeeally wanting to, is half the fun.
Love,
Lola
```

Lola was cranking this morning; she'd come in early to make sure she could leave by 8:07 PM for dinner with Miles. It's Friday, dammit; I'm going to put my overwrought and likely unfounded conspiracy theories aside and get good old-fashioned excited for my good old-fashioned date, she'd thought. She didn't even have her browser open to the Panda-cam.

Generally, Lola and Miles had been doing a solid job of keeping things, such as "things" were, on the down low. And given recent events, Lola had even started replying to his occasional e-mails only in person, like in little flirty walk-bys near the juice bar. She was no dummy; even though—come on, Lola, you crazy lady, no one is digging around—she didn't need her personal e-mails read by whoever was digging around. Or by Douglas, for that matter.

"So how come Doug doesn't have a girlfriend?" Lola heard Ted saying. "Is it because he does odd jobs for women instead of asking them out, like 'my friend' Ted?"

"Hmm, or maybe he's gay." Kat was completely kidding. As if the only two possibilities were either straight-and-attached, or gay.

Not that it didn't feel that way sometimes.

"I don't know about that," Ted replied. "He and I *have* talked a lot about women and their bodies."

"Yeah," Lola chimed in, "but were those women Patti LuPone and Elaine Page?"

•

Finally the clock rolled toward eight. A million eat-your-day-up meetings hadn't hurt. Lola began to pack up. "So what are you guys doing tonight?"

"Play on the Lower East Side. Friend's in it," said Kat. "Theater of Obligation."

"If you fool around with someone you're doing a show with, does that mean you're getting play within a play?" asked Ted.

"Yes," said Lola. "What are you up to, Ted?"

"I'm gonna go listen to a friend that I'm secretly in love with complain about her boyfriend."

"Have fun!" said Kat and Lola.

"OK, I'm outtie," said Lola. She took the east elevator down and hailed a cab.

•

Miles was waiting for her at one of the few teeny round copper tables at "~," the one-table-wide tapas *boite* in SoHo. It had been there forever, but Lola was pretty sure the name used to be longer.

Anyway, Lola was impressed. ~ didn't take reservations; Miles must know someone in order to get a prime table at prime time. He'd probably lived in Spain, where the waiters here actually came from (as opposed to from, say, Yale Drama School).

Miles stood up when Lola entered. Nice. Nothing wrong with feeling like a lady, thought Lola, or a judge.

"Hey." Kiss on the cheek. "I already ordered the *boquerones*," he said with a wink.

Hoo. Note to self. Check PitchingWoo.com; need to send up some sort of flare to Boqueron. Don't I? Lola wondered. Though I feel kind of weird breaking up with him, seeing as how we never went out. Anyway.

Dinner passed in a haze of garlic and dry sherry. Miles told tales of living in—yep—Spain, of private tours of the Prado, of cloisters in Catalonia, of glass-bottomed boats on the Costa Brava, of *Carmen* actually performed in Seville, of camping out in the renegade countryside near Bilbao. "The only thing I ever learned to say in Basque was 'I support your cause!'" he joked.

Lola cracked up. She couldn't help but notice—and this is what she told Annabel in her furtive call from *el baño*—that Miles seemed to have loosened up somehow. Tonight he was even wearing a T-shirt—the nice suedey cotton Banana Republic kind, black, of course—instead of a button-down. He was not only impressive, grown-up, and cultured; he was also fun. This shift made Lola decide not to kill the buzz by confiding in Miles about the recent weirdnesses. It also emboldened her to hold his gaze over curved snifters of syrupy sherry.

His eyes green, mine brown. What did we learn in bio about which color the kids get?

"Hey, let me show you something." Miles signed the bill and raised an eyebrow mysteriously. He grabbed her hand and began to lead her to the back of the narrow restaurant. "Hey, thanks for dinner!?" she called ahead. Miles looked right back at her. "Thank *you*."

They squooshed past the people sitting along the bar—which, in the back, replaced the tables—and stopped at a third unmarked door next to the restrooms. Miles caught the eye of the barkeep, who waved him on.

"There's something I want to show you," Miles said, opening the door to a dark staircase. "Oh, hang on." He stepped back and grabbed a votive candle from the bar.

That's all the light they had as Miles led Lola down the stairs. She could just make out dusty brick walls, massive splintery beams, and—ah, of course!—racks and racks of wine. And big barrels of what must be sherry, or, what do you call them, casks?

"They say this is where Edgar Allan Poe was inspired to write *The Cask of Amontillado,*" Miles whispered at the bottom of the stairs, drawing Lola close. Lola nodded, shivering for many, many reasons. "And they say this is where Miles Farmington was inspired to kiss Lola Somerville." He put the candle on a step, one hand on the small of her back, the other on her cheek, and kissed her much less politely than before. Lola's legs turned to aioli.

•

They had tried to walk to Miles's apartment, but had found kissing and walking at the same time inefficient, so they made out in a cab.

The elevator opened at 19. Only two apartments on the floor. Miles opened the door on the right and flicked on the light. Lola caught her garlic breath.

Most Manhattan apartments, subdivided like movie theaters turned into multiplexes, involved making choices. A study, *or* a common room; a bicycle, *or* a coffee table; a closet, *or* windows.

Miles, for his part, had made different kinds of choices. For the two-story bookshelves, spiral staircase, *and* rolling ladder, cherry or maple? (Cherry.) For the authentic pinball machine, Superman or Flash Gordon? (Flash Gordon.) For the kitchen, a subzero fridge or a restaurant stove? Okay, both.

"Want a tour?" asked Miles.

"Well, how many are there per day? They must take hours," said Lola.

"Or all night, if you want."

"I'm not sleeping with you," said Lola coyly.

•

The morning sun slanted through the blinds, hitting Miles's kabillion-thread-count sheets like big sideways pats of butter. With Miles's arm around her shoulders, Lola felt warm, content, and smug. Sherry and spiral staircase notwithstanding, they had not had sex. Lola felt that spicy before-glow of anticipation, the lustrous pride of restraint. Not sleeping together means we like each other; we have time. Where, after all, is the fire?

"You're so hot," murmured Miles, moving his hand down to her waist.

Oh.

There's the fire.

•

The sun had inched closer to the top of the sky.

No one really knew what to say.

"Hey, Lo?"

"Mmm?"

"Mind if I call you Lo?"

"Not at all."

Long pause.

"Mind if I call you…Lulu?"

"No, but that's also what my parents call me, so you'll also have to call Dr. Freud."

"Right. Mind if I call you…Pooky?"

"Yep."

"Mind if I call you…The Mayor of Casterbridge?"

No answer. Lola couldn't think of a…who was it who was it who was it?…Thomas Hardy comeback fast enough.

"Whoakay! I'll make some coffee," said Miles. "How do you take it?"

Black, like my—"Either just half-and-half, or black, please," Lola replied. This was not the time for idiotic jokes. Today I am a woman.

"Oh, mind if I make it half-decaf?"

"Okay, but you get the decaf half," Lola replied. Okay, that was funny.

Miles laughed and tousled Lola's already messy hair. Yee.

Oh! Tess of the D'Urbervilles! Too late.

•

Lola called Annabel from the cab and got voice mail. Maybe she's on line.

hernamewaslola: yo.
annabel2k: hey! nu?
hernamewaslola: um i just got home from my date
annabel2k: whoa! how was?
hernamewaslola: interesting...
annabel2k: you guys sleep together last night?
hernamewaslola: nope

annabel2k: wowee! what restraint!
hernamewaslola: we slept together this morning
annabel2k: OHHHHHHHHHHHHHHHHH!
annabel2k: bravissima!
hernamewaslola: yes, ma'am.
hernamewaslola: think he'll respect me in the evening?

17

So things with Miles were going according to plan—that is, if the plan was for things to go faster than originally planned. Well, it's water under the bridge now; what's done is done. Lola certainly refused to get all girl-guilty and "What will he think of me?" about it. Though she did catch herself wondering "Why hasn't he called yet?" not two hours after she'd left Miles's place. Ah, vestigial reflexes from centuries of clinging to men for food and shelter.

Half of Lola, the upper half, had indeed kind of wanted to do that lazy coupley Saturday thing, partly to warm-fuzzify what the lower half had done. But—in that weird way that intimacy, *feelings*, is more intimate than intimacy, *sex*—she'd also felt that lollygagging and listening to NPR together or going for brunch or whatever, that *that* would be "too much." Go freaking figure.

And right now, anyway, Lola's inner—well, outer—only child was saying *I vant to be alone.* Of course Lola wanted her life to overlap with someone's, but yeah: overlap. No concentric circles. So this afternoon was finally—though I really should go into the office, she thought—the day to go all FEMA on her apartment and clean up the devastation. Lola looked at the hook where she hung her keys. Funny, huh, how your space is just the one big blob called your *life* until someone else shows up and leans on one side. *Then* it's "your space." *Your* space.

Time to start carving. Lola put on some old music, Boy Georged her way to the window, and plucked a bra from a ficus.

•

"Hello? Achoo!"

"Lola, hey, it's Jordan. Um, bless you?"

Jordan. Riiight. Lola's total non-issue ex-boyfriend from college. He lived in San Francisco now, but they hung out every eight months or so when he was in town. They were supposed to have drinks or something tonight. She'd almost forgotten.

"Jordan! Hi! Thanks!" Lola sniffed, looking around for a Kleenex.

"How are you?" he asked. "Do you have a cold or something?"

"No, no, I was just cleaning my apartment. It's Dust Bunny City, and I'm the Mayor," said Lola. "It's totally gross, but I have found approximately $30 in nickels."

"Put it toward our slush fund for tonight! You still up for going out?"

"Sure," said Lola. Shoot. Part of her really wanted to stay home and putter and nest. But another part of her cleared its throat and read her article 17 of the Single Woman Manifesto: "Do not stay in just because you seem to be going out with someone." All right, all right. "I'm just gonna have to boil myself first," she said.

"Ha ha! Oh, Lo. You were always so funny."

Oh, for God's sake. *Now* I have to say something *else* funny. She thought for a second. Nothing. Oh, fuck it. "Aaaaaanyway," continued Lola, "how about, I don't know, 9, at Nawlins?"

2-for-1 Dixie beers were likely in Jordan's modest zine-publisher price range. "Nawlins? Hmm, actually, I was thinking more like Mmmm."

Well, well, well! Clearly Jordan had some sort of news, not to mention a reservation. Mmmm was the velvet-rope joint *du jour.* Its upstairs lounge was believed to be where Leonardo DiCaprio had gotten fat.

"Works for me," said Lola.

Thank goodness she hadn't had time to take the Cynthia Rowley to the cleaners.

•

hernamewaslola: checking in. going to see jordan.
annabel2k: ah! think he'll wear shoes?
hernamewaslola: we'll see! whassup with rock climber #2?
annabel2k: oh yeah did i mention? he cooks me, HE cooks ME, a romantic dinner of cornish game hens and i don't know what all, then two days later (yesterday) he tells me he's "not ready."
hernamewaslola: oh for god's sake.
annabel2k: yeah. i was like "well you should have told you that."
hernamewaslola: they tell us not to scare guys?! they scare themselves. so sorry, annabel.
annabel2k: yep. he's a real self-startler.
hernamewaslola: haw.

annabel2k: plus, game hens? who serves a girl game hens?
hernamewaslola: right. it's like, there's "i like you" guy and "take no risks" guy, and they're always fighting inside a guy's head...
hernamewaslola: then "I like you" guy does something nice and then "take no risks" guy is all "oh, *great*, you did it again. now i have to make us disappear!" poof. so forth.
annabel2K: yeah. *mind* game hens.
hernamewaslola: yeah. sigh.
annabel2k: onward.
Hernamewaslola: onward.

•

Off to Mmmm.

Oh, look. It was Jordan's grownup brother. The one who'd gotten his act together while Jordan trekked and learned to weave.

"Lola!" he waved, walking toward her. Uncanny how much he sounded like Jordan too.

"Yo, Jordan," said the bouncer.

Oh, my.

"Hey!" Lola and Jordan hugged. "It's so good to see you!" they said at the same time. Lola stepped back.

He'd cut his hair—actually, no, clearly someone *else* had cut his hair; *that* was news. "Business-casual" jacket and slacks, Good Shoes.

Good Lord. What have they done with Jordan?

The two were led right to their table, past models swallowing huge mouthfuls of, well, mainly just smoke. There, they ordered a couple of Mmmm's signature "teeny 'tinis," served in mini-cocktail glasses that you refill yourself from the shaker left on the table. Yes, it was a lot of work for a pun.

"So?! How's Ovum?" Jordan asked.

"You know, it's totally fun," said Lola. "And what are you—"

"So what, have you, like, quintupled your traffic?"

"Well, tripled. Are you—"

"How sticky's the site?"

"Pretty. But right now we're focusing more on growing overall visitors and Jordan if you don't tell me what the hell you're up to these days I will toss this teeny 'tini on your Pradas."

"Oh, Lola, you always were so...determined."

Lola picked up her 'tini, pushed back her chair, and took aim.

"Okay, okay!" Jordan laughed. "I'm founder and CEO of a dotcom."

But of course. "Really, which one?"

"LatexAndNylon.com?"

"Huh. What do you guys do?" Lola asked, preparing herself to hear terms like "systems integration" and "concept forwarding," or "bondage."

"Immediate emergency delivery of condoms and pantyhose."

"Oh my God, that's great! Everyone totally needs that!" Lola said supportively, while thinking, "HOLD ON, SPARKY. WASN'T THAT *MY* IDEA IN COLLEGE?!"

"Evidently they do!" Jordan responded. "Business is booming—and we had a nice little IPO, of course. We're only in the Bay Area and Seattle right now, but we're adding L.A. and New York—that's why I'm in town this time—by next month."

"Wow!" said Lola.

"And once we're set up in those cities, we're also planning to add tampons and duct tape."

"So no more *Loom*, huh?" His 'zine.

"Well, now I finance it."

"Oh!"

A waiter who looked like Beck came over with a plate of beggar's purses. "Compliments of the chef, Mr. Gold."

They ordered. Jordan had the skate in beurre blanc, "without butter," and Lola the steak frites. Isn't that, after all, what models say they eat?

At least Lola knew she couldn't marry anyone with butter issues.

"Yeah, life has changed for me a lot, I guess you could say," Jordan went on, his tone getting ever so slightly misty and mysterious.

Uh oh. Lola's inner third wheel's sixth sense knew what was coming. "Systems integration," indeed.

"I'm engaged."

"Hey! Oh my God! That's wonderful!" Lola gushed.

This. Was. Not. The. Plan.

Lola didn't necessarily want to marry Jordan, certainly not at the moment, anyway. *This* was the plan: she would marry someone else, and Jordan would be bachelor uncle to her children. What, did he miss the memo? When he was, like, meeting with Bill Gates?

"So who's your...partner?" Wait, don't they have gay marriage in San Francisco? There was hope.

"Actually, it's Genevieve Baker."

"Genevieve? You're kidding!" She and Jordan had been buddies in college. Lola had always thought Genevieve would be a gold medalist one day—and that day would be the day they made hackysack an Olympic sport.

"It's true. We were out of touch for a while, but we re-met at Burning Man, and then things really clicked at MacWorld."

"So what's she up to?" asked Lola. Besides starring in an outraged e-mail from me to Annabel later this evening?

"Well, funny, we both wound up going in the same direction. She's a bigwig consultant at TechKnow."

Uh-huh.

Lola ran down the list of questions, cooing and ahhing. Wedding at a Napa vineyard, next April, they'd probably stay out there, blah blah blah. Fortunately, just as Jordan was about to ask Lola to resolve a debate over linens, their food arrived. Lola wanted nothing more than to eat her steak with her hands.

"So, what about you, Lo?" Jordan asked. "You've always had *someone* interesting around. You seeing anyone?

No.

"Yes."

Shut up, Somerville. Jordan evidently knows everyone.

"Really, who?" asked Jordan.

No one you know.

"Miles Farmington?" said Lola.

18

It wasn't the end of the world that she'd spilled to Jordan. It was just the end of *her* little world, the nice bubble-wrapped one where, fingers crossed, only the innermost cabal knew about Miles, where the whole thing still wasn't really Out There. Lola could trust Jordan with a secret, she really could, but still—it was, in principle, a breach of security. Security in all senses of the word.

Yet it wasn't as if she'd told Jordan EVERYTHINGeverything. "Turns out that after all that, Ovum isn't all that. They're already dumbing down the content and thinning out the talent and *cooking* the fish and basically I'm watching my back, which isn't easy when there are cameras everywhere…" was not something she'd felt like shouting up to Jordan's perch on top of the world.

Though actually, it is what I'm going to say today in the meeting, thought Lola, buying the *Times* on Ninth Avenue. The first three things, anyway. Anti-tuna melt platforms were, after all, the stuff of class president election landslides.

Ovum's monthly "Airing and Sharing" meeting was scheduled today in the still-empty proto-day care center, and Lola had spent much of Sunday working up the courage to pipe up about her concerns. On the one hand, given her blurry anxiety, it was the most foolish of moves. But on the other, she'd told herself, if I can't speak up in a company dedicated to honoring women's voices, I might as well intern for Phyllis Schafly. All I can do is what I came here to do, stay true to the larger purpose. And let the chips fall where they may. (Oooh. White chocolate chips in vanilla ice cream—with macadamia nuts? Nah, been done.)

By the way, Lola had also spent much—actually, all—of Sunday not calling Miles. She was pleased with her will power but dismayed that she'd had to employ it for something as lame and dated as Not Scaring Guys.

She reported her accomplishment to Kat when she got in. "For God's sake," Lola said. "They can storm the beach at Normandy, but the phone so much as rings and they're up on a chair, skirts hiked, screaming 'Eek!' I mean, that's what we're told, right?" The Peet's was kicking in. "'Don't scare guys.' 'Don't frighten big brave lumberjacks." Let *them* set the emotional schedule,' 'Wait. Patience. Virtue. Blah blah blah. And they complain about waiting for *us* to get ready."

"Ha. Right," said Kat.

"I'd have to concede that there's *some* legit biology / anthropology in here somewhere, inner hunter/gatherer, blah blah blah." Lola couldn't stop. "But thing is, the longer we're told all this 'give them scare-free space' stuff—especially in all those whopping bestsellers—the more hopeless it gets that anything will change. Ugh! Bite me, E. Ron Wilson!"

"So he didn't call?" Kat asked.

"No, yeah, he totally did, after *The X-Files*."

•

annabel2k: checking in
hernamewaslola: hey. how you holding up?
annabel2k: you mean re that dumb dan quail? oh geez, whatever, fine. you?
annabel2k: you're not feeling bad about doing you know what with you know who, are you?
hernamewaslola: nonono it's cool
annabel2k: <raising eyebrow>
hernamewaslola: ok a little. coulda waited.
annabel2k: coulda is different from shoulda
hernamewaslola: right but whole point is/was for this to be different. call me old-fashioned but i only have casual sex w/people i don't want to DATEdate.
annabel2k: yo. "soon" and "casual" unrelated. sometimes soon=serious. you've said it yourself in column.
hernamewaslola: i know. didn't want to look like a prude. but ok.
annabel2k: also? bet you jordan's entire portfolio that you-know-who is NOT angstily IMing w/his best guy friend worrying re "timing," "right thing" etc.
hernamewaslola: so true
annabel2k: and you are not made of wood
annabel2k: (tho you'd be a better swimmer)
hernamewaslola: LOL. our mothers, tho alive and well, are already turning over in the early graves we may yet send them to.

•

"Guys. Time for—eeuw, I can't say it," Lola announced.

"Airing and Sharing," shuddered Kat.

"Couldn't I just sulk instead?" asked Ted. "It is my birthright."

To the proto-day care center they went. Fresh fruit and cookie dough (eggless), with plastic spoons, were being served.

"Jiminy," said Ted. "I've watched enough women eat cookie dough,"

"At least Lola got you to stop actually baking it for them." Kat said.

"Don't worry, there aren't that many women here anymore anyway," muttered Lola, watching The New Guy walk to the front of the room. It was Angela's replacement, the man from The Man. "Distinguished" gray hair, but a little on the long side; lines beginning to show on his face, dark blue eyes. He reminded Lola a little of Robert James Waller, the author of *Bridges of Madison County,* which Lola had detested precisely as much as Francesca Johnson had loved Robert Kincade. The Man man was wearing a jean shirt with…jeans. Jeans with a *crease.* Nevertheless, someone will be sleeping with him in no time, thought Lola. I am no longer the ingénue.

"Hi, everyone. For those of you who haven't met me, I am Norman Shetland. But my friends call me Skip."

Okay, Norman, thought Lola.

"I have been granted the privilege—and humbling task—of following in the footsteps of Angela Chan as Programming VP," Norman said. "I can certainly never hope to compete with her skill, grace, and achievement, but I do bring years of my own experience and—most important—an open mind to the table."

On saying the word "table," he leaned on the table, which rolled forward. Norman straightened up quickly while a couple of people in the front row pushed it back. "Ahem. Maddy—who, by the way, sends her greetings and regrets. She's keynoting a conference on women in the Balkans in the Berkshires—just wanted me to run down for you some of the things I've done over the years. So let's see. In terms of 'old media,'" he air-quoted, "I was editor-in-chief of *Women's Monthly* for many years. Then I moved into 'the next big thing:' television. I'd actually been at DSBC since long before all the mergers, so I know what it's like to build something from the ground up…to the 'sky.'" He looked up, pleased with his poetic waxing.

"Still, you are the leaders here. I'm just helping with some of the 'heavy lifting.' I mean—heh, heh. I want *you* to show me the way. I want *you* to show me what you think and need. I want *you* to show me the general cluelessness of my gender. Heh, heh."

Ted rolled his eyes. Kat and Lola didn't see because they were rolling theirs.

Lola also hated how he air-quoted things that didn't need quoting, like the people who put an accent mark on the E in "latte." When I am president, she always swore, they will be the first to go. Well, third. After the people who say "irregardless" and "Have a good one!"

"Starting now. Let's get down to the business of this meeting. 'Airing and sharing.' Questions? Comments? Concerns?"

Lola looked around. She was stunned that the great sushi famine didn't send every hand in the company into the air. Never mind the 96 other theses she was about to tack on Ovum's door.

But nothing. Just a few scattered inquiries about matters such as late-night elevator access (West only, starting next month) and whether the rumors of Whoopi Goldberg and Ruth Bader Ginsberg guest-hosting *Chyck* were true. (No.) Brandi Chastain? (Working on it.) Kathi Lee Gifford? (Yes.)

What?

"We should move on. Anything else?" Norman asked.

Now, Somerville, now.

Someone asked a technical question about a new coding protocol.

"You know, I think we'll take that one offline," Norman responded.

Ugh.

"Anything else?" Norman asked.

NOW, Somerville.

"Going, going…"

Go.

"All right, then…"

Now.

"…be sure to finish off the grapes…"

NOW!

"Oh! Hang on. Yes? Forgive me, you are…?"

Lola Somerville, and I was just stretching my elbow.

"Lola Somerville. Hi. Um, I actually have maybe a bigger question." Vague grumbling. People wanted their cookie dough and the rest of their afternoons. So much for the popular vote.

"If you'll bear with me. It's just that…well, I know that a company, especially a new one, has to go through a lot of growing pains. But some of the changes around here—I feel—have been, well, on the painful side. I was…dismayed at Tammy Abedon's getting bumped from her job; I didn't feel that her stand-in was adequately or responsibly prepared. We were left to read the press release about Fern and Angela's departures along with the outside world—and, um, their replacements? And 'Sweat' changing to 'Glow?' What, is the new sport Extreme Going-back-in-time?"

Oops, a little harsh. Lola decided not to mention the sushi at this juncture.

"And still no day care center?" asked Lola, gesturing around. "It's just...it just feels...a little different from the company I came here for. I'm just wondering: what and who are behind some of these decisions? And is there a way to include us in them more meaningfully—or at least alert us to them? And—. Well. That's it. I was just wondering."

Norman made a slight motion toward leaning on the table, but quickly thought better of it.

"Actually, I think I can take that one on." Yee. It was Miles.

"Sweetie, maybe now's the wrong time, but if 'now' is wrong, then I don't wanna be right. Lola Somerville, will you marry me?"

Good Lord, thought Lola, blinking. I am become Ally McBeal.

"...You're right to call them 'growing pains,' Lola, you really are," Miles was actually saying. "And you're right; we need to be better about stopping to communicate even as we're creating at such a breakneck speed. Right?"

Nods among all the higher-ups. "So thank you for raising those questions. Thing is," Miles continued, "we are always walking a fine line, a tightrope even, between what we want to say and what 'they'—our viewers and visitors—want to hear. But we still hold the power—and have the intention—to create change. Take *Sweat,* for example. Focus groups liked the show, but found the title unappealing. So hey, we lure 'em in with a softer, fresher title—and give them the same hardcore badass sports programming we always have. Possibly reaching even more people. So it's not the content—or the intent—that's changing; it's just, and I think, in the long run, for the better, the package."

Lola was so distracted by Miles's saying *package* in public that she forgot to press about Tammy.

"Make sense?" asked Miles.

"Yes. Thanks," Lola nodded, wrenching her attention back. Not bad, actually, Lola thought; she herself had, after all, believed in pressing for change from within the mainstream.

"But let's keep that conversation an open one, you all, okay?" added Norman. "All right. Thanks much, everybody. Have a good one."

Lola, Kat, and Ted headed back to their pod, no one really sure what to say. Ted discovered a bag of M&Ms on his desk with a note from Eva in the promotions department: "Ted—Just wanted to let you know how much I appreciated talking to you. Turns out Brett and I are back together! Thanks!"

"M&Ms make friends," Ted sighed.

"Speaking of friends, Lola, can we talk to you for a sec?" asked Kat.

Uh oh.

19

"Of course!" said Lola. "Anytime!" Except when I hate tension with people I love, which is always.

They pulled up chairs at the table where they held staff meetings. At the last one, they'd talked about AskLola.com plans and projects, but not all the other stuff on Lola's mind. Lola really didn't want to freak them—

"Lo, um, Ted and I have been a little freaked out lately." Oh.

"Oh?"

"Well, I mean, we could tell that there was stuff that was bothering you—we've been talking about it for days and kinda waiting for you to say something. But, like, well…you told Norman before you told us."

"Oh. Yeah. Right. Sorry," Lola said, sincerely.

I suck.

"I mean, we don't look to you for protection—"

"You guys look to me for that," said Ted.

"Right. And you don't have to tell us everything but, you know, we care," said Kat. "Your moods and worries affect us and how we do our jobs. And we look to you as the emotional and political barometer of the place we spend all of our time. So from a personal and professional level, both, we just want you to send up a flare when something's going on. Sometimes we just want to know, but maybe sometimes we could even help. You don't have to do everything yourself. Aside from occasional springs in your step about Miles"—Kat lowered her voice on that one—"it's like you've got the weight of the world—"

"My shoulders are evidently in great demand around here," Ted cut in. "But I'll always keep one free for you and some of that weight."

Lola felt both profoundly touched and severely chastised. "Guys, I'm sorry," said Lola. "I just, like, didn't want to burden you. But you're totally right. You just are. You said it all. And thank you. I basically have nothing to add." (Except "I suck I suck I suck, I am a lame and selfish and bad manager, I suck I suck I suck." But that would be unprofessional.)

"Well…except this." Lola leaned in and told them about Stephanie's crib sheet and the Ben and Jerry's e-mail. They were baffled.

"Of course, it really could be nothing," said Lola. Come on, Lola, show positive, reassuring leadership. "All I want you guys to do is the job you came here to do. I'll take care of the, you know, the hacking."

"Okay, Lola," said Kat. "And, hey, at least they're not trying to turn us into AskLolaHowToSeekMaleApproval.com or something."

"Has Ben and Jerry's done anything in 'Ranch?'" asked Ted.

•

hernamewaslola: i did it
annabel2k: you RULE. you are the RULIEST. howd it go!??!??!
hernamewaslola: ok i guess. MF talked about how it was less about content, more about package. what sells. i mean hey we're still a business.
annabel2k: heh heh he said package
hernamewaslola: ok beavis
annabel2k: but why does it seem like you're the only one upset? are you?
hernamewaslola: dunno. guess for one thing i have more at stake cause i sold my baby
annabel2k: right and also it's STILL SO WAY BETTER than all the other places
hernamewaslola: amen to that
annabel2k: = *a-*, "not" + *-men*, ha ha
hernamewaslola: LOL

•

Mail call. Issues of *Ms.* and *Cosmo*, a package from Starbucks Books. Hmm, what fresh hell? Lola opened it. It was a galley of a forthcoming book.

Like A Virgin: The New Chastity. By Nina Sambuca.

Wait, what?

Nina Sambuca?

20

Lola knew Nina's columns were fabricated, but come *on.* Nina had said in her response to Blake Fox's Literati.com exposé that she'd made things up in order to protect the identities of all the guys she *was* actually doing. But could she really be *this* contrite?

UNCORRECTED PROOF

LIKE A VIRGIN:

THE NEW CHASTITY

Nina Sambuca

—

The reformed "do-me feminist" now just says Wait.

—

"She'll be married in no time."
—Janelle Fine and Laurie Loman, authors of the best-selling *The Canon* series

"Nina Sambuca is one tough Nut. With her honest, canny prose, she shows us how female restraint and modesty will help every Pig — and frankly, our nation — clean up its act."
—Dr. E. Ron Wilson

"This crazy bitch doesn't know what she's talking about. Then again, the sexual daemonism of chthonian nature is an apotropaion, a fecund signifier of the omophagy of a world seeking cathexis. I couldn't put it down!"
—Camille Paglia

In **Like a Virgin,** Nina Sambuca asserts that our *fin-de-siècle* culture has long shunned the classical virtue of female modesty, resulting in loss of respect for women and the institutions designed to protect them from ever-increasing threats and dangers. Offering a personal account as well as a philosophical explanation, with scores of impressive footnotes, this striking Stanford graduate chronicles the new generation of women who are "free" on the outside, yet "empty" on the inside. With piercing insight, she explains that a girl's natural inclination toward modesty is not a "hang-up," but rather a wonderful instinct that has the power to transform society.
Soon to be a major motion picture.

STARBUCKS BOOKS • AN IMPRINT OF DISNEY-SEAGRAM •
8000 AVENUE OF THE AMERICAS, NEW YORK, NY 10019

The press packet also contained am 8" x 10" photo of the roughly 8'10" Sambuca lying on a bearskin rug, wearing only a corset.

"Kat," Lola said. "Get this. Nina Sambuca has written a book about Chastity. "Why, because men are into women with women?"

"No, not *that* Chastity. But Nina has gone to the dark side. The pink dark side."

•

Hiya Boqueron—
Haven't heard from you in a while, but I just wanted to go ahead and say

Hiya Boqueron—
I feel a little silly saying this since we haven't corresponded in a while

Hiya Boqueron—
Can you say you need to stop seeing someone if you've never actually seen them?

```
Hiya Boqueron—
Just wanted to let you know I haven't fallen off
the face of the earth. Have you?

Hiya Boqueron—
I just wanted to assure you that I have been wear-
ing a hairshirt ever since I screwed up our date

Hiya Boqueron—
Just wanted to say hello and let you know that I'm
boinking one of the VPs here

Hiya Boqueron—
Hafta say it's just not the same without your e-
mails

Hiya Boqueron—
```

"Hey."

Lola jumped.

"Miles! Quit that!" Lola shifted so that her head was blocking her computer screen. She hoped. Screen saver, save my ass.

"Sorry. I just wanted to let you know that I'm really proud of you. What you said in there took a lot of balls. Eggs. Ha. Eeuw. Whatever."

Ah. Safe. Screen now totally blocked by swelled head.

"Thank you," said Lola. Being approved of was so totally sexy, in an Electra complex sort of way. "It's just—I mean—I really care about this place. And I—well, you know. What I said."

"Yeah. I know." Miles smiled fondly. He was especially tall and yummy when Lola was sitting down. "And well, I didn't want to be impolitic and snarky in the meeting, but I mean, even with the small changes we've made, there's still no comparison between us and FairerSex.com."

"Right."

Oh, that reminds me.

"Hey, one thing we didn't follow up on? What is the deal with Tammy?"

"You know, that I don't know. I wasn't, like, at the grownup table yet when that happened. That's definitely a question for Angela," Miles answered. "Oh, wait."

"Hah, yeah," said Lola. "Well, actually, do you know how to reach her?"

"I'm sure I have her personal e-mail somewhere. But you know, there must be a 'mailto' link somewhere on her home page."

Of course. AngelaChan.com. "Right. Good call." Note to self.

"Speaking of which, can I call you sometime?" Miles flirted.

"Well, sure, now that you've carried my books," Lola flirted back. Oh, my! Truth: when you're talking to someone you're hot for, "verb my noun" always sounds dirty.

Miles winked and left.

A minute later, Lola's phone rang.

"Lola Somerville."

"Wanna come over tonight?"

•

A minute after that, Lola's phone rang again.

"Hey!" she said, laughing.

"Lola Somerville?" Oops.

"Oh! Yes. Sorry. This is Lola."

"Lola, hi! This is Olive from Penelope's office!" Eee.

"Oh, hi, Olive, how are you?"

"Just peachy, thanks! How are you?"

"Very well, thank you. So what—"

"Lola, I've got great news!" Oh, boy.

"Ooh, I love great news," said Lola.

"We'd like to invite you to be an expert guest on the show next month!" YESSSS.

Finally.

"Hey, wow, that's so great! I'm honored! So, I guess you got my memo with all my ideas?"

"Yes! I did! And they were all great! But actually, we've got a different topic for you to sink your teeth into!"

"Oh! All right! What is it?"

"Office romance!'

21

That's funny, I could have sworn Olive just said "office romance."

"I'm sorry, what?" Lola asked.

"We'd like you to come be our expert on office romance!" Olive repeated.

I've got a better idea. How about I bring Miles along and we just out ourselves on *Penelope?* Or why don't you just shoot live from my bedroom?

This can't be happening. Of *all* the topics! I am so hosed, Lola thought.

"I'd be delighted," she said.

Olive gave her all the details. They hung up.

Okay, I have a month to make sure this is serious, the real thing, thought Lola, without scaring him.

Or myself.

•

hernamewaslola: good news and bad news
annabel2k:?
hernamewaslola: which first
annabel2k: good
hernamewaslola: I'm gonna be on penelope
annabel2k: WHO-HOO!
annabel2k: topic?
annabel2k: bad news?
annabel2k: uh oh
annabel2k: VPs and the busted advice columnists who love them?
hernamewaslola: yep.
hernamewaslola: (ps careful what you say on IM)
annabel2k: right sorry
hernamewaslola: (wonder if keyword filters pick up the words "keyword filter")
annabel2k: so, what, they couldn't get E. Ron?

hernamewaslola: he doesn't think women should work in the first place
annabel2k: good point
annabel2k: look seriously don't worry. they'll have others on to talk about their real life experiences. that's the point.
hernamewaslola: mmm hmm
annabel2k: that's what 'experts' do! they're the ones who don't have any personal experience with anything! they totally won't corner you.
hernamewaslola: maybe there'll be nothing to hide by then anyway
annabel2k: you SERIOUS?
hernamewaslola: i don't know.
hernamewaslola: so, the blue suit or that green dress I wore on Lovephones?

•

Lola gave Ted and Kat the *Penelope* news. They shared Annabel's opinion. Kat said go with the green. Lola wasn't convinced. About the show, or the green. She was leaning toward wearing both outfits, one for each of her two faces. She decided to work on a relatively simple letter to distract herself until her next meeting—a brainstorming session in the tech department about online "tools." Which figured, 'cause she felt like one.

22

Dear Lola,
I hate girls. They all suck. They won't go out with me, and always for some lame reason. I give up. They are weird stupid freaks who live to be mean to us guys. Don't even bother helping me, 'cause there's nothing you can say that will make me like them again, or make them like me. Well, I mean, unless you can think of something.
—Striking Out

Dear Striking Out.
I know you're smarting and I'm sorry. I think a little logic lesson will help. Ready?
1. You're a straight guy. Therefore,
2. You date girls. Therefo—
3. Oh wait, you don't. That sucks. Therefore,
CONCLUSION: Girls suck.

I'm not saying that's true, I'm saying that's how it's playing out in your mind. If you were a girl with the same problem, you'd be writing to me to say boys suck. See? It's not the Girl part, it's the Not Dating You part.

This distinction is important. Because trust me: *hating babes does not make you a babe magnet.* When you think they suck, they can tell. And because they can tell you think that, they will say no.*

So try to hate only the ones who have been specifically mean to you. Which may not narrow it down, I know, because sometimes when girls get nervous and don't know what to say, they get mean and sucky. And don't give up entirely, but maybe

give it a rest for a week or two if you're discouraged. Meanwhile, if there are one or two or girls that you're friends with, enjoy their company. They count as girls too. That way you'll get used to thinking of girls as different, even dumb and weird sometimes, but not as The Enemy. That way, you'll already be better off than most grownups.
Love,
Lola
* Until they get older.

•

Lola picked up some wheatgrass juice on the way to her meeting. Her mother had been sending her news clips about its health benefits since before the Web allowed her to just e-mail the links. Her mother was always right; it's just that Lola never told her that she actually obeyed.

Problem was, wheatgrass tasted like grass, only wheatier. Lola prayed to Martin de Porres, patron saint of public health—she'd looked it up—that just this once, her mother would be wrong, that scientists would come forth and say, "Did we say it lowered cholesterol? Sorry, we meant raised!" Which Penelope would mention on the air, and the ensuing public outcry would cause the FDA to go into emergency session and outlaw wheatgrass altogether.

Lola took another sip of her juice as she sat down. Boy, was she looking forward to her sweet, creamy Peet's chaser. (She'd secretly gone back to real sugar after a few chilling Mom missives about aspartame and fertility.)

"Tools" meetings were where producers brainstormed about what interactive bells and whistles would help make Ovuminc.com the destination women depended on for everything: a full-service portal—with estrogen flava. It was common knowledge that the sites women used most were, well, the same sites that men used: the biggie news sites and portals like TheNews.com and mcmail.com. They were the ones that Ovum—with no small amount of derision for FairerSex.com and her sistren—considered the true competition, or at least where to aim.

Miles wasn't around; it looked as if Doug was leading the meeting. He sat at the tip of the oval table, looking meeting-leadery. He was even wearing a nice Christmas-present-y J. Crewi-sh sweater. The robot cat was curled at his feet.

"Hey," said Lola.

Doug smiled. "That stuff's poison," he said nodding toward her juice cup.

She laughed. "You should know."

"All right," Doug said. "You guys ready to pick up where we left off?" Last week the watchword for the online crew had been "user session;" the word from on high was that the holy mission of all content development was to increase the amount of time users visiting Ovum's websites. They'd brainstormed madly. Okay, enhanced chat features? More on-demand streaming? Or what about—

"Well, forget what you heard about user sessions, Doug said. He looked apologetic. "Now it's all about page views." Whoa. Totally different strategy. "Doesn't matter how long they spend; we just want maximum clickage during whatever time they're there."

Murmur, murmur.

"AskLola.com, by the way, is kicking ass in both areas."

Lola raised her wheatgrass cup and grinned.

Doug talked a little more about the page-view model and passed around some Powerpoint charts showing the top three proven Internet page-view goldmines: couponing, Web-based e-mail, horoscopes. Of course, among those three—and this was so obvious it didn't even merit discussion—Web-based e-mail was really the only option appropriate to Ovum and its mission. "So what we'd like to do is talk more next week about this Ovum e-mail tool: look and feel, special features. Okay? Thanks, everybody."

Did we really need a meeting for that? Did Powerpoint really need to be in such huge type?

Lola caught Douglas on the way out.

"Anything?" she asked.

"Useful in that meeting? Nope!" said Doug.

"Anything…else?" If we're going to be spies, we're going to need some code, Lola thought.

"…er, good happen on *The Profiler?*" Doug said. "Um, no. Nothing yet."

•

Lola headed back to her pod, spotting Cybill Shepherd on the *Chyck* set. Think Andrea Dworkin could have gotten away with more if she'd looked like *that?*

Miles, in a somewhat reckless move, was waiting by her desk. Good thing she'd freshened up before the meeting. And good thing they couldn't kiss right now; Lola Labs had confirmed a clear link between wheatgrass juice and mulch breath.

"Hey!" Lola said, smiling as warmly as she could with her mouth closed.

"Hey."

Then she noticed something on her desk that hadn't been there before, right in front of her keyboard. It was small, but she couldn't miss it, as it was something she, at least in a collective-consciousness Jungian archetype sense, had been waiting for all her life.

It was a velvet ring box.

"So I've got a question for you," said Miles.

23

Well! This isn't exactly how I pictured it, Lola thought wildly. But I guess our workplace does have special meaning, though right here and now is rather public—

"Lo?"

"Mmm?"

"Do you like opera?"

"I do!"

"Do you want to come with me to see *Madame Butterfly* at the Met tomorrow night?"

"I do!" All right, Somerville, funny at first, now pathetic. "That would be really great. Thank you."

"Delighted. Have you ever seen *Butterfly?*"

"Nope." Was that the one in *Fatal Attraction?* Lola did enjoy opera music, especially when performed for an evening picnic crowd in Central Park, but—and this was a matter of grievous disappointment to her parents—she'd never seen one actually staged. Lola felt that they should count their blessings, as she'd also never tried heroin.

"Oh, you'll love it. Well, we'll talk later. I just lucked into the tickets and wanted to make sure you could go."

"Sounds good. Thanks again," Lola smiled.

"My pleasure," said Miles, holding her gaze. "*Quale smania vi prende…*" he sang under his breath as he walked away.

Why did I take French? thought Lola.

Now about that damn ring box.

Maybe it is some sort of something from Miles, and he wanted me to open it when he was gone.

Or maybe it's from my mother, trying to hurry along the process of my marrying an opera buff.

Lola opened the box.

Worse.

It was from a publicist.

Worse still.

It was from the publicist for *The Canon* series.

It had all started with the *The Canon: Your Only Hope for a Husband,* the bestselling guide to scoring a ring by ignoring men and having a life. A busy life, filled with Canon™ reading groups, Canon™ support groups, Canon™ dating journals, Canon™ seminars, Canon.com chats and message boards, Canon™ day spas, Canon™ workouts, Canon™ jeans and—soon to open on 57th Street, near the Hard Rock and the NRA Café—the Canon™ restaurant (no carbs or outgoing calls).

The box contained a teeny weeny pink CD. Lola slipped it warily into her CD-ROM drive. The strains of a rather martial wedding march came up, along with a press release for the series' fifth book (the first four: *The Canon, The Canon II, The Canon for Your Marriage,* and *The Canon for Your Second Marriage).*

THE *ULTIMATE* CANON
Time-Tested Secrets for the New World Order

—

"*These* Nuts, I listen to!" — Dr. E. Ron Wilson

—

STARBUCKS BOOKS • AN IMPRINT OF DISNEY-SEAGRAM •
8000 AVENUE OF THE AMERICAS, NEW YORK, NY 10019

Dear Canon Girls,
One rainy evening, while our husbands had run out for some jewelry, the two of us got together for a Girls' Night In. We made a pot of Sugar-Free Bavarian Creme Rhapsody International Coffee, switched off the ringer, and settled down to watch the royal wedding tape one more time, just to see if we could pinpoint exactly where Diana had gone wrong. But no. Turns out Janelle's husband, while vacuuming, had left the VCR unplugged. Oh, well, we sighed. No tapes tonight. Sockets: not our job.

So instead we decided to brush up on our current events by watching the news. What a downer! People were starving, families were disintegrating, companies were "downsizing" (which, we were surprised to learn, is a bad thing, unless you're in the Loehmann's dressing room!) and unrest in the Sudan (which, we were surprised to learn, is a country, not a supermodel!) was not only destroying a nation, but was also cutting down countless single men in the prime of their lives.

It all seemed so hopeless.

And then it hit us, with all the impact of a Princess Marcella Borghese jumbo powder puff. The Canon™ brings order to the chaos of love — but why stop there? It lands you a husband—why not a promotion? It makes your man behave — why not your children? It brings lovers together — why not nations? In other words, if the Canon™ could find a husband for our dumpy friend Melanie in Mineola, why can't it find a way to fill the power vacuum left by the collapse of the Soviet Union?

Trembling, we looked each other. There was so much more to do. We left our coffee cups and Snackwell crumbs for Janelle's husband to clean up, put on our Sergio Tacchini thinking caps, and got busy.

So now, in our new book, we'll show you how the Canon™ applies to, well, everything.

Compared to this, the empire we built with our first book was the size of Andorra (which, we were surprised to learn, is a tiny country in the Pyrenees, not a fuzzy sweater).

Ready, Canon Girls?

Yesterday, marriage; today, the world.

Luv,

Janelle and Lori

Ye gods. They must be stopped.

•

hernamewaslola: he's taking me to the OPERA (mme. butterfly)
annabel2k: madame supafly! no way! we are all growed up. remember when a date was baskin robbins and ms. Pac Man?
annabel2k: actually out here it still is
hernamewaslola: or when dinner dates involved menus you read standing up? if you know what i mean
annabel2k: LOL. your parents will die and go to heaven
hernamewaslola: mmhmm. think that's actually part of the plot in the ring cycle.
annabel2k: yes, they will forgive you for everything you've ever done, even stuff they don't know about

•

Oh. She kept forgetting. Lola typed "angelachan.com" into her browser window.

404 Not Found.

That's weird. Must be some random server error, Lola thought. Must try later.

24

Tuesday afternoon. Ted appeared at Lola's desk with two tuna melts. Damn, Lola thought. Forgot to bring my own lunch again. Maybe I should keep some stuff in Miles's fridge. Hmm. Would that be a big commitment step up from keeping saline in his bathroom?

"Thanks, Ted," Lola said, glancing at her watch.

"Don't think of our lunchtime as late," said Ted. "Think of it as Euro."

"Good call," said Lola, her mouth already full. "Muchas gracias."

"Sure. Hey Lola, can I get your advice about something?"

"Anytime." It's about Greta.

"It's about Greta."

"Mmm hmm?"

"I really like her, LIKElike her."

"As well you should."

"So I'm trying to avoid becoming her straight gay friend."

"As well you should."

"I did see her Sunday night…"

"Mmm hmm?"

"So instead of, like, talking, or just watching *Sex and the City*, I decided I should do something, like, more boyfriendy, right?"

"Right."

"So I put up a dry wall in her apartment."

"Oh, Ted."

"Not good, right?"

"Well, I'm sure it's a perfectly good dry wall. But yeah, that's what you help with *after* you're the boyfriend."

"But I just like her so much, it's easier to stick to the safe things, like keeping her ceiling from collapsing, than run the risk of actually asking her out."

"I know, but you're gonna have to up the ante somehow, Ted."

"All right, but what am I supposed to say? 'I've been thinking a lot about that handshake we shared the other night'?"

"Actually, that's not bad," Lola laughed. "Also? Why don't you see if there's some sort of afternoon-type thing you can do this weekend."

"Yeah, maybe Home Depot!" Ted exclaimed. "Kidding!"

"Or the Homer exhibit," Lola said.

"On it," said Ted. "Thanks, Lola. I kinda knew what to do; I just needed to hear someone else say it."

"Story of my job."

"Hey, maybe now two of us will have office romances!" said Ted.

"Yeah. Then we'll just need to find some sort of job here for Clive," Lola said, nodding toward Kat, who was wearing her headphones over a floppy hat and didn't hear a thing.

"Mmm hmm," Ted said, on his own roll. "Then they'll turn out to be jackasses and we'll take off and road trip, you and me. It'll be 'Thelma and Louis.'"

•

annabel2k: about rock climber #3
hernamewaslola: yeah??!?!?!?!?!
annabel2k: he asked me to go on a little hike with him today
hernamewaslola: nice
annabel2k: halfway down the mountain he says, "oh, i almost forgot my flute." then he opens his backpack, takes out a recorder, and plays "hey jude." over and over.
annabel2k: I'm going to repeat that in case you were skimming.
annabel2k: halfway down the mountain he says, "oh, i almost forgot my flute." then he opens his backpack, takes out a recorder, and plays "hey jude." over and over.
annabel2k: see, he brought a flute on our hike. to play.
hernamewaslola: i...
hernamewaslola: i...
hernamewaslola: i...
annabel2k: yeah.
hernamewaslola:...take a sad song, and make it bette-e-r?
annabel2k: yeah.

•

Oh yeah.
angelachan.com.
`404 Not Found.`
Damn! I really have to look into—
—getting ready for my date.

•

Miles was waiting for Lola at the Lincoln Center fountain, on one of New York's most magnificent plazas. The water arced up, out, and down from the center like a weeping willow's sparkling cousin, reflecting in the grand glass and marble facades of the surrounding shrines to fine art. Lola felt as if she'd walked out of the subway and into a whole new life, and not just because this was her first time wearing a wrap.

"Hey," said Miles, kissing her cheek and then her lips. "You look amazing."

"That's 'cause of how you look at me," said Lola. She knew she was glowing—and sweating.

Miles offered his arm and they walked into the red velvet palace, Lola floating just above the plaza surface, which was good because her pumps killed.

They were on the early side; Miles bought two flutes of Moet, which they sipped while they looked at exhibits of famous old costumes. Lola wished she had paid more attention to her parents and less to, say, The Smiths. Then again, it seemed like Miles enjoyed explaining things.

"...but of course, no one can hold a candle to Leontyne Price," he was saying.

Lola nodded. Was she the one in "Diva?"

Turned out they had box seats. Box seats. Like the people in movies who peer at their paramours through opera glasses or cast significant glances over the top edge of their fans. Like in *The Age of Innocence*, or *Dangerous Liaisons*, or something.

Wait. *Dangerous Liaisons.*

Duh. What if someone saw them?

"Yo Miles." Lola whispered. "What if someone sees us?"

"Internet people?" he said. "They're all at home watching *Voyager.*"

"Oh. Right."

Just then, the lights dimmed. Miles was probably right, but Lola felt a little safer in the dark.

•

Butterfly! You're still waiting?
But Butterfly! He's a jackass!
Oh Butterfly! You had a child!?
Butterfly, he's not coming ba—oh wait, he is!
Oh, Butterfly!
Oh, Butterfly! He has a *wife!*
No, no, don't make the house all pretty. No, no, don't wait up! No, no—
Oh, Butterfly!
Oh, BUTTERFLY!

By the middle of Act II, Lola was in tears. By the end of Act II, her sobs were nearly audible. Miles passed her a tissue. The curtain fell. Lola couldn't get up.

Miles looked at her fondly, expectantly.

"I have to call my mom," she sniffled.

Back at the fountain, Lola took out her cell phone.

"Mob? It's be," Lola said, nose stuffed, still gasping slightly.

"Oh my God, Lulu, what's wrong?! It's late! Are you stuck somewhere without a designated driver?"

"Mob? Butterfly waited and waited, and then she died!"

"Oh, honey! You weren't in an accident, you went to the opera!"

"Mmm hmm. And Pinkerton never had the slightest intention—"

"Morris?! Your daughter is telling us the plot of Madame Butterfly!"

Lola's dad picked up too.

"Wait, don't tell me she dies," he teased.

"And then? You're not going to believe this, but they had her carry out her son in a sailor suit with stars and stripes on it?"

"Sweetie, they always do something like that," said Lola's dad, enjoying this.

"Lulu? So who did you go with?" Lola's mother asked.

Lola looked at Miles and lowered her voice. "My boyfriend."

Mrs. Somerville burst into tears.

•

"Hope that means you liked it," said Miles as they turned toward Café Lichtenstein for a quick nightcap.

"Uh, yeah," laughed Lola, still wiping her eyes. She looked at her hands. Streaked black with mascara. Oh no. Why hadn't she thought to wear waterproof? She must look like Darth Maul. Lola fished in her bag for a mirror.

Miles stopped. "Well, whaddaya know!" Lola heard him say.

She looked up.

It was Norman Shetland.

With a woman maybe Lola's age.

"How are ya, Skip?" Miles asked.

"Hi, Norman," said Lola, no longer floating above the pavement so much as wishing it would gulp her up right now.

"You two coming from *Butterfly*? Spectacular production, huh?"

"Indeed. I thought Suzuki was particularly outstanding," Miles said. Norman agreed.

"Oh! I'm sorry!" Norman said. "This is Ariel, by the way."

Ariel wore a wide ribbon choker. Your feet bound, too? thought Lola meanly. Then she thought: Okay Miles, stop talking now. Stop now. Stop now. Stopstopstopstop.

Finally.

They waved goodnight. Lola spotted her mascara-blackened hand. Okay, so her boss had just seen the only thing worse than an underling and a superior who appeared to be a couple: an underling and a superior who could have been mistaken for a couple who argue 'til one of them cries.

Then again, we hadn't been holding hands at the time. So least sucky case scenario? Norman thinks we're just friends out on the town—as if—*and* knows that I'm enough of a clueless novice that I still experience opera on the level of plot.

•

Giraffe was ringing.

Wait, Giraffes don't ring.

Plus Giraffe is at home, and I am not.

What is ringing?

"Cllphn," murmured Miles.

Cell phone! Right. Lola leapt out of bed and straight into Miles's titanium mountain bike, having already forgotten that when she's at Miles's he sleeps on "the other side."

Still ringing. Lola followed the sound to her purse. Just in time.

"Hello?"

"Lo? It's be." It was Kat. Crying. Hard.

25

"Kat? What's wrong?" Wait, did *she* just see Madame Butterfly? "Clive," said Kat. "Clive just. Clive just broke up with be." Her voice trailed into a sodden wisp.

"Oh my God, Kat. Oh, Kat. Oh, Kit Kat. I'm so sorry." Oh God. Poor thing. There is nothing like this pain. Nothing. Still, having been on both sides, Lola also sympathized with the burden of the dumper, of having—and hating—to hurt. She was sure it hadn't been easy for poor Clive, either.

"Via e-mail."

I will kill that slacker fuck.

"Oh, Kat. Kat. What do you need right now? What can I do?" Lola knew oh so much better than to do anything but emergency triage. No processing, no rationalizing, no silver lining. Just anything Kat wanted.

"Can I come over?"

"Um…I'm at Miles's. Want me to come there?"

"No, I can't be here. It's not like he's been here in an age. But he's everywhere.

Like, his photos, his poetry, the tuba he's keeping here while he's away…"

"Want me to meet you at my place? Or Florent, or something?"

"Oh God, I can't go OUTout. You should see me! But no one else should. Can I just come there?"

Lola paused.

Anything Kat wanted.

Miles would understand. Anyway, Miles wouldn't even notice, as he would be sleeping over in the other billion square feet of the apartment.

"Sure." Lola gave Kat the address. "Wait, you're taking a cab, right? You're not gonna, like, skate over here or anything?"

"Yeah. Cab. Fifteen minutes. And check your e-mail. I'll forward it."

"Okay. Bye. Be careful. Bye."

Whispering, Lola told Miles what was going on.

"Mmm."

Then Lola said, "Also? David Duchovny is here with champagne and some feathers; he says he wants to see just how ticklish I really am. Okay?"

"Mmm."

Okay, he's really out cold.

Lola ran down to the bodega for some Smartfood and sorbet.

Back in three minutes, she sat down at Miles's computer. It was just asleep, not off. Sort of like her. His browser was open to a web-based mcmail.com account, projectovum@mcmail.com. That was smart, thought Lola; their ovum accounts were a pain to access remotely. Lola was betting that Kat had forward Clive's e-mail to Lola's mcmail account.

Lola switched usernames and checked her inbox.

Sure enough.

That's why I hired her.

FROM: katinthehat@mcmail.com
TO: hernamewaslola@mcmail.com
FWD: RE: We have to talk.

At 4:58 PM clive@czech.net wrote:

<<As an adolescent and early-twenty-something, I believed in perfect romance. Then I whipsawed to the opposite extreme, presuming the natural and relatively swift failure of what the ancient Greeks called *eros*. I suspect that true love lies somewhere in between this Platonic ("Platonic" as in Plato, not as in "friendship," or what the Greeks called *agape)* form on the one hand, and on the other, some sort of inevitable failure, planned obsolescence. Yet I do not know for sure. And as much as I ponder these questions in my poetry, and in long hours at cafes, I feel that I am unable to be in a relationship until I am fully able to comprehend what it "is" that I am "in."

You are magical and inspirational, Kat. I know I have loved and still love you. You have been nothing less than my muse. But that's just it: now I need to find my muse by myself, the one within. Sing in me, muse...and forgive me, my Kat.

```
At 5:11 PM katinthehat@mcmail.com wrote:
  What a load of crap. Have you met someone else?

At 5:57 PM clive@czech.net wrote:
  Yeah, actually. Sorry.
```

Lola sat back in the desk chair and rolled her head around on her neck to give it a stretch. Miles's bookshelf was packed with feminist manifesti from Carol Gilligan to Carolyn MacKinnon to *Tank Girl.* Good boy. Wait, and was that *The Phyllis Schafly Story?* Well, know thine enemy, like I say. And also—weird!—every issue of *Guy,* it seemed, since the Guttenbergs. Well hey, not like I don't read *Cosmo.*

Lola poked around on the desk looking for a piece of paper. Think I'll write Miles a cute surprise note while I wait for Kat.

She opened an average-looking spiral bound notebook and flipped open to a blank page. Which wasn't blank. Lola saw yesterday's date, Miles's handwriting, and the word "feeling." She slammed the book shut.

What did I just see? Is this something personal? If I opened it by accident—not even! With totally innocent, actually very loving intentions!—is it snooping?

Well, yes.

Tally-ho.

Lola opened to the same page. By the blue-gray light of the computer screen, she struggled to make out Miles's thin, slanty writing.

"Haven't forgotten, Nina."

What? Nina? Sambuca? Must be meeting notes. Someone up there must be working on some *something* to counter this whole neo-Victorian trend. Good.

Lola looked back. Her eyes landed in a different place.

"Feeling more strongly about Lola. Oops."

Lola slammed the book shut. I did *not* just see that.

Wait, did he say "Oops?" Or did my conscience?

Lola opened the notebook to fact-check, just as the computer put itself to sleep and snuffed what light there was. Then the buzzer rang. It is St. Peter, thought Lola, coming from the pearly gates to tell me in person to forget about early acceptance. She put the notebook back where she found it and tiptoed down the staircase.

26

Lola opened the door.

It wasn't St. Peter after all. It was Kat's crazy sister, the one they don't talk about, who had evidently just escaped from the attic.

No, actually, it was Kat. She looked awful, which was possibly a first. Ratty sweats, puffy eyes, fuzzy Dalmatian slippers, matted hair. Wouldn't you know, one of the rare times she wasn't wearing a hat.

"Oh, Kat," Lola said.

"I feel pretty!" Kat sang wanly.

Lola gave her a huge hug, the kind that says, "*I* love you—and I know that doesn't count." She led Kat into the apartment. When Kat realized that Miles's place was larger than all the Thursday must-see TV apartments combined, her swollen eyes widened from one millimeter to seven.

"Whoa."

"Yeah," said Lola.

"Well, at least now I'm freed up to meet a boyfriend with an apartment," sniffled Kat. Clive had been couch-surfing in Prague. He said he was "exploring rootlessness."

Lola felt vaguely, evilly, fleetingly smug. But if you still "feel all grown up" because your boyfriend lives in a Real Apartment, does that mean you're not actually grown up? Oh, never mind. Kat.

"What do you want to drink, Kit Kat?" she asked.

"Ovaltine? Or gin?"

Searching Miles's larder, Lola procured an item from each sector of the Despair Food Pyramid: Bombay Sapphire London Dry, sorbet, Smartfood popcorn, Nutela, no chaser. "Here, make sure you drink plenty of water, too," Lola added, not sure why.

She led Kat toward the couch.

"Where's—?"

Lola nodded up the spiral staircase. "Out cold."

"*So is my heart,*" exclaimed Kat, her attempt at maudlin self-mocking backfiring, a little too close to the truth. She burst into tears.

Lola let Kat cry for a while she stroked her hair. "Oh, Kat. It just sucks. He sucks. I know. I know. It all sucks ass." This was no time for Shakespeare. (Rather, Mamet.)

Kat raised her head. "Lo? If he's such a pretentious two-timing dorkweed, then why do I care?"

"Oh, Kat, of course you care! I mean, thank God you care! How sad would it be if you'd spent years with this guy and things ended, however they ended, and you didn't care?"

"Hmm, I guess. But I don't want to care! I hate it! I hate how this feels! I hate it!" Kat shuddered.

"I know. You feel like there's this thing, this gross feeling, this foreign object, that you can't remove...like a cat with tape on its paw? Or, no, like on *The X-Files* when that gross alien oil gets in under your skin, literally, remember, through your *eye?*"

Kat winced.

"Sorry," said Lola. "But um? Unlike that gross alien oil stuff, this goes away. It doesn't feel like that right now, I know, and it won't for a while, but it just does. It just does. Oh, Kat."

Kat was crying again.

"Auuuugh, I don't want to be single! I haven't been single in forever. I don't know *how.* And even if I find someone, *if,* like, in a million years, when I'm *thirty*—"

Ooof.

"...I won't even know what to do then! I mean Lo, everyone says long distance relationships are so hard, but those people don't know what they're talking about. They're *easy.* A cakewalk. I mean, you miss the person, but you don't have to *do* anything. Nothing to negotiate, nothing to discuss, none of that 'When do we hang out with *my* friends' or which parents house for Christmas or 'What if I want to watch *Walker, Texas Ranger* and he wants to watch *Iron Chef'* and you know what I mean. It was like Boyfriend Lite. He was there, but he was over *there.* There was nothing I could mess up."

Lola had never thought of it that way. But now she knew exactly what Kat meant.

"Or wait, I guess there *was* something I could mess up." More tears.

"Kat! No! You didn't mess up anything. Clive was capable of being a pretentious two-timing dorkweed all by himself."

"Then why—?"

"Kat. It was nothing you did or didn't do. People in happy relationships cheat. Studies show. I know."

"So how come—?"

"Kat. I promise. You didn't mess up!"

Kat thought for a long time.

"I love slash hate him," she whispered.

"I know, KitKat," said Lola.

They sat for a minute.

"Why don't you write him a really unmailably nasty e-mail and then don't mail it?" suggested Lola. "Believe it or not, it'll make you feel better."

Kat thought for another long time. She took a sip of her gin and Snapple, and then a deep breath.

"Lo?" Kat said. "I did a bad thing."

"Kat! I told you! If there's one thing I'm sure of—"

"No. Lo. *I did a bad thing.*"

"What do you mean?"

"His e-mail? The one I sent you?"

"Mmm hmm?"

"I forwarded it."

"Yeah. I know. I read it. What a nightmare. What did the Greeks call 'lame,' like, the Platonic form of lameness, you shitty hoser, How dare—"

"No. Lo. Lo! I mean, I forwarded it. Around."

"Around? How around?"

"Everywhere."

"Everywhere?"

"All my friends."

"Well, that's natural."

"All his friends."

"Ohhh—"

"Our college alumni listserv."

"Uh oh."

"And his parents."

Lola fell silent.

"With a note that they should all forward it, too."

Oh, dear. Boy, had she broken house rules against revenge.

"Pretty bad, huh?" asked Kat.

"Well..."

"I kinda wish I hadn't."

Be a therapist, Somerville, not a lecturer. "Why?"

"Because, like, I don't want him to think I actually care that much. I really don't."

"Hmm. How long ago did you send it?"

"Right before I left. Maybe half an hour?"

"From your mcmail account, right?"

"Yeah...?" Kat reached for a piece of popcorn and watched Lola expectantly.

Lola stood up. "It may not be too late. Remember, it is *mcmail.*" Everyone used it, but everyone complained about it. "With *that* crappy network, there's always the chance that mail is all backed up, I mean delayed, and that it hasn't even gone out yet. Especially, um, if you cc'd that many people. So maybe some of your e-mails are still hopping around." Lola was looking for the cordless phone.

"Who you gonna call, Angela Chan?""

"You'll see."

Lola found the phone and dialed. Kat was dipping Smartfood in her chocolate sorbet. While she waited, Lola considered her putative Ben and Jerry's flavor. Chocolate-cheddar covered a lot of bases.

"Douglas!" Lola said into the phone. "Go home and go to bed!" Busted. Still at Ovum. Just as she'd thought.

"Lola? Oh, hey. I would, but Ted and I got sucked into *Sonny and Me: Cher Remembers.*"

"We won't be here long." Lola heard Ted's voice in the background. "Turns out she only remembered an hour."

"Listen, Ranger, I actually need your help pronto."

"Need a loft built or something? You should get Ted," Douglas said. "Ow!"

"No, seriously," Douglas. "How well do you know your way around mcmail.com?"

"Lola, Melanie Griffith could use that system."

"No. I mean, like, inside. Here's the deal."

Lola explained Kat's predicament. "So could you go in and try to unsend whatever you can? Not just from the user interface but from the system itself?"

Lola heard the click of keys over the faint strains of "I Got You, Babe."

"Got your back, babe," said Doug.

"Thanks heaps, Range," said Lola.

Clickety click. "Come on!" said Doug under his breath. "In twenty years, when my brain's hooked up to the Internet, I hope it's faster than this."

"Douglas? Kat says thanks, too." Kat nodded vigorously, her mouth full. Smartfood sorbet was clearly a hit. Lola hung up the phone.

"That's all we can do for now, girlie." Lola tried to sound comforting. "At least about the e-mail situation. Lame cowardly breakups, *that* we could still work on. Also, helping you feel better."

"Yeah, I could use that," said Kat. She was starting to look not just bad, but thoroughly spent.

"Just brace yourself, Kat," said Lola. "It might even get worse before it gets better. It's gonna seem like it's taking forfuckingever. Breakup time, you know, it's like dog years."

Lola thought about that for a second.

"No wait, it's like dog years backwards. One hour of breakup time feels like, like, seven hours. Or wait, is that dog years forwards? Well anyway. You see my point."

"Yeah," said Kat vaguely.

"So, like, all you can do is get through this minute. And then be all, 'Okay cool, I got through that minute. Here's another. Got through that one. Yay me.' That's all."

"Yeah," said Kat, clearly exhausted.

"Kat, why don't you try to get some sleep? You can just crash here." Lola's toothbrush had stayed at Miles's for the first time that night; why not her web-master? "I'll stay down here with you."

"OK," Kat nodded. Lola found some bedding in the linen closet, noting that Miles had a freaking linen closet, and tried to make Kat comfortable on the couch. Where was Giraffe at a time like this?

"Okay, Kat? Just try and rest. You'll feel, well, equally bad in the morning—but you'll be, like, seven hours closer to Over It."

"Okay," said Kat. "Thanks, Lo." She closed her eyes. Lola gave her a kiss on the cheek, propped a pillow up against the couch, and tried to sleep sitting up. It worked in meetings; why not now?

•

"Well!" Miles's voice. Lola opened one eye. Morning. Sun. Miles's face. "I was worried," he said. He looked at Kat. "I still am."

Oh God, does he know I snooped?

Get over yourself, Somerville, he is referring to Kat, who is supposed to get all the attention right now.

Kat sat straight up. "Clive broke up with me last night. On e-mail. He said he couldn't be in a relationship until he really understood what one was," she recited.

"Ahhh. So he's met someone else?" asked Miles.

"Yeah," said Kat.

"Kat, I'm so sorry." Miles came forward and patted her knee.

"Hope you don't mind," said Lola, gesturing at their campsite.

Nina? Feelings for me?

Kat, Lola, Kat. Focus.

"Of course not," he said. "How 'bout I make you guys some coffee?"

Lola talked to Kat while Miles fixed coffee. And defrosted scones from Sarabeth's. And brought everything over on a tray.

Miles comes through, thought Lola. Heck, I should have friends break up more often. She hoped Kat wasn't too jealous. Well, a *little* jealous would be understandable, she supposed, remembering all her years on the other side.

I am going to hell, Lola thought as she stirred her coffee.

27

Lola made sure Kat got home and told her to come in only when she felt like it. "Make sure you stay on IM so I can check on you," she'd said. Thank goodness that smartypants had rigged herself up on DSL, even *before* the Panda-cam. When Lola got to Ovum, she logged into NoNoDontGetUp.com and had some sandwiches and gummi bears sent over to Kat's place. "Poor, poor Kat," she thought. "Wish I could wave a magic wand…and make sure Miles and I work out."

I mean, arguably, what I found in that notebook was good news.

But if I was snooping in the first place, what's already wrong? she wondered. God, Lola, are you your mother's daughter or what? Can't you, for once, *not* look for the catch?

Ted came in. "Boy, is it dark and cloudy outside. Reckon the weather's been engineered by Fox to promote *Millennium?*"

"Hey, you didn't check your e-mail from home or anything, did you?" Lola asked.

"Nope, why?"

Lola told Ted about Kat. "Something about how he *agapes* her, but he doesn't *eros* her."

"Hang on, let me guess. He found a new muse?" asked Ted.

"I thought you said you hadn't seen the e-mail."

Ted shrugged. "Welcome to my nightmare," he replied. "I'll go IM Kat."

Lola checked her e-mail.

Sure enough.

```
FROM: katinthehat@mcmail.com
TO: <undisclosed recipients>
RE: FWD: GET A LOAD OF THIS PRETENTIOUS TWO-TIMING
DORKWEED
```

Also,

TO: lsomerville@ovuminc.com
FROM: dlee@ovuminc.com
RE: "pretentious two-timing dorkweed"

hey. caught some but not all. caught something else too. talk soon? i'll be by.—douglas

Douglas ruled.

Lola fidgeted. Miles's loamy New Orleans roast notwithstanding, she still felt woozy from last night. Can't concentrate, she thought.

Oh yeah.

angelachan.com.

404 Not Found.

Hmm, still down. Lola reached for a stickie to write herself a note to mention this to Douglas, but the Panda-cam caught her eye first. Ohhhh. Mother and child were asleep. Lola closed the browser window. It was cute and all, but she didn't want to get any ideas.

Hmm. Ah. Will buy Douglas an excellent muffin to thank him.

Back at her desk, Lola kept fidgeting. Shoot, was lavender-currant kind of gay? Should I go back and exchange it for something tougher, like sage and…jerky?

You're splitting hairs at this point, Somerville. They're *muffins.*

La, la. Muffins. Puffins. Truffles.

Oh geez! Lola realized that she hadn't yet hidden her PitchingWoo profile—that is, taken herself off the market. Hiding your profile was sort of the "spongeworthy" of the cyberdating set. As in, "He's cute and all, but I'm not about to hide my profile!" or "Janie, it's me. I've got some news: Chad and I are taking things to the next level: mmm hmm, we're hiding our profiles! Can you believe it! Okay, gotta call my mom! Bye!"

But wait, Lola thought. Hiding my profile—isn't that jinxing things, jumping the gun?

I'll think about it while I just clear out my inbox.

Eek! Avalanche! Five messages!

Wait, only five? After a whole week?

FROM: intlmale
RE: Back in the Big Apple, ready to settle down with my soulmate
I've traveled all over the world and spent a year living in the Middle East, where I worked as a

speechwriter for the King and Queen of a small but important country. (I'll tell you which one when we meet.)

"...And then I will have to kill you," thought Lola.
Delete.

FROM: iamsteve
RE: greeting's!
If you're someone who love's dog's and get's excited about everything from loud dance club's to quiet Sunday afternoon's with the Time's, let's talk!

"Hobbies include: apostrophes," thought Lola.
Delete.
Next, an announcement about PitchingWoo.com's next series of singles outings.

1. Join us on a tour of Manhattan's medieval marvel The Cloisters!

There's some irony to that.

2. Special package: pre-theater dinner and tickets to the ground-breaking Off-Broadway smash "Tit à Tit: The Breast Dialogues."

That ought to make everyone good and uncomfortable!

3. PitchingWoo Local Social committees are forming! Come to the next meeting and let us know what events you'd like to plan!

Well, *weddings*, thought Lola. Ha, ha.
Delete.

FROM: nyuknyuk
RE: let me make you laugh
Hello there! I think we'd have a great time together. I think my getting into doing voiceovers over the past five years has contributed to my nuttyness at times. I sometimes slip into different characters to amuse myself and whoever else is listening. Could it be you?

Hmmm, nope, thought Lola, clicking on his profile out of idle curiosity. She'd just remembered she had a Brands meeting in 10 minutes; why start working now?

In his photo, nyuknyuk was wearing a clown nose.

Delete.

FROM: boqueron
RE: Um.

Lola cringed. She still felt lingering lameness and rudeness about their *correspondus interruptus.*

I'd hoped he'd forgotten about me. About *it,* anyway.

FROM: boqueron
RE: Um.
i would ask you out again, but my spider sense—or is it my ego?—tells me you've started seeing someone. please advise. or not if you don't feel like it. in any case i do hope you're well.—b

Ooof. Lola felt terrible.

TO: Boqueron
Spot on. In fact, that very man was in my bed while you were waiting for me at Cafe Reggio. And then, with all the impeccable manners I preach in my column, I said nothing to you, thus destroying any hope of preserving in any form the special vibe we'd begun to establish. Sorry!
Fradulently,
Lola

Typetypetype, *delete*. This exercise made Lola feel infinitesimally better. Her Palm Pilot beeped. Ah, perfect, a meeting—a great place to sit and think about how to respond.

Lola logged out of PitchingWoo.com, forgetting to hide her profile.

28

Lola joined the website producers from *Chyck, Glow, Miss Thing* (Ovum's teen brand) and the other brands that made up Ovum as a whole. It looked like Norman was leading the meeting. Oh, great.

"First on the agenda is Lola's date with Miles last night, after which they tried sex a different way," he said.

Then, in real life, he said, "We've called this Brands meeting to let you know that we're actually not going to have Brands meetings anymore."

Is that good or bad? Lola wondered.

"Now don't worry, this is not a change in content offerings. It's a change in how those offerings get...offered to our audience," Norman went on. "Now, we all know that women are smart enough to ask for directions. Ha, ha. So our concern is that we're not giving them enough. Directions. Direction. Anyway. We feel that it's important for women to come to Ovuminc.com and know where to go. So what we're going to be implementing is simply a new architecture, a new house, if you will, to...house our outstanding content."

Okay, Skipper, and your point is? thought Lola.

"You're probably wondering exactly what my point is," Norman continued. "Well, I mean that once we make these changes, when you come to Ovum's hub site, you will not longer see brand names like *Glow* and *AskLola.* Instead, you'll see keywords like 'sports/diet/fitness,' and 'relationships.' *Penelope* will stay *Penelope*, of course. And those words will lead you to pages that aggregate Ovum's content on those topics. We're not losing the brands or their unique characters, I promise."

Lola's hand had been up for two sentences. "Hi. Did you just say 'diet?'"

"Uh, yes, I did."

"Did you *mean* to say 'diet?'" Titters.

"Uh, yes, I did."

Lola managed to keep a measured tone. "Since when, if I may, does Ovum do the 'diet' thing?"

"Steele, would you like to take that?"

"Sure." Steele was *Glow's* executive producer, and part Borg. She was permanently tanned, frosted, cordial and terrifying. She was the kind of person who said "I have a triathlon tomorrow" the way other people might say, "I have a library book due tomorrow." Journalism was, relatively speaking, the desk job Steele taken after an incident you weren't supposed to mention around her—something about a windsurfer and a giant jellyfish. "Well, apparently focus groups liked our women's team and pro sports content, but felt there was a void as far as feeling like there were ways for them to participate and be involved themselves—so we thought we'd add a service-y fitness component too, including healthy eating—for weight loss if you choose. And, well, it turns out that Internet users are eleven times more likely to click on the word 'diet' than the word 'fitness,'" she finished quickly.

"We're leaving the word 'fitness' there, you realize," Norman added.

"Gotcha," Lola nodded.

"If you have more specific questions about new coding and the like, we'll just take that offline."

Gross.

Lola had a bad feeling—one that told her that this was the road to genericized, watered-down, same-as-it-ever-was hell. Or at least to FairerSex. com.

•

Lola dropped by Doug's pod. They were all in some sort of tech meeting with Miles. "We've really got to make sure to FTP files in binary mode," Douglas was saying. They all turned to look at Lola. "Oh, hey, sorry," said Lola.

I wasn't coming to see Miles or anything, just so you all know.

"DOUGLAS, I was just wondering if you could come by and have a look at my advice filter? It's doing…something funny."

"Sure," said Douglas.

"Thanks, DOUGLAS. Sorry to interrupt."

•

Dear Lola,

My boyfriend broke up with me after seven years. He said he just wasn't ready for a serious relationship.

Now, finally, I'm back on the dating scene, and I feel so green and daunted I'm ready to give up already! I'm confused by all those books out there,

not to mention all those men out there. Well, actually, there aren't that many. Men, not books. So I don't want to mess up. What rules do I follow these days? I guess mainly I'm asking: so what do you think of *The Canon?* Some of it makes sense, but...
—So If I Don't Call Him Back, Does That Mean I Like Him, or I Don't?

Dear SIIDCHBDTMILHOID,
The most interesting thing about *The Canon: Your Only Hope for a Husband*—those hard-and-fast hard-to-get rules that "guarantee" a ring (or at least purchase of the sequel) is not the pro/con debate about it. It's the fact that it's all the rage. It's symptomatic, I think, of a time when the politics of dating look like one huge quicksandy gray area, when people are groping for a black-and-white bar to grab onto for dear lovelife. (That's why it was marketing genius not to call it, say, *The Suggestions.*)

Of course "some of it makes sense." Common sense. Example: don't hurl yourself at someone, repeatedly, who shows no interest. And there's always room for courtship (old-fashioned, even)—*without* mind games, for measuring your responses without egg-timing your phone calls (see Statute no. 6). See, in the Lola Canon, it's not *playing* hard to get; it's *being* hard to get, 'cause you are all that.

So maybe you'd find it more fun (key word!) to hang back, to savor anticipation, to feel the fizz rather than shaking things up so fast they go flat. You can tweak your *approach* without tweaking your loud/direct/true self. Try it, even just to keep things interesting. Let dating frustration break your spirit, and you will break my heart.
Love,
Lola

•

```
TO: cwalters@ovuminc.com
CC: smarlowe@ovuminc.com
FROM: lsomerville@ovuminc.com
RE: my segment
Hey, can I talk about The Canon this week? They've
got a new book. Eeuw. Letter attached w/my posi-
tion. Lemme know if that works for you? Call me
because it would be too forward for me to call you.
Ha, ha. Thanks.
```

Doug came by.

"About that advice filter," he said, smiling, a little loudly. He pulled up a chair.

Right when a *Chyck* camera crew rolled over.

"Hey!" said Terence the Red-Headed Camera Guy, who was so friendly no one could yell at him for leaving his clipboards and pens and drippy coffee cups on whatever desk was near wherever he was shooting. "You kids look like you're up to something interesting! Mind if I shoot a bumper and some extra B-roll?"

Lola and Doug looked at each other.

"Go ahead, Terence," smiled Lola.

"About that advice filter," they said together, half smiling, half sighing.

When on earth would they get a chance to TALKtalk?

29

annabel2k: i was just thinking
annabel2k: has he called you his girlfriend yet
hernamewaslola: not out loud
hernamewaslola: but at least he calls me
annabel2k: is that ok w/u?
annabel2k: ?
hernamewaslola: for now yah. most other guys come thru on words but not deeds. he does latter. so words can wait.
annabel2k: word.

•

Lola and Ted had Kat on speakerphone, just checking in.

"Hey Lola, you know that unmailable e-mail to Clive you told me to write, and then not e-mail?"

"Mmm hmm?"

"I faxed it."

"Hey Kitkat," Ted jumped in, "lemme play hooky and take you to a matinee." Lola gave a thumbs-up. "Hey, there's the new John Woo movie! Lots of fights and chases and explosions!"

"Aw, no thanks, Ted," said Kat. "That'll just make me cry."

•

hernamewaslola: clive dumped kat
annabel2k: i know, i got the e-mail
hernamewaslola: oh, she cc'd you too?
annabel2k: well not exactly

•

"All right, Lola, I'm gonna go do what I do best," said Ted, putting on his cap.

"Serve me blindly?" asked Lola.

"No, that's second best."

"Help a woman move on to the next guy you'll help her move on from?"

Ted tipped his cap and left.

•

hernamewaslola: about that advice filter
douglee: be right over

•

"Hey." Doug had a bag of wasabi peas. Good boy.

"Hey, Ranger."

Doug picked up the remote and turned up the TV a little. It was the three-hour nightly block of *Who Wants to Be Filthy Rich?* During sweeps, all single winners were to be pooled on *Who Wants To Marry Money?*

"Here's the thing," Douglas began. "So I'm digging around in mcmail.com, trying to trace Kat's e-bomb. I figured I should start close to home and make sure she didn't send it to, say, Maddy."

"Hah, right," said Lola.

"So I'm looking for mcmail stuff on Ovum's server, and I randomly find this one weird account that's getting accessed a lot."

"What's weird about it?"

"The name, first of all. ProjectOvum@mcmail.com."

"What's weird about that?" asked Lola, feeling thick. Wait, and why does that ring a bell?

"Well first of all, it's just not necessary, right? I mean, we all work here and we have e-mail here. Why bother with web-based mail, especially with such a big lame ISP?"

"So it's probably just some intern or temp working on something, and IS couldn't give them an Ovum address," suggested Lola.

"You'd think," said Doug. "But I felt like I was totally in the hacking zone, so I kept digging. Just on a hunch."

"Mmm hmm?"

"Well, I couldn't get into the account per se—I'd need a user's password, or Angela Chan's hacking skills. But I could tell what domains, and—inside Ovum, anyway—what users had accessed it."

"So, not an intern."

"Well, the government is famous for plucky interns…"

"The government?"

"Yeah. Lots of action from dotgov."

"Dotgov?"

"Dotgov."

"Is it me, or is that weird?"

"It's not you," said Doug. "As it were."

"Which of these modern painters had a 'blue period?'" asked Regis Philbin.

"Picasso," said Douglas and Lola.

"So what else?" Lola asked.

"Well, as I said, I could tell who internally had been accessing it."

"And?"

"Norman," Doug said.

"Norman," Lola repeated.

"And Miles."

"Miles," Lola repeated. The e-mail address she'd seen in his apartment. Right. Actual computer, actual apartment—not part of that whole dream with David Duchovny.

"Lola?" Doug said.

"Lola," Lola repeated. She ate a pea. Then two. Then a handful, then another, until her nose stung and her eyes watered.

"What is the title of one of television's longest-running most popular shows about a mobile army surgical hospital?'" asked Regis Philbin.

"M*A*S*H," said Doug and Lola.

They sat for a minute.

"Lola, do you have a weird feeling?" Doug asked.

"That these questions are outrageously easy? Yes. Also," she went on, "that something bizarre is going on with Ovum? Yes. Do you?"

"Yeah. Do you know what?"

"No," said Lola. There was a thought in her head that she couldn't quite grab, like that bit of shell in the egg white that keeps slipping out of the spoon. "Do you?"

"No." They sat for a minute. No new thoughts.

"Well." said Lola. "WWNDD?"

"What Would Nancy Drew Do?" Doug asked. Damn, he's good.

"Yeah."

"Sneak into Norman's office to see if the mcmail account password's cookied on his browser?" Doug suggested.

"Maybe," Lola said. "Risky, though. Don't know his schedule, really no excuse on the planet for being in there."

"Sneak into Miles's office to see if the password's cookied on his browser?"

"Well, I know for a fact that tonight's his Euchre night with his college buddies," said Lola. And I am the kind of girlfriend who's "okay with that."

And I am the kind of "girlfriend." Girlfriend. Girlfriend.

"Okay," said Doug.

They sat for another minute.

"Okay!" said Lola.

"Are you sure you want to do this?" Douglas asked.

"Yes," said Lola.

"Is that your final answer?" asked Regis Philbin.

"Yes," said Lola.

30

An hour later, when more employees had cleared out, Lola and Douglas met at the juice bar. In the meantime, Lola had gone down to chat with the security guard. Cameras at and in the elevators, in Maddy's office, and also in the kitchen (though lunch theft had gone down since the switch to tuna); none in Miles's office. Anyway, the guard seemed pretty involved in *G.I. Jane.*

"OK, Ranger, I think we're cool," she told Doug. They headed for Miles's new office, which had walls and a door but no ceiling in the latest "clopen" management style.

Evidently Lola was also the kind of girlfriend who'd sneak into her boyfriend's office. Hrmm. When she'd opened that notebook of his—no matter what it said—she'd opened a *lot.*

But this, this mission, it was different, right? This wasn't about Lola. This lipstick was on a much bigger collar. Of course, Lola knew she could still lose her job if she got caught. Not to mention her boyfriend. But everyone, she thought nobly and dramatically, would lose if she didn't try find out what was going on at Ovum. And, she thought pathetically, I certainly have found a very noble and dramatic way to sabotage my relationship.

"So I'll stay at the door and knock once if something's up?" Doug confirmed.

"Yeah," said Lola. "And then just walk away casually. I'll do the same, the other way. Then we'll regroup when the coast is clear."

"Word."

"Peace out."

Lola slipped into Miles's office and went straight for the computer. It blinked right on when she touched a key to wake it up. Clear desktop, nothing open. Lola clicked on "recent applications;" the usual stuff: word processor, Palm, web browser, Quake. She opened the browser and went to mcmail.com, praying Miles would be facile-movie-plot enough to "leave the keys in the ignition," as it were—that is, to auto-store the password on the welcome page.

No. Hell's bells!

She looked up at Douglas' outline in the doorway. He seemed calm.

Okay. Good thing I know some Miles trivia. Here goes.
Childhood dog's name.
`babbage`
Geek.
`Invalid password.`
Middle name.
`blake`
That is so queer.
`Invalid password.`
Opera.
`puccini`
`Invalid password.`
Coffee.
`peets`
`Invalid password.`
Dumbass wild guess.
`smelt`
`Invalid password.`
Wait a sec.
`lola`
Oh, God. Lola closed her eyes.
`Invalid password.`
Phew.
I mean, damn.
I mean, DAMN.
Wait.
`lulu`
Not possible.
Ping!
She was in.
`lulu?`
Freak out later, Somerville, you've got corporate espionage to take care of.
She scanned down Miles's list of folders.
Inbox.
Zero.
Hmm.
Sent mail.
Zero.
Hmm!

Trash.
Zero.
What the—?
Drafts.
Hmm—
Doug knocked. And vanished. Fuck.

31

Lola hit "sleep," praying that her log-in would time out by the time Miles came back, and stole to the door. Heart pounding, she tried to lean only one eyelash out.

"Lola?"

Lola jumped, bonking her temple on the doorframe.

She'd leaned out right into Greta's face, which was covered with tears.

Casual, Lola, casual. Why, I've got every reason to be peeking out of Miles's office at midnight. What's your point?

"Hey, Greta!" Lola placed her hands on Greta's shoulders and pushed her gently back into the light and out of the danger zone. Perfect. "Are you okay?"

Greta swallowed. "Is Ted still in?"

"I don't think so, kiddo. Is there anything I can do? Do you want to talk?" Please no.

"Oh, no, thanks, um, Ted understands. I'll be fine. I'll find him tomorrow."

"OK, Greta, but I'll be here a bit longer if you need anything." Please no.

"Thanks, but I think I'll go home and watch a movie. He lent me the director's cut of *Terms of Endearment*."

"That should cure what ails ya," Lola smiled warmly. She stole back to her desk.

douglee: darts in fifteen?

Lola didn't usually drink stout, but she wanted something she couldn't chug.

"Sorry to have to sound the alarm," Douglas was saying. "I'm sure Greta's harmless, but…"

"No, of course," said Lola.

"So anyway?"

"Well, I got in."

"He actually stored the password?"

"No, actually…"

"You actually guessed it!?" Lie.

"Happened to know his childhood dog's name," Lola fibbed, following her own advice for once.

"Wow," said Doug, raising an eyebrow. "Good call."

"So. Nothing in the inbox."

"Really?"

"Nothing in the outbox."

"Yeah…"

"Nothing in sent mail."

"Wait, so all of that for a total dead end? Dammit!"

"…*And 9 messages in 'Drafts,'*" Lola finished.

"Ohhhhhh. Wait."

"Mmm hmm. So that way you can leave and read messages without ever leaving an e-trail," Lola said, triumphant. "Nancy Drew, schmancy drew. WWSYD?"

"What Would Scotland Yard Do?"

They clinked glasses.

"So now we just have to read that folder."

"No problem," said Lola, sipping her stout. "Oh wait, the opposite."

"Let's not worry about it right this second," said Douglas. "Actually, Lola, while we're here? I've got something else." He produced yet another printed e-mail and placed it on the table.

Another? Lola started to read.

> Dear Lola,
> I'm a 27-year-old guy in New York City. I'm nice, but I don't have that Friend-Boy problem. I'm smart, but not unable to enjoy the dumber things in life. I'm cute, but not unapproachably so or anything. I'm funny, but not loud funny. I'm outgoing, but not loud outgoing. I'm fit, but not neckless…

Neckless. That made her laugh. Again. Why did this sound so famili—

Doug was looking at her.

"Ranger?! Was this letter from you?"

"Yeah." He smiled shyly. "But I know what your turnaround time is. I figured at this point I could call in a favor."

Lola was touched. "Of course, Doug. Hang on." She reread the letter and looked back up.

"Remember, do not say 'You just haven't met the right woman.'"

Lola said nothing.

"Lola?"

Lola said nothing.

"Lo? Oh, geez..." Doug laughed and pushed up his glasses.

"Rrroo jzt hvnt mut duh rrrt wmmn," Lola said without opening her mouth.

"All right," said Doug.

"You told me not to say it."

"But do you really think that's it?" asked Doug.

"Yes," said Lola. "Definitively. I mean, you? Without a girlfriend? It's nuts. It's an outrage. Why, it's un-American." She sipped her stout. "All right, fine, are you sure there's not some horrible something you haven't told me about?"

Doug shook his head.

"You don't introduce her to your parents on your first date?"

Doug shook his head.

"You don't go in and rearrange her CDs by year?"

Doug shook his head.

"You don't ask a blind date not to shower for three days prior 'cause you're allergic to soap?"

Doug shook his head.

"Oh wait, that happened to Annabel," said Lola. "You don't even crack your knuckles, do you?"

"Nope."

"Doug, look, it's gonna sound corny, but you are special. It's gonna take someone special to match you," Lola said, secretly quoting her mother. "If you're not feeling it with, whoever, you're just not feeling it. You don't have to get all psychology about it, I don't think. You really are—"

"I don't read movie reviews."

"I'm sorry, what?"

"I don't read movie reviews. I refuse. Policy."

"You're kidding," said Lola. "Why not?"

"I don't know, I just don't want to know. I want to judge for myself."

"Based on what?"

"I don't know, the graphic in the ad?"

"Are you nuts? But movies are like fifty bucks a pop! You don't want to know what you're getting into? That's...just weird."

"That's what...okay, that's exactly what Waterfall said. It's basically why we broke up."

Lola looked at Doug funny, then remembered. "Oh geez right, your ex," said Lola. No teasing right now, Somerville, be nice. "Wow, you broke up over *that?*"

"Well, it can't have been *just* that, right? I mean, that's the kind of thing that if you liked the person, it'd be like…just one of those warts as in '…and all,' right?"

Good point. "Yeah," said Lola.

"She said it meant that I was rigid, or closed-minded, or…something. I don't remember specifically. I'm not still hooked on Waterfall at all, I promise," said Doug. "That just stuck in my craw."

"I get it," said Lola. "No Doug, really. Don't force anything. If you give someone a chance and it doesn't take, don't beat yourself up. Bear and forebear." Another Momism. "Just, if you're gonna take someone to a movie, ask me about it first, okay?"

"Sure," said Doug. "Thanks, Lola."

"Of course."

They clinked again.

32

Kat managed to make it in the next morning.

"Bravissima!" said Lola, giving her a hug.

"Yeah, I mean, everything there reminds me of him," Kat said. "Then again, earth, air, fire, water, the *Phantom Menace* and the letter E remind me of him, so what's the difference?" She smiled bravely.

"And Ted helped, of course." Ted had just come in himself. He was taking off his scarf. Good boy.

"Yeah," he said. "I sat and talked to her while she ironed."

"While she ironed!?" Lola asked.

"I find ironing therapeutic," Kat said.

"I don't know, I find therapy therapeutic," said Ted.

"Kat, you can have therapy at my house anytime," said Lola. "P.S.? Why is it so cold outside already? You guys notice? What's with that?"

"I dunno," said Ted. "Hell's frozen over?"

"Oh, a lot's supposed to happen then," Lola said.

I seem like myself, right? Lola wondered. Much as she wanted to keep those two up to date, she didn't want to burden Kat, for one thing; she knew how it felt to be suddenly single. It makes you think thoughts like, "Well, at least you have a boyfriend to spy on!"

"Hey Kat," Lola said. "Did you know that Doug doesn't read movie reviews?" Was *he* wearing a scarf today?

"He what?" said Kat. "He doesn't? Why not?"

"He just doesn't. Isn't that weird? He told me last night and it's been bugging me. What do you think it *means?*"

"I really don't know, Lola." To be fair, she had other things on her mind.

"You know, it's exactly that kind of recklessness that got me mixed up with Kevin Costner's *The Postman,* which grossed $8.50 because of me," said Ted, shaking his head. "I'll talk to him."

•

Lola read the letter she'd asked Ted to pull for her.

Dear Lola,
I'm dating a great guy named Jay whom I really adore. My problem is that while he's genuine and caring both alone and in front of other people, he seems to have a commitment-phobia that comes up whenever anyone *else* mentions it. I'm not in a rush for matrimony, but this guy can't even say the word "girlfriend" in front of anyone. We're completely monogamous, have had the official couple discussion, and we spend much of our spare time together, both alone and with friends. I guess the thing is, he *acts* exactly how a boyfriend should act, except for the avoidance of actually admitting it out loud. Help!
—Jay's GIRLFRIEND. GIRLFRIEND GIRLFRIEND GIRLFRIEND.

Dear Jay's GIRLFRIEND,
On the one hand, as long as he *acts* like a boyfriend and treats you like the tasty morsel that you are, then what's one "girlfriend" among more-than-friends? He sounds great; vocabulary isn't everything.

But on the other, of *course* "labels" matter; it's falsely noble to say that they don't. If they didn't, we wouldn't have trouble saying them in public.

Wait a sec.

Lola made a call.

"Hey, Dad." Professor Somerville was an extremely famous linguist, among the seven or eight people who understood what he did. Lola mainly understood what he did *not* do, such as tape-record aboriginal languages and write books that anyone heard of.

"Hi, Lulu. What's up?"

"Official business, Dad," Lola said. "So there's this guy who won't call his girlfriend his 'girlfriend.' Can I say something about how that means he doesn't think of her as his girlfriend?

"No."

"Wait, so, doesn't, you know, language determine thought?"

"Whoa, no, I'm not going to go there. That's the stuff of six undergrad and grad-level courses in the philosophy of language and the philosophy of thought, or at least a late-night dorm room argument. I'm afraid to get into the theoretical points of—"

"But Dad, come on, can't you just say that, like, words are, you know, how we, like, file things? How we file all thoughts?" Lola was getting impatient. She wished, unfairly, that he would just feed her sound bytes. Used to be: "Why can't you be more like those dads who play soccer with their daughters?" Now it was like, "Why can't you be more like Deborah Tannen?"

"No, no, I can't say that," Professor Somerville said. "There's, for instance, musical thought that can't be explained that way; and emotions are not necessarily encodable, so you can't really make that point—"

"Okay, okay. Thanks, anyway, Dad."

"Hang on, Lu. There's a distinction between his behavior and his words. But his words are also part of his behavior. So you *can* say that there *is* a part of his 'boyfriend' behavior that *is* missing. So, he does *not* in all respects act like a boyfriend."

Lola was typing fast.

"Dad, you rock."

"'Rock.' Is that good?"

"Yes. Love you, Dad."

"Love you too, Lulu."

"Bye."

Ooh, voice mail.

"Lola, it's Molly over at *Chyck.*" Production assistant. Lola had already told Ted she was too young. Remembering the Challenger disaster was the cutoff. "Listen, turns out we're debuting this new celebrity astrology fashion segment called 'It's On the Stars'—"

Wait, what?

"—and the first installment's extra long because we're getting this special feed from Tasmania with Priscilla Presley about this new line of batik stuff that she's doing, so we're gonna have to bump your segment this week. Sorry. We'll touch base beginning of next week."

Lola forwarded the voice mail to Kat, Ted, and Doug to make sure she'd heard right.

It's On The Stars?

I am beyond knowing what to say or do about this, she thought.

Except to just do my job.

Lola went back to her response to Jay's girlfriend and summarized her conversation with her Dad. And then added:

> ...So I wouldn't say the vocab issue is a deal-breaker, but I would say this guy needs to quack like a boyfriend too.
>
> To do: bring this up with him as an inquiry, not an inquisition; tell him hearing that word would make you happy. Maybe he hasn't even realized it's a thing for you in the first place. Or maybe he'll balk. Either way, you'll have more to go on than your thoughts about his language. And if you want us to analyze his grammar, we'll check with Chomsky.
>
> Love,
> Lola
> With Morris Somerville, Ph.D.

Take that, "Dr." E. Ron Wilson. How many MIT professors do you consult for *your* columns?

But needless to say, E. Ron wasn't the only guy on her mind right now.

hernamewaslola: was thinking about what you said
annabel2k: of course you were.
annabel2k: what'd i say?
hernamewaslola: about the "girlfriend" thing?
annabel2k: ah! and?
hernamewaslola: it's NOT ok. Words matter. Words are deeds. quoth the Professor.
annabel2k: ah. dad rules. But does M?
hernamewaslola: we'll see.
annabel2k: lo, do you LIKE him?
hernamewaslola: of course i do. he's my boyfriend.

33

"Hi Lola! It's Olive from Penelope's office!"

"Oh, hey, Olive, what's up?" Just what I need, thought Lola. Exclamation points.

"We're just so excited to have you on the show!"

"I'm looking forward to it." About as much as I am looking forward to that next bout of botulism.

Lola had actually been starting to feel like she and Miles were moving slowly, sensibly, toward Something Real, Nothing To Hide. But now, as far as Lola could tell, they—or at least she—were just tiptoeing in Something Fishy.

Still, she had no proof. Of whatever it was she was supposed to have proof of.

"Well, I hope so! Because there's been a schedule change, and we'd actually like to do the show next week! Would you be available Thursday?"

OK, now she was sloshing through Something Sucky.

"Thursday. Sure."

"Great! I'll be calling you in the next couple of days to go over the details! Thanks for being flexible, Lola!"

"Not a problem." Oh wait, the opposite.

•

"So Kat, how are you holding up?" Lola asked.

"It's On The Stars?!'"

"Hah. That. Yeah," Lola said.

"CELEBRITY FASHION ASTROLOGY?" Kat again.

"It's already so bad I can't even think of a joke about it," said Ted, turning his chair around to join in.

"What's next," Kat asked, "dieting?" Kat asked.

"Oh, I didn't tell you? Yes," Lola replied. She had told them about the whole impending shift to channel-based content, but the damning "diet" detail had somehow slipped her already crowded mind.

"What's next," Kat asked, "foot binding?"

"Oh, I didn't tell you?" Lola said. They laughed. Weakly.

"Just remember our mantra," said Lola.

"Just do our job," Kat and Ted repeated.

"Anyway, yeah, I'm okay, thanks." Said Kat. "I mean, out of sight, out of mind. Clive's mind. I mean, he's out of his mind. Well, you know."

"And you're outta sight," offered Ted.

"Are you OKAYokay, or are you 'No, no, I'm okay!' okay?" asked Lola.

"Well, the latter, but I know I will be the former. I really do," Kat said. "I just wish I could speed up time like…well, I'm sure there's *some* character on TV. Ted?"

"I wish I could *stop* time," said Ted. "Course then I'd *really* procrastinate."

•

douglee: you up for renting "babe" tonight?

That was their favorite movie. Also, code.

hernamewaslola: baa ram ewe!

Reference to *Babe*. Also, code for yes.

•

hernamewaslola: you know doug? get this. He doesn't read movie reviews.
annabel2k: that's weird
hernamewaslola: just doesn't. "doesn't want to know" etc.
annabel2k: really?!
hernamewaslola: doesn't that sound really weird and limiting, and like a little above it all?
annabel2k: it is weird…
hernamewaslola: have you ever heard of such a thing?
annabel2k: well, people have things about stuff. whatareyagonnnado.
hernamewaslola: well that would drive me nuts

•

TO: lsomerville@ovuminc.com
FROM: dawndaley@mcmail.com

Oy. Dawn Daley. A college friend who communicated only in CCd jokes, e-chain letters, and the like. Lola had the chutzpah to confront her enemies on television, but not to ask a friend not to send spam.

FWD: RE: GET A LOAD OF THIS PRETENTIOUS TWO-TIMING DORKWEED.

Sigh. It had to happen.

•

Douglas came by Lola's desk. She had *Beverly Hills 90210* on, just for company.

"Whoa," said Lola. "Is it me, or does Tori Spelling look terrible?"

Doug looked up. "Well, she's standing next to Jennie Garth. That's her first mistake."

Just to be safe, they went to a computer near the mailroom that no one seemed to use much. Lola opened the browser to mcmail.com. Hoping Douglas couldn't see the letters, she typed in the password.

LULU

Invalid password.

Oops, caps lock.

lulu

Invalid password.

Uh oh.

lulu

Invalid password.

Oh God *dammit.*

She tried it three more times, hoping that hitting "return" really hard would make a difference. Nothing. Then Lola tried every other password she'd tried before. Nothing.

"Hell's bells," she said.

"What you said," said Doug.

Then Lola tried

miles

So stupid it's smart.

Invalid password.

password

Invalid password.

ovum

Invalid password.

Lola threw up her hands and sat back. "Okay, now I'm just flailing."

"Well, the Ranger has a plan B," said Doug. "We go back into Miles's office and install a key capture app. Then we go back in—again—and see what he's typed in for the password."

"So we have to go in again, and AGAINagain?" asked Lola. "Oy. Okay." She knew Miles was away speaking at the Mac World convention, and that Norman never stayed past eight. Something about taking care of his live-in aging mom, who at least let him out to go to the opera.

"Do you really not read movie reviews?" asked Lola. "Like, did you used to, and then quit? Was it one in particular that sent you over the edge? Do you—"

Doug looked at her.

"I'll stop now."

•

Fortified with a few orders of tekka maki and unagi, Lola and Douglas ran the same drill. Door sentry, warning knock. Silent high-five.

Lola crept into Miles's office and stood at his desk with the Zip disk Douglas had given her. She popped it in and ran the necessary installer. While Lola waited, her eyes raced around the room, hoping for any password inspiration that might help spare them a return trip. She saw the blank spot on Miles's desk where a framed photo of the two of them (hiking somewhere, or atop the Arc de Triomphe with the Eiffel Tower in the background, or something) would be if this were all not happening in Bizarro World.

World. Travel. Wait.

His Peace Corps girlfriend..

The computer was done restarting. Lola opened the browser to mcmail.com.

No, I'm not even gonna—

tulip

What kind of freaking name is Tulip, any—

Ping! She was in.

34

Shocked, Lola sat down in Miles's chair. On a—what's this? On a *panda.* A little stuffed version of Ping-Pong. With a note so vomitously adorable that Lola would never be able to show it to anyone.

Mmm hmm.

Addressed to her.

Lola didn't know whether to cry, or cry.

Knock.

Fuck.

Or flee.

Flee would probably be best.

Lola clicked "sleep," watching the full "drafts" folder vanish, popped out Doug's disk, and ran on her tiptoes, ballerina style, to the door. She and Tootie saw each other at the same time.

Lola dropped to her knees and said the first thing that came to mind.

"Here, kitty!"

She looked up and smiled as Tootie passed. "Last time Buttercup gets to come to work with me!"

"I'd help you, honey, but I'm allergic," he said.

"Oh thanks, that's okay," said Lola. "She'll turn up. Hey, what are you doing here so late, anyway?"

"Oh, I'm going to a party at Twirly." The latest soon-to-be-closed-for-drug-violations scene in the nearby meat packing district. "But it doesn't start until midnight, and I didn't feel like going all the way home, so I just took a cat nap here!"

"Not allergic to that, huh?" kidded Lola. Har.

"You know it! And I was just on my way to get me some juice with summa that ginko biloba. Pick me right up."

"Sounds good." Lola remembered to look like she was looking for a cat. "Have fun tonight."

Not bad, Somerville. Except now she had to worry that Tootie would tell everyone she was one of those single women with cats.

•

She and Douglas regrouped in his pod.

"Wish we could go to Darts," Lola said. "I could use a drink."

Doug held up a finger. He opened a drawer and pulled out a bottle of pretty good sherry.

"No way," grinned Lola.

They sipped it from egg-shaped Ovum coffee mugs as they whispered.

"So yeah," said Lola. "Password changed. Do you think that's something they'd do automatically, or because they know…?"

"Some people do change them frequently. It could be just that," said Doug.

"All right, but I did get in, you realize, right when you knocked."

"Another lucky guess?"

"Guess so."

"You wanna go back in tonight?" Douglas asked.

"I would, but I'm afraid to push our luck," Lola said.

"Right. I mean, chances are it gets changed, like, once a week or month or something, and we just hit it right between."

"Yeah. That seems logical." Lola yawned. "Listen, Ranger, it's been a long day. Week. Few months. I really gotta go home and—lie awake. Will you keep an eye out for Tootie so I can leave without a cat?"

"Sure, Lo."

Though tomorrow I get to leave with a panda.

What the hell am I doing?

35

Whoooooooooooa.

Lola had gotten as far as her coffee maker when she realized that something just wasn't right.

Tummy? What seems to be the problem?

Tummy? You never hurt. I pack you with gimlets, pork rinds and jalapeño ice cream, and you always stay right there, um, by my side.

So what's this gross gurgly feeling I haven't felt since…college?

O stomach of steel, don't fail me n—

Lola ran to the bathroom.

And then staggered to her couch. She lay right down on top of a jean jacket, an avocado, and an inline skate. The buttons, buckles, and wheels jutting into her back were nothing compared to the swells of pain and nausea rolling from head to toe and back again. Why isn't Miles here to pat my fevered brow? Nothing. Is. Worse. Than. Being. Nauseated, thought Lola. Dear Lord, just send me in for a root canal, or to Hooters, right now, and I swear I'll be good for the rest of my life.

Oh, no.

Lola ran back to the bathroom.

Perhaps it is just as well that Miles is not here.

•

"Mommy?"

"Lulu, what's wrong, have you been throwing up?" Uncanny.

"Mommy, I'm sick."

"Oh, dear, Lo, oh God, why don't you still live in Boston? What do you think you have?"

"I don't know, Mommy, I never do this!"

"That's because you obey me and wash your fruits and vegetables and never eat anything tartare or sushi, other than 'crab stick.'" Mrs. Somerville teased lovingly, yet firmly.

The sushi. Last night.

"Right?"

"I don't know, I just had a veggie burger," Lola lied. "Cooked through," she added hastily. "Hang on."

Back to the bathroom. What on earth was left?

"Lulu, you've got to get to a doctor! It could be *e. coli.* You'd also want to alert the CDC. I have their number around here somewhere..."

"OK, Mom, I will. Call a doctor, I mean." An old editor friend's aunt had a general practice right in the neighborhood and had, in the past, squeezed her in for conjunctivitis flare-ups and the like. "I'll call Dr. Gibson right now."

"Do you want me to get on the shuttle?"

"No, mom. I'll be fine. Really." Please God, make it soon. Lola felt exactly the way she'd described that horrible toxic breakup feeling with Kat, only not metaphorically.

"Call me after you call the doctor."

"I will."

Lola left messages for Ted and Doug (he'd had eel, which is cooked, not tuna—might be okay) and then tried Dr. Gibson. Sure enough, she'd squeeze Lola in if she came in right now. Lola warned the receptionist that "hurrying" was really not an option, but promised that she'd shuffle over as soon as her stomach and its remaining contents, if any, would allow. It was only a few blocks. Lola peeked in the mirror. Sure enough, her skin was gray, like coffee with skim; her hair would soon go in the same color direction, as she had little left to throw up besides pigment. She took—and kept down—a few sips of water, and put on a hat.

•

Made it. Not only without hurling, but also without (as New York Murphy's law would normally dictate) running into an ex-boyfriend with his new girlfriend, or a movie star. A bit of fresh air, chilly though it was, plus having kept down a few sips of water, had actually helped Lola feel marginally better—as if she had just a touch of dysentery, as opposed to malaria *and* ebola. Lola gave the receptionist her ten-dollar co-payment (hooray for health insurance!) and was shown into Dr. Gibson's examining room right away. "Dr. Gibson will be right with you," said the assistant, closing the door. Considering that I have never felt worse in my life, thought Lola, things are really going very smoothly.

Lola pulled herself up, sloooooowly, on the table. She stared at Monet's water lilies until they started to make her a little queasy. Then her cell phone rang. Hmm, who could be—

It was Kat.

"Lo. God, I'm sorry to bother you. How are you feeling?"

"Could be worse. Could have my eyelids pinned open being forced to watch *Les Miz.* I'm at the doctor's right now, actually. What's up?"

"You are? Oh, shit. Well. Okay. I just—I thought you'd wanna know right away."

"Know what?" Is it my delirium, or does Kat sound weird?

"Um, some really bad stuff is happening over here."

"Like? What? Now it's just, what, Bugles on Tuesday?"

"Lo, Ted just got laid off."

36

The water lilies turned black and bilious. The room spun. Lola's hand started to shake.

Then the rest of her.

"WHAT?! They can't—He's not—How can—WHAT?!"

"Along with a bunch of other people doing Internet stuff. Greta, Janet whatshername, lots of people at Miss Thing—"

"Wait Kat, how is Ted?"

"Dealing. You know Ted."

"OK. Kat wait, look at my phone. Any message light?"

Pause. "No. But Lo? Norman's been looking for you."

He *better* have been looking for me. "This is off the fucking charts. Tell Ted I'm coming in. As soon as the doctor amputates my torso." Lola struggled to hold the phone to her ear. Her heart was racing at StairMaster Level 23,427.

The nurse came in. "Hi!" she grinned. "Just need to take your blood pressure!"

•

Food poisoning, Dr. Gibson guessed. "Just go home and rest. Your body's doing what it needs to," she said. Purging? Like my company?

"Thanks so much, Dr. Gibson," Lola said.

She hailed a cab and headed for Ovum, praying that she'd get a driver who'd obey the laws of physics. On her way, Lola checked in with Ted (who joked wanly about the loss of his shoulder to the office cryers), lied again to her mom ("Yes, I'm heading home!") and left messages for both Annabel and her lawyer. Hellish as she felt right now, Lola would never not get a kick out of having someone she called "her lawyer."

A few more blocks. Lola tried to focus on one steady spot. Jesus. We haven't even been there a year. Phone rang again. Kat.

"Lo, you almost here?"

"Yeah Kat, just a few blocks. What's the latest?" She heard a sniff. "Wait

Kat, what's wrong?"

"Lo, I've been…'reassigned.'"

"WHAT?"

"I'm the Production Manager for the new, um, lifestyle channel. It's called 'Cycles.'" Lola's stomach could barely keep down water; how was her brain supposed to process this?

"Dear, sweet Jesus. Kit Kat, just sit tight. I'll be right there."

How the fuck do they expect me to do my job without Kat and Ted?

•

Lola stormed into her pod, but then steadied herself on a desk, realizing that she couldn't storm very hard without steadying herself on a desk. The desk, of course, started to roll. Lola barely caught her balance. It was not a strong entrance—and it took place in front of Miles.

"Lola," he said with the expressionless look of someone trying to look expressionless. "Could you join me in Norman's office?"

"Could you give me a minute?" asked Lola, standing up taller. "I need to talk to my staff for a moment." My *former* staff. Jesus.

"Sure. But as soon as you can?"

"Yes, Miles." She didn't even look at him.

Lola felt faint. Oh, *that's* what I haven't eaten today. Food.

"So," said Lola, looking, heart sinking, at Ted's pre-labeled boxes. There was a folder on his desk labeled "Facing the Change." Wow, they work fast.

"What the fuck?"

Kat and Ted were numb, at a loss. They told her what they'd been told: that the streamlining of the content into channels required an analogous streamlining of staff. That the Internet, while still a strong and here-to-stay sector, was not proving to be the cash goldmine that was expected. That "everyone was going to have to trim, here and there, in order to stick with it for the long haul." Blah blah blah.

"Guys? I don't know if I can change anything," said Lola. "But I can start by making it clear that no one gets away with treating you guys like that. Going around me? I can't even…."

"Nobody puts Baby in a corner!" said Ted, who'd seen *Dirty Dancing* a few too many times.

"All right," said Lola. "Here I go."

"Fight the girl power," said Kat.

Group hug. Kat was crying, Ted was trying not to. Lola walked off.

Wait a sec. Where's my head? Oh, that's right, I barfed it up. Hello, Lola: The e-mail. The Miles-gate break-in. Jesus. Am I busted? Am I more busted than I've ever been in my life?

Lola stopped briefly at an empty (recently emptied?) desk and dialed Doug's extension. "Ranger."

"Holy moly, what a bloodbath. I just heard. What's going on?"

"Have you heard anything about, you know...Babe? Anyone been asking you anything?"

"No, nothing."

"'Cause I just got called into Norman's office."

"Jeez."

"Yeah. It's either bad, or worse," said Lola. "Maybe I should get something to eat so I can throw up on a full stomach."

37

"You rang?" asked Lola, glaring at Norman, not even looking at Miles.

"Hi—why don't you close the door and have a seat," said Norman.

Lola obliged. Wait, who was that woman? She was wearing a suit, a frumpy one. No one wore frumpy suits at Ovum.

Oh my Lord, she must be a cop.

"Lola, this is Lorraine from Human Resources," Norman said.

Ah.

Wait, that's still bad, right? Like in *The Right Stuff* when the man in the black suit comes up the pilots' wives' front walk. Right?

"Hi," said Lola.

"First of all," said Norman, "I want to apologize, personally, for the way things have been handled so far. You should have been notified first. We had a lot of unpleasant stuff to do today and we got some wires crossed. I'm sorry. Oh—are you feeling okay?"

"Tip-top," said Lola. She was feeling better, but also worse. That *X-Files* alien-oil feeling was crawling under her skin again.

"So Lola, we're sorry to deliver bad news...badly." This time it was Miles. That is, it was the pod person who looked just like Miles.

"Go on," said Lola.

"You know, of course, about our structural shift from brands to channels," Miles began.

Lola nodded.

"We'd thought, originally, that it would be only a matter of architecture, and not of the, let's say, furniture inside," Miles went on. "But, well, the market's not doing what we wanted it to, and our readers aren't wanting what we thought they would."

"I cannot do my job without Ted and Kat," Lola stated.

Miles paused. "Right." Paused again. "Lola. Your job's been eliminated."

Dear Lola,
My boyfriend just laid me off. How do I react?
—Lola

Dear Lola,
My boyfriend just laid me off. How do I react?
—Lola

Dear Lola,
My boyfriend just—

Lola?
Lola?

Ahem.

Dear Lola,
For now, you just become that person who, fueled by pure adrenaline, hoists the tree trunk off her leg.
You can do it.
More later.
Love,
Lola

"So you're going to, what, just make my columns into searchable archives?" she asked.

"That's a super idea," said Miles. "But no, actually."

Lola waited. Did Pod Miles just say "super?" Cover blown. Since when would the real Miles say "super?"

"We really need to make sure we have new content, but of course, well, we no longer have the creative staff to do that."

Lola waited.

"So after about a two-week transition, we're going to start syndicating some content."

Lola waited.

"From Dr. E. Ron Wilson."

Lola stood up and left.

Lola got as far as the juice bar—hardly noticing that Ovum's usual bustle had ground to a hushed halt, motionless clusters of murmuring employees dotting the floor—and stopped.

This is happening. This is happening. This is happening, she told herself. Kat. Ted. Miles. Pod Miles. E. Ron Freaking Wilson. Think think think think think. Is this payback for the snooping? But if they knew about that, why didn't they bust me? And why did it have to be Miles?

"Lola." Speak of the Devil.

"Lo, I'm so sorry. I feel awful. Just horrible, horrible, awful. I—"

Lola looked at Miles. God he's hot. Shut up, Lola.

This better be good.

"It was out of my hands. The big picture, I mean," he said. "But um, I actually offered to, um, do the deed."

So far, not so good.

"I mean, Norman can be kind of a jargony cad. I just—I just didn't want to sit there and watch him make things worse."

Worse than your boyfriend firing you? Plus you said "super," you hoser.

"Lo?" Miles took a step toward her. She noticed that his right hand was behind his back. "There was nothing I could do. I feel…I…this is just…"

Lola had never seen Miles speechless before. His right hand came forward, holding the panda.

"Lo?" Good God, was that a tear in his eye? "Will you still be my girlfriend?"

38

Now he says it?

Come on, Lola. Snappy comeback. Think Rosalind Russell. Katharine Hepburn. Mae West. Dorothy Parker. Come on.

"I…I don't know, okay?"

All right, Molly Ringwald—the best one could expect under the circumstances, really. Lola turned and walked away, leaving Miles holding the panda.

Kat and Ted looked up, waiting. Doug had come by.

"So Ted, what time do we have to be out of here?"

"Six," said Ted. "Wait. 'We?' *What?*"

Doug's jaw dropped.

Kat fell into a chair.

Lola shrugged, her face a bust of itself.

"But…you don't have a folder," Ted offered weakly.

"Whatever," said Lola.

"Do you need me to get you one? I'm your assistant for about five more hours."

"No," Lola smiled. "Thanks, Ted."

"Lola, are you, like, okay?" asked Kat.

"Yes. In that 'No, no, I'm okay! sort of way," said Lola. "At least I discovered something worse than nausea." Lola vaguely noticed she was famished.

"But Lola, there can't be an AskLola.com without you!" said Doug.

"That is correct."

"So no more site?"

"Guess not."

Everyone took this in.

"What are they going to do for relationships content? They have to have something," Ted said.

"Well. I'll give you a hint," said Lola. "Let's see. Right now, the Pigs are Fixing, and the Nuts are Sharing."

"And the Lolas are kidding," said Ted. "Please."

"The Lolas are wishing the Lolas were kidding."

"That nincompoop is going to work here?" asked Kat. "Nindotcompoop? Sorry."

"No. Syndicated content. Blah blah blah," said Lola. "I guess this isn't a place I'd want to work anymore." She saw Kat and Doug's faces flicker.

"Lo," Kat whispered. "I can't afford to leave right now."

"No, Kat, you shouldn't," said Lola. "Truly. Don't you guys dare pull a Jerry Maguire. If anything, I need you—and you," she said, turning to Douglas, "on the inside."

"Roger," said Kat.

"'Strike me down now, and I will become more powerful than you ever imagined,'" quoted Ted, wielding an invisible light saber.

"I need to call my mom," said Lola.

•

"Mommy?"

"Lo? How is your stomach? Wait, did something happen at work? I can hear it in your voice. Oh, I *knew* you were going to go into the office."

"Mommy, I just got laid off."

"What? Lola? You're not—it isn't Canadian April Fool's Day? How could—? What happened? Oh, baby, are you okay?"

"Yeah. Right now I am. Yeah," said Lola. "I—I have to pack up my stuff. I—I don't know what to say."

"Do you want me to get on the shuttle?"

"No Mom, no, thanks. I'll call you in a little while. I—I have to pack."

"What about that boyfriend of yours? Can he help?"

"I—I don't know, Mommy."

•

hernamewaslola: m called me his girlfriend
annabel2k: no way! yay!
hernamewaslola: right after he laid me off
annabel2k: **WHAT?**
annabel2k: ARE YOU OK?
annabel2k: LO?
hernamewaslola: no but yah. yah but no. you know.
hernamewaslola: what do you say when your boyfriend lays you off?

hernamewaslola: can't i just give the company more space?
hernamewaslola: "it's not you; it's the economy, stupid"
annabel2k: lo? i see you're "dealing with things through humor"
hernamewaslola: just doing my job. OH WAIT.
annabel2k: really lo, you ok? what can i do?
hernamewaslola: geez. dunno. numb. right now i actually just need to pack. i have help.
annabel2k: ok. i'll be right here. love you. i know that doesn't count.
hernamewaslola: yes it does

•

"Lo?" Douglas.

Oops, how long have I just been sitting here?

"Lo, let me help you pack. Kat and Ted have their hands full. I'll, like, label boxes and all that stuff. You shouldn't have to think about it."

"Thanks, Doug. Yeah, there's something else I have to do."

39

Dear Everyone,

You know how I always tell you that even great relationships end, that relationships that end are rarely a waste of time? That they are, rather, a part–if not the whole point—of life?

I'm afraid, right now, that this relationship–mine to you, mine to this site–must end. For once this is true: "It's not you." Sometimes–and I've told you this, too–it just must end, for reasons that no one can ever satisfactorily explain.

I am so sorry, and I am so grateful to you all for your amazing letters and your awesome trust. Please keep treating each other as equals, and please keep having fun. Because if relationships aren't fun, then I quit.

Oh, wait.

Love,

Lola

"Hey, Ranger?" Doug looked up from Ted's computer, where he was inventorying Lola's stuff on a spread sheet.

"I'm gonna e-mail this thing to you, this, um, farewell—" Lola's voice caught "to my readers? Big Brother, Sister, whatever, has probably already changed the server passwords and stuff. Can you do me a favor and just make sure it gets posted somehow, somewhere, during the transition? It's in Ovum's best interest, and it could not possibly be more important to me."

"Of course," he said.

"Thanks."

Doug walked over. "Lo, are you okay?"

"Yes," she said, clearing her throat.

"Oh wait, the opposite," they said together.

"Let me know if there's anything at all I can do," Doug said. "I'm here."
"That's plenty," Lola said. "Thanks."

•

I wonder if I should tell—
angelachan.com.
404 Not Found.
Dammit. Can't deal with that now.
Lola opened her e-mail. Good grief. Seven messages with the subject line "press inquiry." Insidemedia.com, TechTalk.com, PinkSlipsToday.com. That was a new one. Ping! More kept coming in. Ping ping!
Lola dimly remembered signing something draconian, some non-disparagement something she'd never imagined would be relevant; she began forwarding all the inquiries to her mcmail.com account, cc-ing her lawyer while she was at it. Ping!
Forward this, forward that, forward forward forward.
Wait a sec, what's—

TO: lsomerville@ovuminc.com
FROM: boqueron@mcmail.com
Hi. Long story short, I heard what happened, and I wanted to say I'm sorry.
All best,
Still a Fan

Holy moly. Boqueron?! How did he find—? How did he figure—?
I cannot think about this right now, thought Lola. But wow, was that nice.
"Lo?"
Kat, with a big delivery bag from NoNoDontGetUp.com. She peeked in. Gummi bears, dried figs, wasabi peas, a pink stuffed "Babe," plus a flyer from the company announcing its purchase by LatexAndNylon.com.
Choosing to ignore that development, Lola read the note from the sender.
It was a care package from Annabel. Lola burst into tears.

•

At six, they were ready. A security guard "just happened" to stop by, looking uncomfortable. Lola spotted Miles hovering, too.
"Let's just make this unceremonious," said Lola. "I really can't deal. Okay?"

"Yep," said Ted. "Let's call it a night. Mare."

Kat and Doug nodded. They stacked the last of the boxes for the delivery guys. Kat grabbed Lola's right hand, Ted the left. Doug trailed. They walked toward the elevator. Lola cast a glance back.

"Bye, me," she whispered.

40

Lola woke up, partly. It was still dark out. There is some reason I really, really don't want to wake up, she thought foggily. Then it hit her like a cartoon anvil.

Oh, that.

And that.

That, too.

Many anvils. Lola closed her eyes tight. And lay wide, wide awake.

Normally pretty organized, if not actually neat, Lola didn't know where to file all her piled-up feelings. Should Ovum go under C for Conspiracy, or P for Paranoid—or just T for 'Tis Better To Have Sold Out and Lost…? Should Miles go under M for Miss, or H for Hate? She wished, wished, wished that her feelings overall could just nicely, simply—if terribly sadly—go under L for Loss. Unfortunately, though, it looked like there was lots of room under B for Betrayed. Lola groaned aloud and rolled over. Giraffe wasn't sure what to say.

At precisely 9 AM, the phone started ringing. Lola made like a Gap employee—hah, it could come to that—and put on her cordless headset. She shuffled to the coffee maker. Having collapsed into bed the night before without setting up the machine and the timer, Lola couldn't remember the last time she'd awakened (alone, anyway) to no coffee ready.

Ring. "Hello?" Lola filled the pot with cold water.

"Lola, this is Nancy Noonan. I'm a reporter for PinkSlipsToday.com. We just launched yesterday."

Oh yeah. Lola had heard something about that on a radio show in the cab. They'd given the site a week.

"Just wondering how you're holding up," Nancy was saying.

Lola scooped some Peets into the machine, getting grounds on her knuckles as she reached into the bag.

"I'm…I can't tell you. I mean, not as in 'I can't tell you how upset I am,' I mean, as in, 'I CAN'T tell you how upset I am—I mean, I'm not allowed. Not that I'm not upset. Crap, I said too much. Um, I haven't had my coffee." Lola pressed the ON button. Hard.

"Oh, so you have a gag order?"

Eeeuw. It didn't sound so sucky when it was called a "non-disparagement agreement."

"I guess so, yeah."

"Can you talk off the record?"

"Maybe. But only when I'm on the caffeine."

"Can you refer me to anyone else who could talk?"

"Um, would you mind giving me a call later?"

"Sure Lola. Sorry. Sorry about everything. Call you in like an hour?"

Oh, God. "Fine."

Beep. Call waiting.

"Lulu, you OK?"

"Hi, Mom. Yeah. I guess."

Beep. "Mom, hang on a sec?"

Click. "Hello?"

"Lo, it's me. Miles."

"Lo?"

"Lola?"

"Miles, may I please call you back? I'm on the other line with my mom."

"Sure. Just wanted to say I hope you're O—"

Click.

"Hi, I'm back."

"Are you doing okay, Lulu?"

"Well, you know. Yes. No. No. Blaaargtpp."

"I know. Did you manage to get any sleep?"

"Sort of. I guess. Mommy, I'm just numb. Mommy, Lola isn't Lola anymore."

"Oh, Lulu."

"Mommy, I think I've lost everything."

"Lu, you still have your friends, and your father and I who love you."

"I know, Mommy. But everything…else."

"Do you want me to get on the shuttle?"

"No thanks Mom, it's okay."

"All right, Lulu. It's okay to be numb right now. Of course you are. You don't have to make any big decisions. In fact, you shouldn't. Just get through this minute, then the next minute, then the next—"

"Okay, Mom."

"—And then sue their asses."

"Mom!" Lola laughed.

"Or whatever you think is appropriate. I don't understand all the details yet anyway."

"Me neither."

Beep.

"Hang on, Mom."

Click. "It's me." Kat.

"Oh, hey! Hold on."

"Mom, I'm gonna take this one. I'll call you later?"

"OK, Lu. You're doing great. Your father and I are proud of you no matter what. Love you."

"Love you too." Lola choked up.

Click. Deep breath. "Hey, Kat."

"How are you? Stupid question."

"No clue. You?"

"Lo, I'm lonely. It's so weird and bad here. It sucks. I hate it." Kat was starting to sniffle, too.

"Oh Kat, I'm so sorry. Look, um, you've got Doug," Kat said.

"Yeah, that's true—I can actually see him from my new desk. Mmm hmm, he just picked up the phone."

Beep. "Kat, I'm sorry, hold on."

"Lola! It's Doug,"

"Ranger! Hold on one second, okay?"

"Haah, Kat, it's Doug. Funny, huh? Lemme tell him I'll call him back," Lola said.,

"No, that's okay, I actually gotta go," said Kat. "My department is having some sort of 'feelings circle' to 'process' what happened yesterday."

"Oh. Who-hoo!" said Lola grimly. "Guess they've gotta do something—I mean, it's not like Maddy's been around to hold people's hands."

"Yeah, well, surprise. Anyway, talk to you later? In like a minute?

"Yeah. Thanks, Kat. Hang in there."

"You too."

Click.

"Hey Doug. Sorry."

"No problem. How are you holding up?"

"I'm...holding." Lola poured her coffee and added half and half.

"Well, um, is now a bad time or anything? Am I interrupting anything?"

"Douglas," Lola laughed ruefully, "for the first time in three years I have absolutely fucking nothing to do." Pause. "Except listen to whatever it is you're about to tell me."

"Right, well, yeah." Doug lowered his voice. "Can you hear me?"

"Mm hmm?"

"Angela Chan called me," he said. "Looking for you."

"Angela? Looking for me?" For a moment Lola felt popular.

"Yeah, I actually knew her kinda well. She said she heard about what happened and really wanted to speak with you but all she got was voice mail or a busy signal. She wanted to know if I had your cell number or something."

"Couldn't she just hack into Sprint or something?"

"Probably, but it's easier to just to pick up the phone." Fair point, thought Lola.

"Anyway," said Douglas, "One thing led to another and I wound up telling her about the stuff we'd found. Point is, she wasn't surprised."

"Really?"

"Yeah. Lo, she knew something was going on here."

"What kind of something?"

"Something about how Maddy's actually not running the show."

"Duh. She's never there. Norman, Miles—," something in her stomach went clunk, "it's those guys. Emphasis, *guys.*"

"No, I mean, she seems to think it's, like, someone else. Someone above her. Someone outside."

"Who, Skull and Bones?" The secret society at Yale whose alums, like Penelope, ran the world, only from inside the Pentagon.

"Well, you know how Angela used to be this hacker goddess? She talked me through, well, *into* that projectovum@mcmail account."

"Yeah?"

"A bunch of those drafts had been deleted, but there was one new one. We read it. It just said 'Well done. Onward.'"

"Hmm. Well, that's not much to go on."

"Lo," said Doug. "It was from Senator Vestibule."

41

"Wait, WHAT? I can't even—*Senator*—?"

Beep.

"Jeez, Doug, hold on."

Click. "Hello?"

"Lola? *There* you are! This is Angela Chan."

"Uhhh, hi! We were just—"

"Lola, I'd like to talk to you. Douglas gave me your cell phone, but I wanted to try land again just in case—

"No problem, Angela. Can you hang on just a—"

"Actually, in person would probably be better, and not one of our apartments—someplace where we're not likely to be spotted."

Good lord, the drama, thought Lola. This can't be my life. She made arrangements with Angela and told Douglas she'd talk to him later.

Ring.

"Lola, it's Nancy Noonan."

"Oh, Nancy, so sorry, can I call you later—?" Later this century? Oh, wait. Later this millennium? Oh, wait. Later this—forget it.

•

"Um, I guess I'll have the Pikachu Pesto," Angela said.

"I'll have the same, please," said Lola. They'd met at the Pokémon theme restaurant on West 57th.

Angela looked terrific, of course, in just jeans and a black sweater. Lola felt like a huge frump in comparison, even though she was wearing the exact same thing.

"So," said Angela.

"So," said Lola.

"Lola, the stuff that's going on, the stuff that you and Douglas started to pick up on? It's big."

"Big how? How big?"

"Dotgov big."

"I don't get it. I mean, I know about that e-mail, but what does the senator have to do with...whatever it is that he has to do with?"

"Well, he may have tried to destroy the National Arts Endowment, but it looks like he's involved in some creative ventures of his own."

"What, did someone dig up a book of really bad haiku poetry he'd written under a pseudonym or something??"

"Well, no, that's not it."

That was five syllables, Lola thought. Hmm. "I'm—not—sure—I—fol-low—you." Seven!

Angela looked around. "Ovum, Lola, *Ovum,*" she said.

Wait, that's six syllables.

Focus, Somerville. Angela is not playing your live haiku game. "Wait, what? What, Ovum. Ovum, what?"

Angela waited.

"I mean, what could the senator possibly want to have to do with Ovum, of all places? We're—I mean, *they're*—his worst nightmare. They *were,* anyway, until everything started going to 'diet' hell," Lola said. "OH."

"Yeah," said Angela. Their pesto came. Lola salted hers in silence, buying herself time to figure out why she'd just said "OH."

"So yeah," said Angela. "Given everything we've dug up, I don't know what else to think except, well, that Ovum is somehow...involved with the government."

Okay, that's why I said OH.

Wait, what?

"Isn't this where I say 'I think we've been watching a little too much *X-Files?*'" Lola asked.

Angela waited.

"I think we've been watching a little too much *X-Files,*" Lola said. "I mean, like, well, for example, is Maddy complicit in this whole thing?"

"Lola, there is no Maddy."

"What do you mean, there is no Maddy?"

"Have you ever seen her?"

"No, only on screen—"

"You know that chatbot thing Douglas helped develop? He didn't know what all its applications would be..."

"You're kidding."

"I wish I were, especially because I fell for it."

"Wait, you took your job without ever having met Maddy?"

"Well, I fell for what they told us at the time—only a few of us were in on it. The executive board told us that since this business—and the pipeline to it—was so new, there really wasn't a woman qualified to run such a high-level, high-profile technology company. Well, actually *I* am, but they needed a figurehead with more mainstream crossover appeal; they didn't want people to be able to say, 'see, feminists are all lesbians.' But they also didn't want someone less than qualified to subject herself to such a high risk of told-you-so failure. I mean, this is all what they told me, anyway. I don't really need a 'career-builder' job, or even a salary really, so it wasn't a Life Choice with a lot of cautions and cons. Bottom line, I believed so strongly in the mission that, even knowing what I knew, I went for it. Frankly, I also figured that once we—they—got established, Maddy could 'retire' and I could go ahead and step up."

"Then why did you leave?"

"Same reason you did, sort of."

"It wasn't exactly up to me."

"Well, me neither. I mean, I am going to have a baby, but I wasn't planning on leaving because of that. I thought I'd be able to use the company day care."

"Which should be ready right about when Angela, Junior goes off to college."

"Not even, Lola. One day I got worried about some old insulation that had gotten exposed in the area, but whatshername in Facilities? She wouldn't answer my e-mails about it. So I just went and looked up the contractors listed on the permit, figuring I'd call them myself? Turns out Osgood Bros. construction doesn't even exist. I complained to the board and—well, I guess I was on to something, because they basically threatened to out me unless I left quietly."

"Whoa," said Lola. "But, um, you're kind of out, aren't you?"

"Well, yeah. But let's just say I'm still in the closet about a little affair I had—"

Lola raised her eyebrows.

"—with Senator Vestibule."

"Ohhh," said Lola. Okay, eeeuw. Though it was refreshing to learn that even a supercool smart gay woman had made at least one foolish choice.

"It was a long time ago, and I have no idea how they knew, but I wasn't sticking around to find out."

"Wow. Okay. So. Wait." Lola struggled to assemble her thoughts. "So we're saying that the senator is trying to destroy Ovum. No, no, that Ovum's obsolescence was planned all along. Bait and switch, yes? Rally the feminists—the cool ones who pose the biggest threat—flush them out, then bring them down…and wind up feeding women the same old crap." Now Lola had her game on. "So the senator, and God knows who else, wants to keep us in our place. And he, or they, are working with people on the inside. The board. Norman. And—"

Duh. Viva denial.

"—Miles," Lola said. The pesto in her gullet turned to paste.

```
Dear Lola,
My boyfriend isn't supportive of my career. In
fact, it appears that he dated me specifically in
order to destroy it. What should I do?
—Lola
P.S. Why do I feel like something similar happened
to Nina Sambuca?
```

Lola lifted her glass for a sip of her water just as the busboy began to refill it. Ice cubes rafted into her lap.

"Oh! God! I'm so sorry!" she exclaimed. They scrambled to dry up the mess.

"Angela, you know, Miles and I were, you know."

"Duh," Angela said with a thin smile.

"But, I mean—" Lola told her about the Stefanie Marlowe memo, about how the only show she'd been invited to do for Penelope was about office romance. "…But discrediting me was taking too long—well, okay, plus I was getting a little testy—so they just got rid of me," she finished. Wham, bam, thank you, Ms.

I hate them. I HATE them. This brought "being used" to a whole new level.

"Speaking of Penelope, I don't think yours is the only love life they think is expendable."

"What do you mean?" asked Lola. "Did they bring her in to bring her down, too?"

"I doubt it," said Angela. "She's just way too powerful. At first I thought they were just using her for her huge cachet, but now I think they're *really* using her."

"What do you mean?" asked Lola.

"Well, it's something Leo Cameroon spilled to me at the party," Angela replied. "He was drunk as a skunk, actually. What was in that blue punch, anyway?"

Lola shrugged. Oh, just my innocence.

"Well, I didn't take it seriously at the time, but he told me that someone had offered him money, a lot of money, to propose to Penelope. On the show. Specifically, he even said, some massive sweeps-time extravaganza they're setting up about the blessed institution of traditional marriage and conventional gender roles. *The Canon* women, E. Ron, the senator, the whole gang'll be there. She'll be cornered."

"But why would you have to pay him to marry Penelope?"

"Oh, didn't you know? Leo's a huge queen."

Oh, for God's sake.

"Okay, so, right: if they can't beat Penelope, they join her…in holy matrimony. Like, no more of this non-traditional shacking. They need her as a *de facto* spokesperson. Right?" asked Lola.

"That's what I'm thinking."

"So," asked Lola, "isn't this where I say, 'We've got to find a way to stop them!?'"

42

"Yep," said Angela. "And *this* it's where I say, 'and you're the only person who can do it.'"

"Me?" asked Lola "I mean, 'I?' Well, you know."

The waiter came by. Lola and Angela said they were still working on the pesto they'd left nearly untouched. In Lola's case, not only because she was completely distracted, but because it really wasn't very good.

"You," Angela said. "Who else is Penelope going to listen to?"

"Penelope would listen to *me?*"

"Are you kidding? She writes to you."

"She *writes* to me?" asked Lola, who would have dropped her fork if she'd been holding it.

"Oh, sure. I once overheard her on the phone to Leo saying, all happy, that you'd said they didn't have to do that whole 'I *feel* that you…'thing anymore."

Well, then. "But wait. Aren't you two friends?"

"Hardly. She knows about me and the senator. She's never forgiven me."

"Ah," said Lola. "Well. I feel…that we've got to warn her."

"Mmm hmm," said Angela.

"And somehow, in the process, get her to expose the whole plot," said Lola, on a roll now. "I mean, her show is the perfect place."

"Correct."

"So when's this particular show?" asked Lola.

"Let's see if it's listed yet," said Angela, taking out her Palm XII to check the TV schedule.

Tap, tap, tap. Tap.

"Lola," said Angela. "It's tomorrow."

"Angela," said Lola. "It's Norman."

Norman Shetland had just walked in with a boy who must have been his nephew. New York, Lola thought, is tiny. She bent down as if to pick up her napkin and dived under the table.

"The table trick works better when there are tablecloths," observed Angela, looking straight ahead.

"Right. Well." Lola was new at this. "At least this way he won't see me from the door."

"And at least this way I'll have to explain why I'm eating alone at Pokémon," said Angela. "I know you're a big proponent of taking yourself on 'dates,' but…"

"We'll be out of here before he see either of us," said Lola, passing a twenty up to Angela. "Can you see him?"

Lola saw Angela's legs shift as she turned slightly. "Yeah. They're sitting by the door, but he has his back to it."

"OK, go ahead. I'll catch up with you."

"Actually, hang on."

Lola waited, admiring Angela's shoes. Angela passed down a napkin on which she'd scribbled: "Set up a new mcmail account. Not on your home computer. Then e-mail me at secure@angelachan.com. I had to take the site down for a while and reencrypt the whole thing, but now it's secure."

"Gotcha," said Lola.

Angela pushed her chair back and got up.

Lola waited a minute, hoping the restaurant's service would continue to be sluggish.

"Lola?" A familiar voice came from behind her. Whuh? She turned around, bumping her head.

Jordan was under the table next to hers.

"We've got to stop meeting like this," he said.

Lola stared.

"I—I came in here because for once I didn't want to be recognized," he said. "And who should just walk in but my ex, the one who hates me, with her niece or something. I'm hosed. She'll tell everyone I was here eating alone. Um, and you?"

"Same thing, only replace 'ex' with 'boss.' Actually, ex-boss.'"

"Oh, that. Yeah, I know, Lo. I heard. I was thinking of calling you while I was here but I didn't know if you'd want to hear from me. I'm sorry about what happened."

"Make it up to me by walking out with me."

"Done."

They emerged from their respective hiding places. Jordan gave Lola his arm. They walked out, faces blank, not knowing who saw what. Let 'em talk.

•

Lola sat on the subway, her brain clogged. Take your own advice, Somerville: one thing at a time.

1. Get in touch with Penelope.

2. Get her to believe that there's some sort of male plot behind Ovum, with its ultimate goal the re-fifties-ification of gender roles. Oh, which is also why they're paying her boyfriend to propose.

3. Get her to expose all of this on her show.

That seems so much easier now that I'd made a list. Oh, wait, the opposite.

All right, back to number one.

How am I going to get into the building? Ah, I will hide in some sort of large laundry basket and Kat will push me where I need to go. Or I could bonk a security guard on the head and wear his uniform. Or hello, I could just *call* Penelope. What do you call that, Occam's Razor? To start with the simplest solution? Lola had learned that in college philosophy, or else from Fox Mulder.

When she reached her stop, Lola called Ovum from the first available pay phone. Which was the fifth actual pay phone; the first four she tried either had no dial tone, no cord or no place on the receiver that was not covered with gum. The anti-cell phone people should refocus their campaign, she thought.

"Olive Estrada, please," said Lola. Olive likes me.

"Olive, this is Lola Somerville."

"Hi Lola! How are you? We're so excited to have you on the show! Oh, I mean—Oh, dear! I'm sorry!"

"No problem," said Lola. "But actually, Olive? I was wondering. Is there any way at all I could speak with Penelope, do you think? It's actually kind of urgent. I wouldn't ask if it weren't, of course."

"She's in a meeting right now, but I can certainly leave her the message! I know she's very fond of you! And that she takes very seriously what you have to say! So I'll see what I can do!"

"Thanks, Olive." Lola left her home and cell numbers. "Today, do you think? I mean, thing is, it really needs to be before tomorrow's show."

"Gotcha," said Olive. Lola heard other lines beeping.

"Okay 'cause it's urg—"

"Gotta go! Have a good one!"

Lola was pretty pleased with herself so far.

Then she stopped at the local Internet café. Deserted. She ordered a Caesar salad from the teenager at the counter and then set up the account anchovy@mcmail.com.

Oh! *Boqueron.* Hang on Lola, you and Miles haven't even officially broken up yet. Hah, maybe I'll just get Penelope to announce that it's over on the show—save me the trouble. Anyway.

To: secure@angelachan.com
From: anchovy@mcmail.com
Re: P.
Hi—have a call into P. she should get back to me today.—L

•

While I'm at it.

Lola clicked on literati.com and searched for Blake Fox's byline. Only one piece.

Nina Sambuca Puts Out…Fiction

By Blake Fox

Exclusive to literati.com

Notorious bad girl Nina Sambuca, it seems, has a soft spot for good guys. I knew her a long time ago; recently, she agreed to meet up with me again. I gave her a few cold drinks and a warm shoulder. Amazing how quick she opened up…her mind. Soon she was slurring. "You're the kind of guy I can *talk* to…" she murmured. Soon after that, she was talking herself into a corner—and into my tape recorder. "All that stuff in my column? I make that up," she said….

Hmm. What a lousy trick. Also, a lousy writer, thought Lola.

•

Home again.

hernamewaslola: hi
annabel2k: how you holding up
hernamewaslola: fine! just taking care of numero uno! girly spa day, green apple candles, etc. not thinking about decline and fall of entire life etc.
annabel2k:…the opposite?
hernamewaslola: mmmhmm.

•

"Ted, it's me."

"Hey, Lola. How are you?"

"All right, I guess. You?"

"Hanging in. Say, hang on for a sec and lemme save this level of Tomb Raider?"

"No no, that's okay. You play. We'll talk later."

"Okay. Lola? I miss…us."

"Me, too, Ted."

•

Lola turned on the TV and clicked through the channels to Ovum while she puttered around. FairerSex was showing the she-spense movie *Baby Monitor: Sound of Fear.* Wait, I was sure I'd tuned into Ovum. Lola clicked the remote. Yea, verily, this movie *is* on Ovum. Good Lord.

•

"Kat, it's Lola."

"Hi. How's it going?"

"All right, I guess. You?"

"Lo, it's going from worse to worser here. Remember way back whenever when they did a segment on oppression of women in Afghanistan?"

"Yeah."

"Well, I saw more women in chadors today," said Kat. "But Lo? It turned out they were doing a *fashion segment.*"

"What? Eeuw!!! What's the segment on, 'modesty chic?'" Lola snarled sarcastically.

"Um, actually, yeah."

I hate them.

•

to: anchovy@mcmail.com
from: secure@angelachan.com
okay lola but you really might want to start thinking of a plan B.
—AC
PS meanwhile I'll work more with douglas on getting into that acct.

to: douglee@mcmail.com
from: anchovy@mcmail
hey ranger. just wanted to say hi and thanks and hi.

43

Duh, thought Lola. Guess I was still so high on the notion that I could conceivably get Penelope on the phone that I forgot that I probably won't.

So, let's revisit.

1. Get into office.

Well, that's pretty easy; Kat or Doug can meet me with their ID.

Wait.

1. Get into office at prime time, unrecognized.

Hm.

Phone.

"Hello?"

"Lo, it's me." Miles. Dude, you have so lost your "it's me" status.

"Miles?"

"Yeah."

"Can I call you back?" I'm on the other line with my conscience.

"Well, I—sure."

"Thanks." Click.

His solicitousness was becoming oppressive.

Oppressive.

Wait a sec.

"Ted? It's Lola."

"Hey, Lo. Hold on. 'Lara, baby, wait for Ted just a second, kitten—'."

"Come on Ted, this is important."

"Okay, but you realize Lara Croft is *hot.* If I were a cartoon, I'd totally do her."

Lola smiled and ignored him. "Ted, Don't you have a friend in wardrobe, someone who wants to date someone *like* you, just *not* you?"

"Oof,"

"Just quoting you quoting her," said Lola. "Doesn't she owe you a favor?"

"Megan," said Ted. "Yeah. She's cute, but she's no Lara Croft. More like Pocahontas."

"Can you call her?"
"You tell me."

•

Lola hung up with Ted—having switched to the miraculously functioning pay phone outside the corner bodega (which Lola referred to as "My Refrigerator")—and then left a message for Annabel. "Listen, disregard basically whatever I say on Instant Message, OK? I'll explain when I get you in person. Ciao, bella." Then she called Kat, then Doug. "Could you just e-mail secure@angelachan.com—yeah, it's safe—and tell her Lola has a Plan B? Thanks. I'd do it, but it's just—the Internet café is way too depressing."

•

Cell phone voice mail check. "Lola, it's Mi—"
Lola hit "3." Erase.

•

Lola got ready for bed.

Nothing, nothing, nothing from Penelope, even when Lola turned on/off and reset her phone to make sure it was indeed functioning properly. Note to self, invent phone with "Yes, it's working" indicator light. She stirred up a cup of vile instant Suisse Rain Forest something or other that must have belonged to her cupboard's previous renter. Why couldn't it be like the good old days, when she would sit, hands cupped around a favorite steaming mug, rain pattering on the window like the shattered bits of her breaking heart, waiting in vain for the love of her live, whatshisname, to call? That was way better than sitting, hands cupped around a favorite steaming mug, rain pattering on the window like the shattered bits of her career and identity, waiting in vain for the leader of the free world, Penelope, to call—and wishing that whatshisname would just freaking leave her alone.

Yeah, nothing from Penelope. What did you expect, Somerville?

Well, frankly, a little more from someone who supposedly sets so much store by me. I mean, geez. If she had taken the kind of advice I've given to people like that Ultimatum Frisbee, this secret government cabal—"secret government cabal?!"—might never have had the chance to use her as its pawn.

"Use her as its pawn?" This is unreal. Lola stared at the ceiling until sheer drama and self-righteousness wore her out, and then she slept. The phone did not wake her.

Meaning that, she realized when she checked voice mail the next morning, it hadn't rung.

Plan B.

Lola grabbed some quarters and made some calls.

Then she changed into the nice Ann Taylor sportswear she wouldn't be needing for her new job scooping Tofugurt.

Drink coffee, read paper—changing your ritual will only throw you off your game.

Oh, boy. Page one.

Nuclear Families Continue Meltdown

Lawmakers, Experts Wring Hands, Practically Hand Out Rings

WASHINGTON (Reuters)—The number of Americans living alone has grown rapidly this decade and for the first time less than a quarter of all households consist of married couples with children, the Census Bureau said yesterday.

According to figures released from the 1999 census, the number of American single-person households amounted to 26 percent of all households, while households with married couples and children under 18 dropped to 23.5 percent from 25.6 percent in 1990 and 45 percent four decades ago.

The new figures suggested that living together without getting married is no longer taboo, with the number of unmarried people living as couples increasing by 72 percent to 5.47 million in 2000 from 3.19 million in 1990.

Demographers attribute the shift from the traditional nuclear family to several factors, such as couples delaying marriage and childbearing, a higher divorce rate, faster growth in the number of single-parent families than in those made up of married couples, and women being picky.

Senator Helmsley Vestibule—who, along with the authors of the popular bachelor-baiting handbook *The Canon,* will today appear on *Penelope* to discuss these figures—voiced dismay. "What we are witnessing is no less than the destruction of the American family, which itself is no less than the destruction of American society. Of course, women have made great strides over the years, strides that have allowed many lovely young ladies to contribute greatly to my own office. But traditional roles became 'traditional' for a reason, did they not? We must also acknowledge that feminism has encouraged women to price themselves out of the marriage market, ditch their husbands, endanger their children, practice witchcraft, become lesbians and eschew training in the skills our society depends on, such as dusting."

Who says we can't have it all? thought Lola.
She tore out the article and headed for the subway.

44

Kat met Lola outside the warehouse/gallery across the street from Ovum, as planned. She was carrying a big brown bag from Bloomingdale's.

"Hey," they said, giving each other a big hug.

"Ready?" asked Kat.

"Ready," said Lola.

They went into the gallery, which was currently featuring sculptures of the Virgin paper-mache'd entirely of articles about Mayor Giuliani. Nigel, the front desk guy, was buried in a worn copy of *Harry Potter and the Sorceror's Stone.* They'd all made friends at various Darts outings; when he saw Kat and Lola, he waved them right into the restroom, as planned. "This better mean I get to meet Penelope," he called.

•

Nigel whistled at Kat and Lola as they left, which was ironic on many levels.

The two made it through the first checkpoints with only a few sidelong glances. Carrie Walters met them outside the *Chyck* studio. She didn't work for Penelope, but it made more sense that she, rather than Kat, would be escorting a guest. She was not exactly sporting, but they'd told her they'd repay her this little favor with some interesting information about the future of the day care center she'd come there to direct.

"Hi," she said, looking Lola up and down.

Doug showed up. "Wow," he said, looking Lola up and down.

"Here you go," he said, holding up a manila file containing several printouts. "I wanted to mark it TOP SECRET but I thought that might defeat the purpose."

"Right," she said. "Thanks. You rock so hard."

"Ready, Lola?" Carrie asked.

"SSHH," everyone said.

"Right," said Carrie.

"'Ready as I'll ever be,' as they say," Lola replied.

"Okay. I can get you as far as Penelope's outer offices. Beyond that you're on your own."

"Save the world!" whispered Kat. "No pressure."

"We still think you rule no matter what," added Douglas. He handed the file, discreetly, to Kat, who reached under some folds of fabric to hand it to Lola.

Lola beamed under the veil of her chador.

•

Lola followed Carrie across Ovum's main floor. Penelope's studio was actually in a new space out of the way, on the floor below, but only the studio audience entered that way. Lola felt like she was wearing the Princess Leia costume her grandmother made her for Halloween 1977, and also like she was having one of those dreams where she's invisible. Mmm hmm, there's the juice bar, there's the Incubator, there's our old pod, with—good grief—new people already totally moved in. And there's…Miles. Up ahead. Lola knew this could happen. Just. Keep. Walking. Just. Keep.

Miles walked right by, without giving Lola so much as an up-and-down glance.

Asshole.

They reached the studio door. The On-Air light was off. So far, so good.

"This is where I shove off," said Carrie. "I've aided and abetted enough."

"Thanks, Carrie."

"Hey, whatever I can do, within reason of course, to bring down those…those…day care fakers. Good luck with whatever crazy stunt you guys are pulling." Carrie sighed. "Off to tweak my resume."

Lola opened the door and slipped in. Now she felt like Obi Wan Kenobi sneaking around the Death Star.

Help me, Tootie, you're my only hope.

Lola beeped him to her cell phone.

It rang back right away.

"Tootie, it's Lola. Listen, the worst thing about leaving this place is not having you to do my eyebrows. So, well, you're gonna totally kill me, but I went to this local place? Total disaster. I can't even go out in public. It's so bad that I snuck in and now I'm somewhere in your studio. Can I come find you real quick, please? Knowing you, it'll just take a couple of plucks…"

Tootie, suitably horrified, told Lola how to find him.

"But hurry, I'm about to do Penelope," he said.

"I'll be right there."

Phone again. Damn.

"Hello?"

"Lo. Miles."

"Hello? Anyone there? Hello? Sorry, it's a bad connection. Call me back? Thanks."

Lola hung up and turned the damn thing off. Not bad, Somerville. Good thing I am not Fox Mulder—one time they found him hiding in the Mojave desert by tracing his cell phone.

Lola stole around a few corners. Eek! Someone with a digital camera. Must be the guys who do the behind-the-scenes simulcast at http://penelope/ovuminc.com. Camera Guy passed Lola, going the other way. She peeked back around the corner. Aha! Bright makeup lights streaming out of a half-open door.

She tiptoed over, pushed open the door, and stepped in. Tootie looked her up and down, but that didn't count.

"What—?"

Lola lifted off her veil. "Oh honey, you're right! Total eyebrow apocalypse!" Tootie exclaimed. "Who did this to you! I'll stab them with my tweezers!"

But wait, I didn't actually—oh, well.

"Thanks, Tootie," Lola said uncomfortably.

"And I don't think you even want me to ask you about this fashion choice, am I right?" he asked?

"Correct," said Lola, looking at her watch.

"So, you poor thing, I didn't even get a chance to say goodbye. I'm so sorry about what happened. You doing okay?"

"I'm holding up, thanks. So when's Penelope due in?"

"About five minutes. Not time for the full amputation you really need, girl."

Ow. Lola let Tootie, furrowing his brow, attend to hers.

The door swung open. It was Penelope. She looked radiant—without makeup—but, Lola cautioned herself, this was really not the time to hate her.

"Oh, excuse m—Lola?" Penelope asked. "What on earth are you—?"…doing here?…wearing? Many possibilities.

"Don't mind us," said Tootie. "I'm just saving her eyes. I mean, ass. Well, both."

"Um, hi, Penelope. Please forgive the intrusion, I just really need to talk to you," Lola ventured.

"Didn't you leave me a message?" asked Penelope. "I would have gotten back to you."

"Well, thanks, but it's urgent." Tootie, befuddled, had backed off.

"It better be," said Penelope, looking at her watch and gesturing for Lola to get out of her chair. "In fact, could you just e-mail me about whatever it is and I'll read it right after the show, promise? Go ahead, Tootie."

"It's about the show," said Lola. "Actually, it's about something bigger than that. Something pretty huge, and bad, that maybe only you have the power to stop right now."

"This wasn't really about your brows, punkin, was it?" asked Tootie. No one responded. He suddenly got really busy sorting some sponges.

"Lola, with all due respect, I really can't handle this right now. And I don't have to tell you it's not right for you to just barge in here "—Penelope cast her eyes up and down—"no matter how modestly you may be dressed."

"Penelope, please, I can prove—" Lola waved her file.

"Lola, please, I can call security," Penelope said, reaching for the phone.

Lola took a quick breath. And a monster gamble. "It's also about Leo, Penelope. Or should I call you 'Ultimatum Frisbee?'"

Tootie dropped a Q-Tip. Penelope sat back.

"Go on, Lola," she said warily.

45

"All right. It's going to sound a little crazy," Lola began.

"Going to?"

"OK, OK. Um. I'll start small," said Lola. Deep breath. "Today's show, about marriage and traditional gender roles and all that? Penelope," Deeper breath. "Leo's going to propose to you, on camera."

Penelope's face lit up, then fell dark, as if someone were messing with her inner dimmer. "He's gonna—?! Hey, muchas gracias for ruining the surprise! Damn, Lola. It's like when that girl who wrote to you snooped into her boyfriend's Ebay account and found that he'd bid on a ring? And I didn't even snoop! You did! Lola?!"

"Penelope," said Lola. "I know this is what you've been waiting for."

"No shit, kid! I mean, if you must know, I didn't even follow your advice in that letter."

Oof.

"I mean, I knew I should, but I was too chicken. That's—well, honestly? That's kind of why I'd been avoiding you and all your damn show topics and everything. I just—I just couldn't look you in the eye, Miss MyConscience.com. Hah. Sorry."

"That's all right," said Lola, attempting to submerge her personal huffiness in socio-political homiletics. "I mean, hey, in 1998 lots of huge political decisions were made—some say bombs were dropped on Libya—in order for someone to avoid confronting relationship problems. It takes a village."

Penelope went on. "Then Norman pretty much insisted that we do a show on office romance, so whatever. But anyway, it looks like I won't have to issue any ultimatums!"

"Penelope," said Lola, leaning forward. "*You can't say yes.*"

Penelope sat straight up.

"What on earth are you talking about?"

Lola opened her file and pulled out the top sheet. How hard did Douglas rock? She handed it to Penelope without a word, then got up and read over her shoulder.

```
FROM: HVestibule@mcmail.com
TO: <undisclosed recipients>
RE: penelope today
All systems go. Stop.
Leo on board. Stop.
Cayman Trust at the ready with the wire. Stop.
Good work, everyone. Stop.
HP
PS Say, Farmington. Don't forget the damn ring.
```

Old coot kept forgetting he wasn't writing a telegram.

Penelope shook her head. "From the *senator?!* Miles? The Caymans? This doesn't make sense."

"I know," said Lola. "Shouldn't guys want to marry terrific women like us without getting paid?"

Penelope frowned. Oops. "Penelope, look. You are, as you know, a massive role model. Evidently there are people, I don't know who, or how high up, who want to have more control over, uh, the roles you model. They're working on you and they've also been working on Ovum. I mean, come on, would Angela Chan have OK'd the switch from *Sweat* to *Glow?*"

Penelope scowled so hard she looked almost unattractive. Okay, wrong person to have invoked. Lola handed over the rest of the file. Penelope read. Her eyebrows flew back up as if she were doing some sort of "MAD!" "SURPRISED!" exercise in drama class.

"See? Replacing me with *E. Ron?!*" Lola, antsy, narrated. "And see, there are more e-mails like the first one. Penelope, you've got to say—"

"Wait, what's this from Ben and Jerry's? Why is this here?" Penelope asked, still reading.

"Oh! I never received it. It was deleted before it got to me. Penelope, you've got—"

"You're *kidding.*" Penelope frowned and looked up. "What about something with hazelnut?"

Eh, overrated, Lola thought. She took the chance to jump back in. "Penelope, you've got to say no to Leo and you've got to bust the senator on the air. Look, whatever's going on here, it also involves E. Ron, the *Canon* harridans and the other horsedorks of the apocalypse; I'm practically sure of it," she said. "You and Harry Potter are the only people powerful enough to stop this, and Harry Potter is a fictional character."

Smoking e-mails, ice cream, flattery. Lola could tell she was getting there. Come on. Come on. But Penelope was stuck on one more thing. "Does this mean Leo doesn't love me?" She blinked.

Tootie, wisely, kept his mouth shut.

"Maybe he's just not the marrying kind," said Lola. "Some men just aren't. Could be that this, like, dowry just somehow sent him over the edge," said Lola, grasping. "I mean, is everything else you said in your letter true—the way he treats you, all that?"

Penelope nodded.

"There you go. *Actions*. You can't fake that, can't fake them. Not with you. Not for this long," said Lola. Bet *he* called her his girlfriend, and he's *gay*. Anyway.

"I know this is painful, Penelope, and I'm so sorry, but listen, I've got to make myself scarce," said Lola. "Penelope, please. You trust me online; please trust me offline. I don't know how to tell you what to do, but I will tell you that if you don't do anything they *will* turn us all into Pigs and Nuts."

The door swung open. Another Headset Girl ushered in the Canon Women and their husbands. The women were wearing black miniskirts and various feral prints—more evening wear than day, really, but whatever—and their husbands sported fancy satin sweatsuits. Everyone looked at Lola, who didn't really have a fashion leg to stand on at that point. Husband number two, recognizing Lola's face, stepped protectively between her and his wife. Lola rolled her eyes and ignored him. Now she really had to get out of here.

"Thanks, Tootie. Have a great show, everyone!" Lola cast an imploring glance back at Penelope, and then closed the door behind her.

I guess I've done everything I can for now, she thought, pulling down her veil and turning down the hall. Now, where to hide until the show st—

Clunk.

"Oh! Dear! Young lady, please accept my apologies."

Lola had walked right into Senator Vestibule and his aides: two khaki footsoldiers—one girl, one guy—plus his powder-blue-suited, bearing-and-forbearing wife, Harriet.

"No trouble," Lola said, trying to make her voice sound funny. She tried to take a step past. The senator and his entourage were still in her way.

"So tell me, young lady, about your plight in your homeland." What an idiot, thought Lola. Also, I'm hosed.

"Gladly, sir, though I am also concerned about the plight of single women here," is what came out of Lola's mouth. Not now, Somerville.

Tootie's head popped out of Makeup. "There you are, Senator," he said. "Ready for your close-up?"

"Be right in, homie!" said the senator. Wow.

An aide led Mrs. Vestibule away, presumably to the green room.

"Pleasure to make your acquaintance, young lady." Senator Vestibule turned back to Lola. Eeuw. "Such a shame to hide that pretty face. There ought to be a law." He winked and swept into the makeup room.

Go, Lola, now. Go. Lola started hurrying down the hall, trying to look like she wasn't hurrying.

"Miss? Miss?" came a voice.

Shit. Shit.

"Miss? Miss?" the voice caught up. It was one of the senator's various girl wonks. "The senator wanted me to give you his card with his private number. He requests that you call him before you leave the country."

Eeuw. Eeuw.

Shuddering, Lola took a mental Silkwood shower. She watched two Headset Girls pass in the hallway ahead, waited a few seconds, and followed them. Ah. The door marked "GREEN ROOM," right next to "BACKSTAGE." Oddly, the latter might actually be safe—once you've gotten that far no one asks questions. As long as you stay out of the way, everyone's too busy to notice you. Lola pushed back her hood and veil, then opened the door.

46

Lola found herself backstage, stage right. The set, which she could see from the side, was a multi-leveled mauve-and-silver expanse, with *Penelope* scripted on the back wall—like a tasteful space capsule that had landed in, well, a garage. Behind the stage: unfinished walls, ladders, beams, cables and plenty of nooks and crannies for spies in chadors. Lola positioned herself between an unused light board and some sort of utility cabinet, and waited.

It wasn't long before the studio audience was ushered in. They seemed subdued, hushed with awe, so you'd think they might have dressed better. Who wears a "...This Lousy T-Shirt" T-shirt on national television? And clamdiggers? Dude, lose the cap! What, was the Hootie show sold out?

Then the door on Lola's right swung open, and another Headset Girl led in the guests. The *Canon* ladies first (of course), then the skanky senator with the same Girl Wonk (who stepped away and stood on the opposite side of the door, ahead of Lola where she couldn't see her), then frosted brunette Nina Sambuca (whose legs seemed to go right up to her neck the way Lola's Barbies did when she removed the torso section and put their heads on their waists), then, of course, the apple-cheeked, middle-parted, knit-sweatered E. Ron Wilson, trailed by his own wonky Mini-Ron, Smithers to Wilson's Mr. Burns. Wilson always amazed Lola by evidently having gotten this far without a stylist. They were all followed by a digital video girl doing the backstage web-cam thing.

While Robin, the stage manager in painter's pants and a ponytail, had the audience practicing how to applaud—on TV, you do it double-time—the guests took their seats on the set, where the sound guy fiddled with their mikes. They settled, they smiled. Then Penelope entered through the door behind Lola and stepped up close to the stage entrance. Lola tried to read Penelope's face, but it was hard to do though the back of her head. Uproarious double-time applause as Penelope emerged onto the set.

Please, God, thought Lola.

Final adjustments, and then they were three-two-*live.*

"Good afternoon," said Penelope, all poise. "Today we're here to talk about the plight of an endangered species: married people. Our guests are, first

Janelle Fine and Lori Loman, authors of the best-selling *The Canon* series. They contend that women aren't getting married because they're trying too hard with the wrong guys. We also have E. Ron Wilson of *Men are Pigs, Women are Nuts* fame, who claims that women are focusing on their careers—dare I say 'Nut jobs?'—at the expense of their...duties. He'll tell us why—sigh—we're still talking about this. And we also have Senator Helmsley Vestibule, who intends to introduce legislation to help turn around the state of unions in our less-than-perfect union. Finally, we have Nina Sambuca, who has recently declared that she is now at least *like* a virgin and who has called for a return to feminine modesty. Welcome, everyone."

Nods, smiles. "Always a delight to see you, Penelope," gushed E. Ron. Shut up.

"Always a delight to start with you, Dr. Wilson," smiled Penelope. "So let's see. Isn't marriage—legal marriage, that is—by definition, a partnership between a man and a woman? So when it comes to the causes of these demographic shifts, why all the focus on women?"

E. Ron Wilson was ready. "Why, it's because women hold all the *power*—am I right, gentlemen? Heh, heh! So it's up to you to use it right." Shut up shut up.

"That's where modesty comes in," murmured Nina, Sharon Stoning her bare legs.

"See, women's lib has left women confused," said Lori Loman.

Women's lib?

"We're told that we can do what we want, that we have full choice in all matters, but then we find that those choices don't work. That some of those choices scare men. So if we do and say everything we want all the time, we die alone and childless. Which is *not* what we want, am I right, ladies?"

If Lola hadn't heard this all before, she might have run away screaming.

Penelope let her guests establish their positions—unchallenged so far—and then went to commercial. Lola could see Penelope bantering with the guests and with the front rows of the audience.

Lola waited. As the stage manager prepared to go back live, the door next to Lola opened again. It was Leo.

Aha. Bring on the ring before Penelope can go in for the kill. Oh, Penelope, please kill back.

Leo was accompanied by a hot Headset Guy carrying a dozen roses from—Lola recognized the wrapping paper—the shop next door that supplied flowers to the galleries. There was also another digital video dude with his camera off, just for now, so as not to ruin the surprise..

Action. Applauseapplauseapplauseapplause.

"Welcome back to Penelope," said Penelope. "Before I forget, Janelle and Lori, don't you have a new book on the way?"

"As a matter of fact, we do," said Lori. Lola saw on a nearby monitor a screen shot of the cover of *The Ultimate Canon*. Lori went on: "And I'm glad the senator is here, because if there's one thing the feminists got right, it's that,"—she air-quoted—"'the personal is political.' So in our new book, we outline, for example, The Canon for U.N. Engagement. 'If a superpower calls, act unavailable. Don't seem like you *need* a peacekeeping force—let those adorable blue berets come to *you*. At your first meeting, don't spill your guts about 'lack of arable land'—"

"Excuse me, Penelope? Sorry, Lori." It was stage-manager Robin, who occasionally appeared, aren't-we-jaunty-and-accessible-style, on camera. Now she was on stage. Here goes, thought Lola. She glanced at Leo. He had broken a sweat. Headset Guy, standing by, mopped his brow.

"Sorry to interrupt you, but we have a special surprise guest today who'd like to ask you something right now?"

"Oh, my!" joked Penelope. "Is it George Clooney?" Damn, she's good.

"Nope, just me." It was Leo, with the roses. Applauseapplause.

"Well, honey, what a lovely surprise indeed!" said Penelope, beaming.

"Princess, I've got a question that just couldn't wait," said Leo, looking hotter than George Clooney. "I mean, I've waited long enough. Penelope," he said, kneeling in front of her, "will you marry me?"

47

The *Canon* women beamed as if watching their own daughter. The senator beamed as if watching his own daughter—that is, if he were King Lear in Act I, scene I.

"Oh, Leo," said Penelope, looking radiant. "Let's—

Lola thought she could see her heart pumping inside her burqa..

"Let's—"

Oh NO. She looks really fucking radiant.

"Let's—take this offline?"

Right, right. Penelope always looks really fucking radiant.

"And, we're out." Robin, clearly obeying higher orders, went to commercial. Applause.

Penelope was stroking Leo's arm and whispering in his ear. The senator was clearly trying to remain calm. Dr. Wilson, Nina Sambuca and the *Canon* women were, for once, struck silent.

"Senator?" said Penelope. "Would you mind explaining what's going on here?"

The audience was rapt.

"Isn't it self-explanatory, Penelope?" the senator replied. "Someone just asked you the most important yes/no question of your life, and you said 'maybe.'" He shook his head. "Picky, picky, picky."

"You're saying you had nothing to do with what just happened."

"How could I possibly—"

"Hey. Come here," Penelope gestured to the senator's Wonk Girl, who was backstage on the other side. What is she doing? wondered Lola.

Wonk Girl's eyes were wide as coasters, but that could have been due to the sheer force of her headband. She obeyed Penelope before the senator even had a chance to think, because you obey Penelope. "What's in your pocket, Miss Thing?"

The Wonk Girl's face said, "You're not the boss of me!" Meanwhile, her hands said, "But you are the boss of us!" and produced a few items from her pockets: half a pack of Mentos, the senator's "special" cards, and a crumpled slip of paper.

"May I see that, please?" Penelope unfolded the paper. "Hmmm. 'Milk, eggs, marshmallow rice cakes'...Oh, sorry. I—"

For the first time in history, Penelope floundered.

Hell's bells! Think, Lola. Think like it's going out of style.

Out of style.

Wait.

Lola waved frantically at Penelope, catching her eye just as the senator, shaking his head, reached to unclip his mike. Lola cocked her head to the side; Penelope followed her gaze and raised her eyebrows. Lola nodded.

"Hold it," Penelope raised one hand at her guests and pointed the other toward backstage. "You." Mini-Ron stepped forward.

Pigs may not empty their hearts to Nuts, but they sure as heck empty their pockets to Penelope. Dental floss, a tiny cell phone, and a crumpled slip of paper. Please, not a shopping list, or Kat's number, thought Lola.

Penelope looked at the paper. "Hmm. Harold's Blooms, the florist around the corner," said Penelope. "A receipt, dated *today,* for"—she looked at Leo—"*one dozen roses.*"

Gasp.

"Mr. Wilson, would you mind explaining to me why on earth you would have anything to do with my personal life?"

"Yes, actually, I would mind," replied Wilson. "When Pigs are in their Thinking Cave, Nuts should leave them alone. Everyone's happier that way."

Even the *Canon* women rolled their eyes. Lola was sure of it.

Penelope, herself again, didn't miss a beat. "All right, Mr. Wilson, we'll get back to you," she said. "Senator, would *you* mind explaining your role in Ovum Inc.'s striking programming changes?

"I don't know what you're talking about," said the senator.

"Then maybe you can tell us what you were writing about"—Robin placed a file in Penelope's outstretched hand—"in these e-mails."

"E-mail? Never touch the stuff."

"'Change Sweat to Glow,' add horoscopes and fashion ASAP, 'AskLola just answered her last question'"—Penelope flipped through the sheets—"all from an account with your name, signed with your initials."

Gasp, double-time. One was the senator's.

"I *told* them telegrams were safer," he muttered.

48

Now the audience was beginning to churn in indignation and disbelief. They didn't really know what Penelope was talking about, but they felt that they should begin to churn in indignation and disbelief.

Canons and Wonks, nonplussed, said nothing. This was all a bit more than they'd signed on for, or could follow. Nina, for her part, appeared unruffled. She crossed and uncrossed her bare legs again, but for once no one was looking.

"So you don't deny this?" demanded Penelope. "That somehow, somewhere, our own political leadership set out to, wait"—she thought hard for a second—"*was behind Ovum from the very beginning?!* I feel...that you set us up to bring us down. Did you not?"

"Goodness, no, not the *whole* government, young lady," said the senator, struggling. "Just me, actually."

Right, thought Lola. I knew it. That whole conspiracy theory of ours was a little too *X-Files* and not enough *Wall Street Journal.*

She'd written about this herself: "the government" is not going to back this retro-agenda; America *needs* a thriving scene of successful single women. Women buying their own cars and homes and twenty-dollar cocktails—without Bridget Joneses, they can't keep up with the Dow Joneses. It's the economy, stupid.

But this bizarre little men's club could afford to see things a different way, as the senator was now affirming. "Just me on Capitol Hill, that is. But my team and I—captains of industry, computer whizzes, the Promise Keepers, young men who've had their hearts broken in the prime of life—were all guided by the knowing hand, and the bottomless coffers, of my good friend Dr. Wilson."

People on talk shows are, somehow, compelled to spill their guts. People in the process of getting busted are, somehow, compelled to spill their guts. At this point, Senator Vestibule—and now Dr. Wilson—were both.

"All right, yes!" said Wilson. "We were behind FairerSex.com, too, which, I may point out, commands more than 75% of the market and has a number two rating at MediaMetrix. We had all *those* women worried about fat grams instead of fair pay...*then* we just had to bring down you...you...wily feminists."

Wily? Hee, hee. Share on, Pig.

"Mmm," said Penelope. "If I know one thing, it's that this just stopped me cold from investing in the Internet."

"Oh, and reprogramming Nina Sambuca? Us, too," offered Mini-Ron proudly. "Whole thing was his idea, soup to nuts. I mean—well, you know."

"How did you two hook up in the first place?" asked Penelope, at this point genuinely interested.

"Skull and Bones."

"But Dr. Wilson, you didn't go to Yale."

Mini-Ron piped up. "When the organization went co-ed,"—Vestibule shuddered at the thought of that dark, dark day—"they hired Dr. Wilson as a consultant to smooth the transition. You might say we bonded. And then—"

"Oh, the heck with it," Wilson interrupted. "I *did* go to Yale. I am indeed a Bonesman, but I invented a new background early on, on the advice of a professional image consultant. You see, I've got the brains—enough to build *two* empires, the second, in the shadows, supporting the first—*and* the looks: the folksy, un-fancy image that people will love and trust.

"The 'E' stands for 'Eli,' as in Eli Yale," said Mini-Ron, clearly trying to be helpful in any way he could.

Wilson was done. "Perhaps you consider this all a confession, but I couldn't care less. We're still on commercial break. No one has heard any of this, except these, these..." he gestured dismissively at the audience.

"*Tourists,*" said Senator Vestibule.

That meant war. The audience rose to its feet, hurling the Wilson paraphernalia they'd brought in hopes of an autograph, and chanting "Free Harriet Vestibule! Free Harriet Vestibule! Free Ha—"

"HOLD IT!" boomed a voice. A woman's voice—much, much louder than the beige suit beneath it. Striding out from the wings, massive wedding ring glinting in the spotlight, was Harriet Vestibule.

What on earth next? People shushed.

"First of all," she said, "it's *Mrs. Helmsley* Vestibule." She adjusted her cuffs. "Well done, gentlemen. Perfect articulation of the story we agreed to tell if captured—but I could not just sit there and let you take the fall. No, let me amend that. I could not just sit there and let you take the credit."

"Yes, dear," said the senator. Dr. Wilson nodded.

"Ladies and gentlemen," said Mrs. Helmsley Vestibule, "these gentlemen work for *me*. My husband may be a senator, but *I* am president. Of the small-but-powerful, heretofore secret organization known as 'Ladies Against Women.'"

49

Too much. Too much irony, too much everything. Lola's brain was plum out of RAM. She wasn't alone. The room was silent again.

"*I* wrote those e-mails. Everything these gentlemen helped execute—I schemed it up. With the help of my"—she looked at Penelope—"perhaps you would call them 'sistahs?'"

"Perhaps not," Penelope whispered, Lola reading her lips.

"Other Washington wives, certain well-known actresses, one or two Promise Keepers, Ms. Sambuca, of course."

Nina gave an insouciant salute.

"Nancy Reagan helps out when she can." Mrs. Helmsley Vestibule turned to the to stunned *Canon* women. "You've been terrific, too. Thanks."

"Us? We didn't know!" shrieked Lori.

"We thought my grandmother had some good points, that's all!" Janelle cried. "We just wrote one little pink book, and it's all spun so out of control—"

Penelope interrupted, fixing her gaze on Mrs. Vestibule. "But *why?*"

"You feminists have been making things far too complicated for far too long," she replied calmly. "And the liberal media establishment had utterly failed to discredit you on its own by not reporting your radical goals or your vulgar language. On television, you wear dresses and use terms designed to evoke unthreatening housewares, such as 'glass ceiling.' Why, *Time* magazine even declared your movement dead—but if you were *that* dead, why not a small obituary instead of a cover story? That so-called news actually *helped* your cause."

She had a point. Not a dim bulb, Mrs. Vestibule. Lucky for her American women were permitted to attend school, thought Lola.

"On you go, exchanging horror stories about men, magnifying little slights into grievances, until women blame 'society' or 'all men' for their own failures, mistakes, and disappointments," Mrs. Vestibule went on. "It was one thing when you just had *Ms.* and mimeographs. But today? On the information superhighway, women—feminists—are very dangerous drivers. 'My girls' and I—oh, and him too," she waved a hand at her husband, "—decided it's high time you reached a dead end. Because you know, we were fine before you came along. We knew where we stood. *We want that back.* Do you think I worked my way up from secretary to deputy Energy Secretary—and then gave everything up for my husband—for nothing?" Mrs. Vestibule pulled herself up taller than ever in her square-heeled pumps. "We do not want our daughters to have to make *choices.*"

"I see," said Penelope, folding her arms across her chest. "Well, the American people will have some choices to make after they see what's happened here today. Ladies, and women, and gentlemen, meet Lola Somerville."

Penelope turned to face backstage, toward Lola.

Who had gotten everything on digital video.

And thus streamed it live to millions of viewers on the worldwide web.

Dr. Wilson went white. Whit*er*. Mrs. Helmsley Vestibule went beige.

Applause, double-time. Applauseapplauseapplauseapplauseapplauseapplause.

Even *Canon* and Nina looked pleased.

Note to self: Somerville, *you rule.*

Lola turned the camera on herself for a moment, waving and grinning. Okay, finally I can say I've been on *Penelope!*

Oh. While I'm at it. "Senator? I have a question," said Lola, stepping forward. The other digital video girl was rolling now. "What about Valentine's Day?"

The senator sighed. "Oh, actually, Valentine's Day *is* a government conspiracy."

"Really?" asked Penelope, genuinely surprised. "It's not Hallmark?" asked Penelope, genuinely surprised.

"That's what we wanted you to think."

•

Lola gave Penelope a thumbs-up and left her to salvage the rest of the show, not to mention her relationship. "Thanks," she said, handing the camera back to the DV girl. She walked out the stage door—and right into Miles, who was holding a ring box, and a panda.

"Lo?"

Lola waited, wishing only that she was wearing a better outfit. At least her eyebrows were good.

"Lo. I just wanted—" You can't fool me with that ring box, you…fool. I know it's the one for Leo.

"I just wanted—Lo, *mea culpa.* I *was* sent here to do to you what I did to Nina..."

Nina. Lightbulb. *"Haven't forgotten, Nina."* His notebook.

Bigger lightbulb.

"Miles, you're 'Blake Fox,' aren't you?"

"...Yes," he said.

"Miles, did you and Nina used to date?" Lola asked.

Miles blinked. "Yeah. She dumped me. Then, right then, I *knew* that women had far too much power," he said. "That was tenth grade." He ran a hand through his hair. "I tried to forget about her, to get over it, all through college and with all that traveling and stuff I told you about..."

Ohhh, those dreamy dates. Maybe I should give him one more cha—Lola? Are you high?

"But I just couldn't," he said. "I mean, I kept dating women, and it kept not working out."

You dumbass, thought Lola. That's life, not women. That's life, life until you find the one, or *a* one, or whatever. Didn't you read my freaking column? Dumbass.

"So when I first went to work for Wilson, just developing geek stuff like the branded GPS, oh, and the watch-communicator"—Miles looked proud for a moment—"well, when he recruited me to bring her down, *there* was the opportunity for revenge I'd been working and waiting for."

Tacky, tacky, tacky.

Of course, at some level, Nina was probably working out similar boy-blame issues. Which is so much more interesting a thought than what Miles is saying right now. Anyway.

"So yes," Miles went on, "things started out as a bit of a conspiracy. But then, my heart...conspired against me...and I fell in love with you."

Have to say he's cute when he's contrite.

Oh, well.

Too late.

"I understand exactly what I did wrong. You are totally, completely right. I humbly ask your forgiveness."

Men Are Pigs, Women are Nuts, page 173.

"Lo?" He was holding out that darn panda.

"I can change," he said. "I met Mary Matalin at a party once. We can find out how she and Carville make it work."

"Hey Miles?" Lola said.

Last chance, Ms. Parker.

"Pencil me in for *never.*"

Lola walked right past Miles. And the panda.

"Got it!" said the girl with the camera.

•

Lola rounded a corner near the exit and bumped into Nina Sambuca coming out of the bathroom.

"Oh. Hi," they said. They stood uncomfortably for a moment, Lola particularly uncomfortable to have found herself at the precise level of Nina's breasts.

"Nice work," said Nina.

"Thanks," said Lola. "Um, Nina? What was Miles like in high school?"

Nina looked at her. "Geeky. *Smart.* Into, you know, the Hobbit, and I think he had a ham radio. Did I mention geeky? Of course, so was I."

"Why'd you break up with him?"

"Oh God, who remembers? I guess when the A/V club started to take over my life, I just lost interest."

"Guess he took it pretty hard."

"Uhhh, yeah," said Nina. "Yeah, sometimes I feel bad for toying with his feelings. But whatever, he's hot." She grinned at Lola, gunning for one of those sisterly slutty moments.

"Wait, what?"

"Oh yeah, we hook up whenever I'm in town," said Nina.

Okay, I did *not* just feel jealous.

"But what about your new book?" said Lola, feeling stupid by the time she said the word *about,* but continuing anyway. "That chastity stuff's not true either?"

"Hey, you gotta get a gimmick," Nina shrugged and looked down at Lola, who at this point felt like the naïve newcomer being trained by the head geisha.

"You think *The Canon* would have sold more than three copies if it had been called 'The Suggestions?'"

"Guess not." Wait, didn't I say that?

Yow.

As she'd walked away from the studio, Lola had sensed a dark blur around the edges of her giddy glee. And somehow, the brief Evil Marketing 101 moment with Nina brought that unpleasant feeling into clear focus. Lola now knew that when she opened the door back to Ovum, she would walk into a world totally new to her. A world where business is...business, if not worse. A world where people cannot automatically be trusted. A world that does not necessarily, like the stock market, reliably right itself over time. A world where things are, simply, *not* what they seem.

God, was the Panda-cam even real?

Of course, when it came to pain and drama and supreme unfair suckiness, Lola had seen it all. But she'd seen it in the letters in her *inbox*, not in her *life*.

Yes, indeed. It had now all been confirmed. This world was a dangerous place.

Boy, did Lola feel safer knowing that.

"So I'm sticking around through the weekend," Nina was saying. "You wanna grab coffee sometime?"

Lola smiled sincerely and looked Nina in the eye. "Not really."

"Yeah, me neither."

They laughed and shook hands.

50

Lola opened the door back into Ovum's main studio, not caring who saw her, since at this point the whole world just had. Douglas and Kat were right there.

"LOLA! We saw everything!" they exclaimed.

"We mean, *everything,*" said Kat.

"And look at *this,*" Doug said, switching the nearest TV to CNNfn.

"Today, immediately following a disparaging remark by Penelope on, ironically, her show's web cast, dot com stocks took a tumble so hard that the entire new technology sector may never recover," Maria Bartiromo was saying as Penelope's earlier words, "...this just stopped me cold from investing in the Internet," crawled across the bottom of the screen. "I'd even call it a dot crash," said Bartiromo.

"Whoa," said Lola, only beginning to get it.

"We called Ted," said Kat. "He's on his way. We're going to Lombardi's to celebrate your triumph—and our last day at Ovum."

"Your what?"

"Mmm hmm!" Doug and Kat both nodded. "Like we could stay here after that."

Lola, who is never speechless, was. The moment she regained her faculties, she left messages for Annabel and her parents.

•

Ted joined them and they headed for Lombardi's, the best pizza in town. Lola insisted that the BESTbest was Grimaldi's, but evidently Brooklyn wasn't "town."

Her cell wouldn't stop ringing, She shut it off as they settled into their seats.

"Can we please, please get at least one half with anchovies?" Doug begged. He looked hard at Lola. She looked back.

They all talked about what to do next.

"How about something without the words 'dot' or 'com'?" Kat suggested.

"Well, I don't know," said Lola, "it's not like the technology *per se* isn't here to stay. I'm thinking we could re-launch the site, small scale, as, say, really nicely navigable archives."

"With a special section for letters from Penelope," said Douglas.

"You know, it would also be nice to do nothing," said Ted, "but there's no money in that."

"Yeah, but you know what? Let's do it for now." Lola suggested. They ordered a bottle of Chianti.

•

"OK, now I need a nap," said Lola, who had drunk most of the Montepulciano herself. "It's been kind of a big day," she said. "I'll talk to you guys in an hour or so?"

"First come with me to the bathroom?" said Kat.

"Sure," Lola said.

In front of the mirror, they gave each other a big hug. "Oh, Kat."

"Lo, you know, you didn't really like him."

"What? Who? Miles? Well, I'd like to think I could tell that he was, oh, trying to sabotage my career and the progress of my entire gender."

"Me, too," said Kat. "But I still don't think you LIKEliked him. You weren't yourself around him."

"Well, being nervous around someone is kind of how you know you like them, you know?" said Lola, fixing her lipstick.

"Yeah, but not necessarily. There's *excited* nervous and there's NERVOUSnervous. Butterflies-in-your-tummy nervous and gut-feeling-something's-off nervous. You just weren't yourself. You talked fast and you laughed weird, like a little too loud."

Oof, thought Lola. That's the worst.

"You were like Bizarro Lola," Kat went on. "I just don't think you liked him, Lo. Though you sure tried."

"I did try. Yeah," said Lola, zipping her makeup case and turning to Kat. "Guess that's the problem. Like, *engineering*. As opposed to *chemistry*."

"Yeah," said Kat. "And *that's* like that song India played at the party, remember? 'I Just Want To Hang Around You?' That song totally made me think. *That's* really what it comes down to. Finding someone you just naturally dig and want to hang around with—with flaws that bug you, but you don't *care*. You know?"

"I do now," said Lola.

•

Kat and Lola met the guys out front. Big hugs all around. They parted ways. Douglas and Lola did that thing where you both look back.

Lola passed a newsstand. The evening version of the Post had a big new headline. Plastered everywhere.

"OVUM CRACKED."

Oh, my.

51

One million messages.

"Lola, this is Jan Benjamin at Kennedy, Kuntsler, Rockefeller, Roosevelt, Vanderbilt, Puff Daddy and Associates. We saw everything. Just wanted to let you know that we're filing papers demanding that Ovum revert the rights to AskLola.com to you, free and clear. It doesn't normally work this way, but given what happened today, it shouldn't be a problem. Oh, and no charge to you. We'll keep you posted."

Beep.

"Lola, this is Dixie Desmond at Dixie Desmond Literary Agency. We saw everything. Perhaps you're soured on the whole Internet thing and would like to turn your advice into a nice old-fashioned book with ink and pages? We'd love to represent you. Please let us know when you'd like to take a meeting."

Beep.

"Lola, it's Mom. We saw everything. We're getting on the shuttle. We'll call you from the Algonquin. We're so proud of you."

Beep.

"Lola, this is Dylan at Indie Street Cred Films. We saw everything. We'd like to feature you and your exposé of Ovum in our new 'Fuckyoumentary' series on Bravo. Please give us a call."

Beep.

"Lola, this is Zack Eager at DSNBC. We saw everything. We'd like to invite you to be the host of our new show, *Who Wants to Marry His Mother?* Please give us a call."

Beep.

"Lola, it's Jordan and Genevieve. We saw everything. After what Penelope said today, our dotcom's tanking too. And we just wanted to thank you. We're overworked and underappreciated and we're quitting. Getting out of the whole dotrat race. And finally, finally, going backpacking in Bali together. We'll e-mail you. Thanks again."

Beep.

"Lola, this is Jonas Ingall at Ben and Jerry's. We saw everything. Listen, if you can get the rights back from Ovum, which we're sure you can at this point, we'd still like to talk to you about branding your own flavor. We're thinking something with figs? Anyway. Please call us at your earliest convenience."

Beep.

"Lola, it's Tammy Abedon. I saw everything. And now I've heard everything. From Tootie, of course. Mrs. Helmsley Vestibule? Guess who *she* sees on the side!? *News America* columnist *Simon Snood.* Just thought you'd like to know. Call me."

Beep.

"Lola, it's Penelope. Everyone saw everything. Thank you. And about Leo, well, if you get your site back up, you'll probably be hearing from me. In the meantime, maybe I'll just track down your friend Ted. He seemed nice."

•

annabel2k: I saw everything. *BRAVISSIMA!*
hernamewaslola: thanks ☺
annabel2k: so, so proud
hernamewaslola: so, so thanks ☺! so, like, what does this mean about being a single woman: trust no one?
annabel2k: it doesn't MEAN anything lola. who was it who said that no matter what, every relationship, even if it ends, contributes to—even reshapes—our lives in some lasting way? o yah that was you
hernamewaslola: o yah, i did say that
annabel2k: and miles gave you...?
hernamewaslola: a panda? oh wait, not even that
annabel2k: how about opera? don't you totally love it now?
hernamewaslola: actually yeah. which also means my parents totally love me now
annabel2k: so.
hernamewaslola: so.
annabel2k: plus you didn't really like him in the first place.
hernamewaslola:?

annabel2k: you were trying to talk yourself into it, 'cause you DECIDED it was TIME. I know 'cause you never talked about the things that annoy you about him but you don't care 'cause you like him
hernamewaslola: ohhh
annabel2k: yeah. at the end of the day, he wasn't the guy you wanted to…hang around with at the end of the day.
hernamewaslola: did you talk to kat?
annabel2k: no why?
hernamewaslola: never mind.
annabel2k: ps date tonight
hermamewaslola: ooh! rock climber #3?
annabel2k: nope, surfer #1
hernamewaslola: in colorado?
annabel2k: so he'll have a lot of free time
hernamewaslola: hurrah! call me from the cabana? oh wait, getting another IM

douglee: lola? it's me
hernamewaslola: yo ranger!
douglee: no i mean lola? It's *me*
douglee: BOQUERON
douglee: that was my gaming name too
douglee: can i come over?
douglee: lo?
hernamewaslola: baa ram ewe
hernamewaslola: yes

52

hernamewaslola: are you sitting down?
annabel2k: why would i be standing at my computer?
hernamewaslola: boqueron? Is DOUGLAS
annabel2k: WHAT?!
hernamewaslola: mm hmm and he's COMING OVER RIGHT NOW
annabel2k: holy MOLY.
hernamewaslola: i'm skeered
annabel2k: why? you already know he rocks
hernamewaslola: that's why i'm skeered
annabel2k:?
hernamewaslola: because that's what i realized with this miles thing—I'm the EXPERT, i have to make it work, i have to know what I'm doing. no pressure!
annabel2k: lo, much as i love you you're not as unique as you think you are
hernamewaslola:?
annabel2k: EVERYONE has a reason to avoid relationships.
hernamewaslola: oh.
hernamewaslola: right.
hernamewaslola: did i say that?
annabel2k: no, i did. now get offline and go floss.
annabel2k: CALL ME FROM...YOUR BATHROOM
hernamewaslola: roger. EEEEE! And THANKS.
annabel2k: love ya. so does he, i bet
hernamewaslola: you both count xoxo

Lola left a message for her parents that she was exhausted and going to bed, but that she'd meet them for breakfast, anywhere but Caffe Reggio.

•

Buzzer. Lola opened the door.

"Hey," said Lola.

"Hey," said Douglas, looking the same but different. Different but the same.

"Are you taller?"

"Than you? Much. Than before? No."

"I know," Lola laughed. "It's just—you figured it out a while ago, right? How did you know 'Truffle' was Lola?"

"You forwarded that hilarious e-mail from the Russian guy that time?" Doug said. "Plus you're the only person I know who says 'Hell's bells.'"

Lola laughed, looking up into his glasses. "Come on in."

"Wait," Doug said. "Have you considered the long-term chiropractic implications?"

"No," said Lola, "but I've got some pretty good sherry."

"I've got *Babe*," Douglas said, holding up a DVD.

•

Sunlight. No alarm. Weekday. Nothing to do. Wait.

Where's Giraffe? Pat, pat. Here's something soft, but not fuzzy, and a little bony.

This is not Giraffe.

It is a human hand.

Attached to an arm coming from somewhere behind me.

And *not* wearing a dumbass geek watch used to communicate with Mrs. Helmsley Freaking Vestibule. Ranger is no one's bitch, thought Lola, crazily.

"Glad we followed your advice," Douglas whispered in her ear, chin on her pajamaed shoulder. "That thing about how sex is better when you wait? I don't know, somehow I feel like...we got a while."

"Yeah," smiled Lola, suddenly, giddily, awake. "Me too."

```
Dear Lola,
Things have been amazing for nine hours. Is it too
soon to take down my profile?
—Lola
```

"You know what's so great?" asked Doug. "I already know what annoys me about you."

"Hurrah!" said Lola. "Wait, what?"

"I'm not gonna tell you now!" said Douglas. "It totally doesn't matter, anyway, which is the point."

"Uh uh, no. You can't do that to me! You have to tell me!" insisted Lola. "I have to know to not do it, or to do it, depending."

"Okay, okay," said Douglas. He paused. "It's how you sometimes deflect tough stuff with humor and hide your true feelings."

Lola resisted, mightily, the reflex to do it right then. Instead, she said, "but you don't care, 'cause you like me?"

"Right," said Doug. "I mean, 'I'll take it.'"

"And I already know what annoys me about you," said Lola, kissing his fingertip.

"The movie reviews," said Doug.

"Yes," said Lola.

"But you don't care, 'cause you like me?"

"No, I care," she said.

Doug looked at her.

"Oops, I did that thing I do that annoys you but you don't care 'cause you like me," said Lola. "Oops, I think I'm still doing it." She took a breath and looked right at Doug. "Yes. I like you." There. "How about some French Roast?"

"Sure," murmured Douglas.

"How do you take your coffee?" she asked.

"Like my…women," he said, smiling with his eyes closed.

Lola kissed his forehead. "Equal?"

About the Author

Lynn Harris is an author, journalist, comedian and commentator on matters of gender, culture, relationships, and "the deal" with Ben and J. Lo. She is perhaps best known as co-creator (with supergenius Christopher Kalb) and alter-ego of the cultishly popular superhero Breakup Girl (BreakupGirl.net), who helps men and women through breakups, makeups, hookups and beyond.

Lynn Harris is author/co-author of four books, most recently *Breakup Girl to the Rescue! A Superhero's Guide to Love, and Lack Thereof* (Back Bay, 2000). She was co-producer of the *Breakup Girl* television series (directed and animated by Chris Kalb, with Mike Lee) and co-writer and star of *Breakup Girl LIVE*, Gotham Comedy Club's longest-running variety show.

Currently *Glamour*'s "Dating Dictionary" columnist, Lynn also writes for *Salon.com, The New York Times, The New York Observer,* and many more. She has appeared on *Good Morning America, Today, ABC News, CNN, Queen Latifah, Montel Williams,* Lifetime, and numerous other talk and radio shows. Her 2002 Off-Off-Broadway two-woman show *Lynn Harris on Ice*, with Betsy Fast, played to sellout crowds.

Having survived a bad dotcom breakup, Lynn lives in Brooklyn with her husband.

0-595-28776-X